The LENS *of* GOD

A Novel

The LENS
GOD
of

CARRIE DUGOVIC

XULON PRESS

Xulon Press
2301 Lucien Way #415
Maitland, FL 32751
407.339.4217
www.xulonpress.com

Unless otherwise indicated, Scripture quotations taken from New International Reader's Version (NIRV). Copyright © 1995, 1996, 1998, 2014 by Biblica, Inc.®. Used by permission. All rights reserved worldwide.

Printed in the United States of America.

ISBN: 9781545610732

DEDICATION

To my children, Geoffrey, Emily and Seth Retemeyer, for every "Mommy, tell me a story …."

And to God, for giving me your words when I prayed each time before writing. May this offering of work be pleasing to you.

ACKNOWLEDGEMENTS

I STARTED WRITING *The Lens of God* 15 years ago, and two hundred pages in … life happened, as it does to most of us. The pain overwhelmed me. I shut down, except to do what was necessary to provide for my kids and to survive. After healing, my book kept calling to me over the years. The characters were unfinished, waiting impatiently for their story to be told. Last year, I exhorted a dear friend to put her beautiful words into a book. She conquered her fears and wrote her book. And then she asked me to edit it. The day we submitted her book to the publisher, my friend looked me square in the face and challenged me to finish my book. I paused. What excuse did I have? None. Debi Massey, I thank you for encouraging me, believing in me and giving me the wonderful gift of you.

After I finished my book, I loved it. But, honestly, I wondered if anyone else would. Along with Debi Massey, I am grateful to Emily Retemeyer, Peggy Jenkin and Marilyn Tamazi for reading the raw manuscript. I anxiously awaited their feedback. When I heard the words from all four of these lovely ladies that "I love it," and "I can't put it down," or "I'm staying up too late at night to read," and finally, "It was so good, you have to publish it," my heart was full. Your positive responses gave me the motivation to go through the tedious editing process.

I must sincerely thank my editors. I couldn't have asked three people more qualified for this time consuming and meticulous task. Kirsten Sweeten, teacher and avid reader, your questions and suggestions for the content were spot on. You caught me on details that I overlooked or needed clarification. Randi Esau, University Curriculum and Catalog Specialist, your eye for detail such as punctuation, a missing word, capitalization and quotes is amazing. I think fondly of those little red marks throughout, and am thankful for every one of them. Lisa Allison, Advanced Placement and Honors English teacher, after 30 years of grading papers, thank you for grading mine. Your command of the written English language is exceptional. The large pile of tiny post-it notes, each one representing a mistake or suggestion, helped to make my book into a work worthy of discerning readers.

Finally, thank you Kiley Keas for the exquisite cover photograph of Gretchen, my daughter's 1965 Volkswagen Beetle.

PROLOGUE
BOULDER, CO
2002

TASHA WOKE to the annoying sound of her alarm clock. The irritating noise was persistent and continued its increasingly loud chirp. Groaning, she rolled over and pounded on the nightstand until she found the offending item. Suddenly her eyes flew open as she remembered she had a very important meeting today. Quickly she shut them again when the bright morning sun shone directly into her face.

The warm rays felt good as she luxuriated in the soft sheets and spooned her body pillow. Monday morning, she thought, humming a few bars of a song played on the radio about it being "… just another manic Monday." The alarm dutifully went off again, and Tasha rolled over to silence it. Her beloved cat, Penelope, sat on the white wicker nightstand observing with a slight look of amusement on her whiskered face.

"How opposite we are," she mused. The large cat was beautiful, gray with long silky fur and brilliant green eyes. She purred and leaned over to rub her cheek against Tasha's wavy light brown hair, tousled from a night of heavy sleep. Her hair used to be blond, but it had grown darker over the years. Tasha rarely felt beautiful and sighed as she got out of bed and walked to her overflowing closet filled with clothes she never wore.

"My favorite jeans and sweatshirt won't do today." Tasha gently rubbed her stomach trying to calm the fluttering from nerves and anticipation. Penelope brushed against her leg, and again she faced her intimidating closet. While the guest house she rented in an old established neighborhood was small, the builders didn't skimp on the closet. It was big and deep with built-in floor to ceiling redwood shelves and sturdy rods of varying heights for hanging clothes that no longer fit.

The blue suit? No, it was too formal.

"Should I wear slacks or a dress, Penelope? Something extravagant or modest?" The cat turned with a flounce, tail high and slowly swishing. Tasha envied her that she never had to choose what to wear. After a few minutes of searching for the perfect outfit, she sighed and turned away from the overwhelming task. Everything seemed wrong for the meeting she had in just two hours.

Still undecided, Tasha followed the cat into the bathroom and turned on the shower. She decided to pamper herself with a lavender scented natural shampoo and body wash. The generic brand she usually used was fine, but today she wanted to feel special. She stepped into the shower, warm water cascading down her hair and body settling nerves and washing away her fears.

She thought of God and how central he used to be in her life. When had she walked away? Today she really needed his reassurance and attempted an awkward prayer.

"God, I know I've been absent lately, and I'm not really sure how to ask this. I mean, why should you listen? If you're really up there and care, I could use some help today. Please, help me get out of the door without trembling. Don't let me make a fool of myself. Give me the right words and please help these darn butterflies fly away. Thank you. Oh, and God?

I also need courage to accept the outcome whatever it might be. Thanks again."

Tasha rinsed the soap from her hair and body, enjoying the lovely lavender scent. She turned off the water and wrapped up in a big soft towel. Some items in life just had to be nice, and she prioritized towels, sheets and toilet paper in her tight budget. Penelope looked up at her quizzically and meowed. "Okay, salmon and tuna occasionally for you too, girl."

Tasha spent extra time on her hair and makeup, thinking again of the meeting in two hours as she put on her watch. She looked at the time and realized now she only had one hour before her potential life change. She rushed back to her closet and peeked inside. There it was! A long sleeve cream colored silk blouse under a soft brown denim jumper, and neither were too tight or needed ironing, a miracle. Sliding on sheer hose and a pair of brown pumps, she looked longingly at her jeans and sweatshirt and promised herself in a few hours, she could change back into them.

The one-inch heel didn't do much to make her taller like the magazine models she envied. Why had she stopped growing in the ninth grade at just over five feet? She longed to be tall, thin, and graceful with long swinging blond hair. She walked over to the mirror and looked at the short and slightly overweight woman. While not tall and slender, her extra efforts paid off today. "Not bad."

"If I lost the 10 pounds I started on two years ago, these darn pantyhose wouldn't cut into my waistline," she grumbled to herself. Penelope meowed again and moved toward her legs. "Oh no you don't, I don't need your fur covering my dress. How about a little salmon treat?"

The cat responded by running ahead of her to the kitchen and waited impatiently by her bowl, meowing loudly. Tasha quickly opened the can and placed the fish in the cat's bowl. Salmon for breakfast wasn't exactly appetizing, but Penelope looked up for a moment as if to give thanks, then dug into her breakfast. Tasha grimaced and wondered how to teach manners to a cat. She glanced at the clock and noticed she only had 45 minutes before her meeting. The bus ride would take at least 15 minutes, so she quickly shoved a plastic spoon, a container of strawberry yogurt and a banana into her bag, and hoped she wouldn't make a mess of her dress on the bus. Carefully tucking her prepared portfolio under her other arm, she ran to the door. Could she open it today? Would the fear ever go away?

"God?"

"Perfect love drives out fear."[1]

"Now I'm hearing voices," Tasha muttered to herself and slowly opened the door, tentatively placing one foot over the threshold and then the other. "Okay, I can do this." She felt a slight fear, but so far not a panic attack. Breathing deeply, she called "Bye Penelope, be good, and please, please don't leave me a dead mouse on my pillow today!" The cat was now studiously cleaning her face after the gourmet meal and didn't bother to respond.

The short walk to the bus stop was uneventful. It was a beautiful morning. Tasha looked around with appreciation at the blue sky, flowers planted alongside white picket fences and mature shade trees. The smell of freshly cut grass was pleasant and refreshing. Birds chirped, dogs barked and children laughed.

This is a good day, she started humming the manic Monday song. "Not today," she firmly said to herself. The bus came around the corner and stopped with a squeal of brakes. Tasha gave Jack, the bus driver, a huge smile and confidently stepped up the bus steps putting her tokens in the slot. "How many tokens have I put in that slot?" It didn't matter. She liked riding the bus, experiencing the everyday sounds of people and meeting someone new occasionally, as long as they were what she considered safe. Grandmothers, moms with little kids, they were safe. Men, teenage boys, rough women, definitely not safe. She had a little beige Volkswagen bug from her high school days, but it broke down a few years ago, and she never bothered to fix it.

Jack attempted a smile back, Tasha was one of his favorite riders and he treated her with extra kindness. The smile wavered and Jack's eyes watered, though the tears didn't run down his rough cheeks before he got them under control. Tasha reached over and gently squeezed his shoulder, "Was it a rough night with Millie?" Jack nodded a bit, but she could tell he didn't want to talk about it, nor did he have time right now with a busy schedule to keep. Tasha leaned over and quietly whispered, "Jack, you are making a difference, and while Millie might not call you by name or treat you kindly, deep down she trusts you and knows you love her." Jack gave a slight nod, put the bus in gear and headed toward the next stop.

Tasha sat down and thought about Jack and Millie. Millie was in the final stages of Alzheimer's, and Jack was not only worried, but exhausted caring for her. Then she started to think about the events that brought her up to this day.

No, Tasha shook her head. Today she was not going let her mind go back there. It's in the past. The anxiety started, but with years of experience, she knew how to manage it. Today of all days, she did not want to suffer through another terrifying attack. She forced herself to take several deep breaths and think of good things to force her mind elsewhere.

Tasha looked out the window and tried to focus on the pretty neighborhood. Listening, she heard a baby laughing in the back row of the bus and toddlers arguing over who got to sit next to the window. With God's help, he brought her through the dark days and she would not, could not ever go back there again. She frowned, "But what about the fear? Would it ever go away for good?"

The bus always had interesting smells, some not so good, but someone peeled an orange in the next row and it made her mouth water. She wondered if the passenger had a cup of coffee and chocolate to go along with it. Thinking of how soft Penelope's fur was, she felt the anxiousness lift and breathed a sigh of relief. When she got home she would dust off her Bible. She remembered a verse in there somewhere about thinking on good things. That's what she would look up first.

Tasha's hands were clammy and her stomach full of flutters. She was so nervous, but she also knew she was as ready as she would ever be. Jack called out strong and clear, "County Courthouse, First and Main." Tasha knew her stop was next and realized she hadn't eaten her breakfast. Oh well, at least the panty hose wouldn't feel so tight, though she hoped her stomach wouldn't growl during the interview. She gathered her things so she would be ready and Jack wouldn't have to wait any longer than necessary to proceed to his next stop.

The bus brakes squealed and the arguing toddlers got off the bus with their exasperated mother. Tasha overheard her saying, "Be grateful you have a brother. If it was just one of you, who would you play with and spend the rest of your lives caring about?" Tasha agreed, and wished for the thousandth time that she had a brother or sister.

The bus took off for its last run before her stop. Tasha leaned her cheek against the cool window and reflected on the normalcy of life. Shopkeepers were redressing their windows with pumpkins and fall colors even though it was just now August. A jackhammer drilled into the street to prepare for a new stoplight, and Tasha was grateful she wasn't the one having to hold onto the vibrating machine all day. She thought he must have a royal headache at night, wondering if he went home to a nice wife and children or was alone with a dog or cat like her each evening.

"Downtown, 27th and Mapleton," Jack called out. Taking a deep breath, she tightly grasped her bag and portfolio and headed toward the front door. This time Jack gave her shoulder a gentle squeeze and said, "Thank you for the encouraging words, they helped." Tasha nodded, gave him a smile, then turned toward the door and stepped down onto the sidewalk.

She knew exactly where she was going. She'd walked by the business many times before, but never dreamed she would be going inside, especially for an interview herself. The address was 2040 Mapleton Street, just a few blocks down. It was a charming street. Quaint offices filled the old two story brick houses. She passed a lawyer and a stockbroker, a title company and a used bookstore. She almost stopped at a bagel shop advertising its wares with the delicious smell of fresh baked bread, but firmly walked by before stopping in front of her destination.

The house was a two story brick like the others on the street. Tasha opened the gate and breathed in the heady fragrance from white gardenia flowers as she walked up the brick path. Two huge maple trees on each side of the path stood guard for the old house and offered refreshing shade for those who cared to stop for a moment.

The house had a wide front porch with wicker chairs and a mismatched table. An open magazine and half-finished cup of coffee sat on the table. A gentle breeze turned the pages as if someone unseen was sitting there. The sight was homey and comforting.

Tasha walked up the stairs, and saw hanging white and green baskets filled with pink fuchsias. She envied the healthy plants' caretaker. She had never been able to keep a fuchsia alive for more than a month, much less through a hot summer. Wisteria climbed up the side rails, its vines reaching toward the second story windows. It was too late for the lovely, sweet smelling purple blooms, but Tasha knew it would be beautiful come spring. She took a deep breath, called up one more *"Okay, Lord, here we go,"* and rang the bell.

It was a beautiful bell, not an apartment buzzer or the ring of a newer and modern home. The bell gave a distinguished and resounding chime, its tone carrying on far longer than most rushed and harried people would consider necessary. Tasha anxiously tapped her foot and finally heard firm footsteps coming towards her. She smoothed her skirt, licked her lips and tucked an errant strand of hair behind an ear. The gesture was a nervous habit and she realized it just as the door swung open. It was too late to put the hair back in place, and she was sure she looked like a girl just coming in from a windy school recess break.

Oh well, first impressions aren't everything, and it's too late now to look grown up and sophisticated. Her boss commented on her 27th birthday that she still looked 16, but today she wanted to look at least a seasoned 30.

The man on the other side of the door smiled. He stepped back while holding the door open and with an open hand sweeping toward the inside foyer gestured that she was supposed to come in. He didn't say a word, and neither did Tasha. She was afraid her voice would croak and she would sound like a frog, or worse yet, squeak like an adolescent boy going through puberty.

The man still stood there and smiled for a painfully long moment. Finally, in a rich, deep voice that reminded her of the door chime asked, "And you must be Tasha McCleary? You're right on time, even a bit early. That says a lot about you already." Tasha realized she had no idea of the time as she hadn't checked her watch in the last half hour, but she didn't dare look now.

"Would you like something to drink, Miss McCleary before we get started? I have tea, or, well, he looked perplexed, I have tea. Would you like some tea?"

Tasha thought about the coffee on the front porch and realized she had yet to say one word to the man. She thought he might be Stephen Banks, the owner of the studio she had come to interview with, but he looked so young, barely older than herself, and a little ill at ease. He was tall, at least six feet, with short brown wavy hair, and kind brown eyes. His smile was warm and friendly, and she thought it odd he seemed to feel awkward and unsure of himself. Wouldn't someone so successful be more self-confident and commanding? Certainly, he wouldn't offer to get her tea himself?

Tasha replied, relieved she didn't sound like a frog or an adolescent boy. "Yes, tea would be fine, um Mr.?"

"Ah, I didn't introduce myself, I'm Stephen Banks. Your tea is coming right up. Would you like milk and sugar, or honey and lemon? Please make yourself comfortable in the front parlor just off to your right through the open door there." Stephen Banks pointed toward the open door and rushed off in the other direction presumably to get her a cup of tea. Tasha thought it odd he seemed to be very nervous and realized he didn't give her time to answer his question about how she liked her tea. She fretted about him going to too much trouble to make her a cup of tea she didn't want.

He didn't even look like a tea kind of person to her, whatever they were supposed to look like. He looked like he should be off to a ball game or a walk in the park in his casual jeans and Colorado University sweatshirt. She really was dying for a strong cup of coffee, but didn't want to offend her host, or rather potentially her future employer if the interview went well today.

She headed toward the front parlor, enjoying the lemon scented polish on the beautiful golden wood floor and staircase. The wood wasn't oak or pine, but she couldn't place what type of tree was used, perhaps maple? It would fit with the majestic trees in the front yard. She briefly considered that she wasn't afraid, but didn't want to think about why, concerned she might become afraid. It was a maddening cycle. Taking a deep breath, she continued down the hall, her curiosity reminded her of Penelope and how the cat loved to explore.

The walls were painted a soft cream and covered with breathtaking matted and framed photographs. There wasn't a common theme, rather it appeared to be a collection of the artist's favorites. She saw family portraits and wedding photographs alongside still life and stunning landscape shots. Each one was special in its own way and she couldn't believe one artist could be so versatile. Most were color photographs, though some dramatic black and whites adorned the walls as well. She felt rude staring, as if intruding upon someone's secret thoughts and turned quickly away so she wouldn't get caught before Mr. Banks returned.

Tasha entered the front parlor and gasped when she saw the photograph on the opposite wall. She dropped her precious portfolio on the wooden floor with a resounding slap. Some of the photographs fell out; she didn't acknowledge the accident or bend to pick them up.

Tasha took a few more steps until she was in the center of the room. Tears fell unnoticed down her soft cheeks as she slowly turned around and drank in the photographs displayed on the walls. Her heart hurt terribly as if a knife had pierced it, yet it was a bittersweet feeling. She felt like she was in the middle of a fragmented dream, terrifying but with comforting moments as well. Such was her life since that horrific experience in high school.

Tasha had been inside every one of these scenes. They were all landscapes. How had Mr. Banks been to the very most private places of her life and photographed them? How did he know? Who was this man? Nobody knew about these places, yet each one was so familiar. She saw each detail in her mind, smelt the scents of every refuge and felt the breeze, water spray or grimy dust on her face as she unwillingly stepped into the photographs and remembered ....

Tasha had no idea how much time had passed before she stumbled over to the nearest chair and sank into it, not trusting her trembling legs. She started hyperventilating and immediately recognized the familiar signs. Talking herself through the panic attack, she tried to take long, deep breaths instead of short shallow ones she knew would cause her to pass out. She closed her eyes for the photographs on the surrounding walls were too disturbing. It didn't help. The images were still firmly imprinted in her mind. Should she run out of here and never come back? Should she be angry that Stephen Banks had penetrated her most private sanctuaries? Her thoughts raged back and forth, knowing that he would be back any moment with a cup of tea that she didn't even want. Tea of all things!

Tasha continued her deep slow breathing, trying to get her turbulent emotions under control. She took one last deep shuddering breath and gained the courage to open her eyes. Stephen Banks sat directly in front of her, close enough she could smell the fresh scented soap he used to shower this morning. He must have slipped in quietly for she hadn't heard him enter the room. She wondered why she hadn't noticed the soap smell before and how long he had been watching her, but didn't really care. This wasn't about an interview today, this was about her life, either losing it completely or saving it. Curiously distant from herself, she contemplated which it would be.

Stephen Banks leaned forward, elbows resting on his knees with his hands cupped on each side of his clean-shaven face. He was obviously concerned at her strange reaction, the tea forgotten as he sat quietly and watched her. His eyes displayed enormous compassion as if he knew exactly what she was experiencing, though there was no way he could know what seeing those photographs in his front parlor cost her. His face became blurry as the tears welled up in her eyes again.

They both sat quietly for several moments, looking at one another with unspoken questions. "How did he know, and where did he find these places?" He asked her with his penetrating gaze, "Trust me. Will you let me explain?" They both started to talk at once. He whispered "Please, don't go," as he saw her start to rise while she groaned, "I can't stay here. I'm sorry. This was a huge mistake."

Tasha heard the plea in his voice and sat back down. She tried to wipe the tears from her cheeks with the back of her hand, though it was a futile gesture as they continued down her face, dripping onto her carefully chosen dress.

Stephen breathed a sigh of relief. "I see you have a lot of questions, understandably so. Will you please let me explain? The photographs you see on these walls are not mine ... they are yours."

Tasha sniffled and her eyes widened, "Mr. Banks, how ... when ... who would give these to you without my knowledge? I don't remember seeing these exact photographs, though I have several that are similar."

"Please call me Stephen. I feel like I know a little bit about you already through your photographs and a very good mutual friend and mentor. And after this morning, I think we've stepped beyond the bounds of polite manners." She sniffled again and nodded as he continued. "Tasha, we have more in common than you know." His smile was bittersweet as he continued.

"Several years ago, I was also a graduate of Colorado University. Dr. William Guenther, Professor of Photography, mentored me, as he did you. You were starting your education just as I finished mine. Dr. Guenther saw in you what he saw in me."

"When Dr. Guenther realized he had taught you everything he knew, he thought about the possibility of us working together. He knows my work, and he considered asking me to offer you an apprenticeship. But I was just starting out on my own so he decided to wait until my business and reputation were firmly established.

"Last week Dr. Guenther sent me your photographs, knowing they would speak for themselves. While you were in his classes, after you finished in the darkroom, he waited until you left campus, then went in and took the negative and photographs of a few of your shots."

Tasha gasped, her face hot with anger that her beloved professor had betrayed her, even stolen her work. Yet Stephen quickly continued, and she could not stop his explanation for she had to know how her photos had come to be on his gallery walls.

"Dr. Guenther justified his actions that you had taken so many photographs of each place, you wouldn't miss one here and there. I don't know the facts behind that difficult time in your life. Dr. Guenther told me your emotions were in such turmoil from your personal life that when you went to the darkroom the next day, you probably didn't even notice the missing photographs." Tasha nodded, recognizing that she hadn't missed them with the tumultuous thoughts raging through her mind.

"With good intentions, he planned to surprise you with a portfolio of your best work that you could use to apply for employment. Then you got the job taking school pictures, and he decided to wait, hoping you would get bored and ask for another recommendation. Rather than giving the portfolio to you, he gave it to me without your knowledge, knowing he could trust me with them.

"These are the photographs you see today on my walls. When I saw them, I knew I had to step out of my own comfortable solitude and ask you to apprentice with me. Something is drawing me towards you Tasha. It must sound very strange, but I think we're supposed to work together. I framed and hung your photographs yesterday. No one besides Dr. Guenther, yourself and I have ever laid eyes upon them. Regardless of how our meeting turns out today, please take them with you. They're yours, and they deserve to be in a gallery."

"They're not perfect, but I see you in them. A photographer's true gift is to let her audience inside, to share with them what you see and allow them to experience the same awe you feel from capturing a perfect moment in time. Please trust me and let me teach you beyond what Dr. Guenther offered. See the moments through my eyes, and let me see them through yours. I owe it to you, myself, and of course, our God. Let's learn together. You have things to teach me as well. Our photographs together will be even more beautiful."

Stephen stood up and walked toward the window gazing at his lovely front yard, yet not seeing it. He couldn't bear to see her rejection from his plea in the turn of her head, mistrust in her eyes, or tightly folded arms. He needed her as much as she needed him. He had no idea how similar their painful pasts were, but surely they could help one another and at least be friends?

Tasha finally spoke, her head down, eyes closed, not caring that she sounded like the frog she was so worried about a lifetime ago. She said, "Mr. Banks, uh, Stephen, do you believe in God? I mean really believe that he is real and cares for us?"

Stephen took a deep breath, turned toward her, an unexplainable peace flowing through his body and quietly said, "Absolutely." Tasha raised her head and looked into his eyes and could see that he believed, not a trace of doubt showed on his face, and though quiet, his answer was firm and strong.

"Then Stephen, will you pray for me?" Tasha whispered, fresh tears streaming down her cheeks as she stood up and walked back through the beautiful front entrance, leaving the photographs on the walls and her forgotten portfolio scattered across his lemon scented wood floor.

He heard the front door quietly close and watched the distraught woman walk down his path, most likely, out of his life forever. Stephen let his thoughts drift as he sunk into the old rocking chair his mother loved. The beautiful day and his ambitious plans forgotten as he remembered ....

CHAPTER 1
SPOKANE, WASHINGTON

"STEVIE, TIME to get up," his mother called in her sing-song voice. He jumped out of bed, because today was Saturday and sure to be full of fun. His mom made Saturdays special, and Stephen never knew what to expect. At ten, most of his friends didn't want to be around their moms, preferring to play soccer, basketball or just hang out. But Stephen loved being with his mom.

Last Saturday, they went to the Bowl and Pitcher along the Spokane River and had a picnic. They climbed and explored through the secret passageways in the big rocks and caught a lizard that she let him bring home. She even looked under rocks with him to find crickets and other tasty insects to feed the newest member of their small family. When they got home, she dug out an old aquarium and found a broken screen to make a cover. Together, they made a really cool lizard sanctuary. He gathered broken sticks and leaves while she raided the fridge for lettuce leaves and gave him one of her prized tropical plants for the lizard to hide under.

Yes, today would be special like every Saturday. He hurriedly dressed and haphazardly pulled his bedcovers up in some semblance of making his bed. The adventure started once his room was clean. He quickly shoved dirty clothes in the basket, closed his dresser drawers and hid unfinished homework under library books, making sure they were neatly stacked.

Stephen yelled, "I'm coming mom," as the delicious waffle and fresh brewed coffee scents filled the house. He ran down the stairs two at a time, picked up the old grey tabby cat, who protested mightily, and skidded into the kitchen on the worn linoleum just in time to see her take two waffles out of the even older iron. She turned and gave him a mischievous smile. "Is your room clean and your homework done?"

"My room is clean, and I only have, um, maybe 10 or 15 minutes more on my homework, but I can do that tomorrow after church Mom."

"Stevie, I saw your light on at 1:00 a.m. when I went to bed last night. What were you doing if not your homework?"

"Oh, Mom, I just had to finish my book. I only had 40 more pages, then I wasn't tired so I started another one. This one is about four kids who get lost on a mountain and …. " His mom laughed and said, "It's okay, Stevie, you can finish your math tomorrow. Read, my son; let your imagination take you places we can never afford to go to in real life. Except no later than 9:00 on a school night, understood? And your homework has to be done first. We'll go back to the library on Wednesday after school to replenish your insatiable thirst for adventure, okay?"

Stephen grinned, went to the fridge, poured them both a glass of orange juice, got out the half and half and fixed their coffee exactly the way they both liked it. He measured hers carefully with one half teaspoon of sugar and three teaspoons of cream. For his, he scooped in a heaping teaspoon full of sugar and enough cream for the hot liquid to be cool enough to drink and match the light brown color of a Jersey cow. He loved Jersey cows, especially their big brown eyes. His friends' moms didn't let them have coffee, but on Saturdays Stephen's mom did, and he loved her even more for it.

Stephen knew better than to ask what they would do today, for it was always her surprise and she liked secrets. To be honest, he liked them too and didn't really want her to tell him of their plans. The waffles were delicious. He generously spread real butter over the small holes, watching it melt into little droplets before adding pure maple syrup and lots of powdered sugar.

His mom was a counselor for a non-profit organization and they were on a shoestring budget, but Saturdays were special and it was worth scrimping through the week to have extras on this one day. Stephen felt bad when his pants became too short or his toes hurt in the too-small shoes. He tried not to say anything, but she noticed anyway. His mom made shopping fun, and thrift stores and garage sales were an adventure. They never knew what treasure they would find along with cast-off Seattle Mariners sweatshirts and Levi jeans for school. There was no better Mom than his in the world, anywhere.

Cathy finished cleaning up the kitchen while Stephen ran upstairs to brush his teeth and get the winter jacket and boots she requested he bring along today. Some days felt like spring was just around the corner, but a lingering winter storm could still surprise them. She sighed and brushed her long auburn hair out of her face as she leaned down to put the old waffle iron away. It used to belong to her Aunt Louise who gave the unusual gift to her as a wedding present, remarking in a gruff voice that a good seasoned waffle iron was much better than a new one. Louise was right. The waffles never stuck to the iron and came out beautifully golden brown every time. Still, she smiled as she remembered the horrified looks from the other wedding guests as Louise gleefully pulled the ugly appliance out of a used shopping bag.

The gift was one thing Rich couldn't take from her, that and their son, though it was hard to think of Stevie as Rich's child. He decided not long after their marriage and Stevie's birth that Cathy wasn't as sexy as she used to be with a baby tugging at her breast every time he thought his desires were more important. She frowned as she remembered his cruel remarks that her body looked like a deflated water balloon and when would she stop lazing around and get herself back into shape? Before the baby's birth, he had asked if she was going to join a circus as the first human blimp, and it wasn't a kind remark. Her doctor was very happy that she had gained just 25 pounds throughout the pregnancy, but obviously, her husband was much more critical. It had only been two months since the baby's birth and she tried as hard as she could, but nothing she did seemed right.

Rich started complaining about the same old meals every night, the stack of folded laundry on the couch and dusty blinds. Why couldn't he see that taking care of a newborn baby was exhausting? He never once offered to help and he refused to hold the baby, stating "it" only laid there and didn't do anything.

Every time she started to plan a nice dinner or dust the inconsequential blinds, Stevie woke up needing to be fed or just held. She would stare in awe and wonder at his perfect little mouth and fingers, and the way his long dark eyelashes lay against downy soft cheeks. She listened with pleasure to his little sighs as he sucked contentedly at her breast for both physical and emotional nourishment. As she watched the little miracle drift off to sleep after filling his tiny tummy, a nagging in the back of her mind told her to get up and clean house, but she knew deep inside this early bonding was much more important. Cathy would lay the baby on her breast and stroke his back until she too drifted into a pleasant and dreamless sleep.

As the baby started to nurse less often, she worked harder, making sure she looked nice for Rich by vigorously brushing her hair and putting on fresh makeup in the late afternoon. She sat Stevie in his infant seat on the bathroom counter and talked to him continuously about what fun they would have when he got older. "Just wait until you can sit, little guy. We'll go to the carousel and ride the pretty horses. When you can walk, we'll go see the most wonderful waterfalls, and when you can run, we'll race up a mountain together. But right now, let's just get to know each other, okay?" He would look up at her with big brown eyes and smile a huge toothless grin, and Cathy's heart overflowed with love and gratitude that she was indeed his mother.

Rich didn't seem to notice that she took care to make sure the laundry was put away and that she got her Betty Crocker cookbook back out to help her make delicious, yet economical dinners. The blinds remained dusty, but the house was picked up. Smooth jazz played softly on the stereo, and the young wife scrimped and saved in order to keep a lovely smelling candle lit every evening.

However, nothing she did seemed to matter. Rich started coming home later and later after work, smelling of cigarette smoke and beer. He sat in front of the television, turning up the volume to overpower the jazz and watched sitcoms or sports until late in the night, drinking beer after beer until he passed out on the couch. Cathy cried and pleaded with him to stop, but he just callously laughed and said the beer was a lot more fun than she was. Soon she didn't even want him to come home and was glad he didn't come to their marriage bed, but also feared if he left there would be no way to support herself and the baby.

Marrying soon after college and quickly becoming pregnant, she never had a chance to gain experience in a career. Her degree in Psychology seemed worthless as she thought about her relationship with Rich. How could she have so grossly misjudged him? Was his attraction to her only that, a surface attraction? She thought about his attentiveness to her, hanging onto every word with interest and laughing at her small anecdotes. He was the perfect gentleman, opening doors, one light kiss on the cheek at the end of a wonderful evening and deferring to her wishes at every turn.

Cathy thought his marriage proposal was a bit soon after only six months of dating, but she loved being with him. Her parents had retired and started traveling two years ago. She'd only seen them once as they were passing through to yet another National Park. Her brother was studying for a graduate degree in some scientific field in New York. She was lonely, and the idea of marriage and a family sounded perfect.

She said yes, and within a month they were married by a Justice of the Peace. Rich had no time for churches, and Cathy had never been in one herself. It didn't take long before Cathy realized that not all was bliss. Rich still listened to her, but he seemed bored, and he definitely was not happy when she announced she was pregnant. "I thought you had taken care of that," he said with a frown. Cathy said she did, right before they got married, but she didn't tell him that it was hard to remember to take the little pink pill every night, and sometimes she forgot. She was disappointed with Rich's reaction, and tried not to let it affect her own happiness at the good news. As the baby grew inside her, kicking and turning, regularly getting the hiccups, and calming down when she went for short walks, Cathy anxiously waited to meet the new little one.

Stevie was born on the first anniversary of their marriage, but Rich was working that day and asked the nurse to tell her he couldn't get away. He was absent from both his child's birth and their anniversary celebration. The hospital brought a congratulatory cake, and Cathy cried both bittersweet and joyful tears that night as she held their newborn son and ate it alone.

Cathy planned to become a high school counselor as soon as she could get a job after college. She wanted to help troubled young teenagers. Her own childhood was filled with a loving home, caring parents and an irritating younger brother. Her best friend did not have the same luxuries and often came to school with bruises on her back and ribs where they didn't show, except to Cathy who shared a P.E. locker and cried every time she saw Jenny's wounds. She would hug her friend oh so gently and beg Jenny to come live with her, but the girl was too afraid of what her father would do when he found her. Jenny did finally escape and waitressed at Denny's to support herself. The years of physical and emotional abuse took their toll, however, and Jenny had no close relationships other than Cathy.

She decided that she wanted to help kids in troublesome homes or those who made poor choices and needed guidance to deal with their problems. Now with a newborn baby, how could she go to work? Who could she trust to take care of this precious little one she had fallen desperately in love with? Would it even be possible for her to leave him in the care of someone else? Her heart ached.

Cathy's fears were soon realized as Rich started taking long weekend business trips and came home smelling like perfume along with the smoke and beer. She routinely saw lipstick marks and short blond hairs on his clothes when she did the laundry. At first, she was hurt, then angry and finally apathetic, relieved when he didn't come home at night.

Maybe she did look like a deflated water balloon, even if the bus driver, reference librarian and butcher's eyes lingered on her now trim figure, clear green eyes and long silky hair. Her smile was easy and contagious, not aware of their appreciative looks or obvious interest. She loved talking to people and made a point of offering sincere compliments whenever she could.

The young librarian was very helpful finding articles on teaching babies sign language before they could talk, and she made sure to thank him and comment on his extra effort. The bus driver never failed to help her with the infant seat and diaper bag as she boarded the bus, so she naturally gave him a smile and look of gratitude. The butcher generously added a bit more hamburger or an extra chicken breast to the already weighed order, laughing when she asked him how he would stay in business if he gave everyone a bit of extra charity like her. They all knew she was married and respected her wedding vows, so they carried the flirtations no further than a kind act they would give to just about anyone. The quickening of their pulses and slight blushes on their whiskered cheeks they could not control however, and the involuntary actions occurred every time the new young mother crossed their paths.

Rich moved out when Stevie was six months old, stating this wasn't the life he signed up for and told her she could have everything, but not to expect any alimony or child support as he had his own needs to take care of. As she looked around the small apartment, everything wasn't much, but she was grateful he didn't kick her out. In fact, it was a relief to not worry about when or if he would be home and what kind of awful mood he would be in. She looked at Stevie, just now beginning to sit up on his own and thought about the carousel ride. How could she afford to take him, much less eat, buy diapers and pay the rent? At least she was still nursing so she didn't have to buy expensive formula. She sat down on the floor, dejected, yet filled with a tiny glimmer of hope that they would be okay. She didn't know where the hope came from, and wondered about their future. "One day at a time, that's all I'll worry about for now, she thought."

Two weeks later, Cathy swallowed her pride as she balanced the checkbook and looked woefully at the $5.31 balance. The day after Rich left she went to the bank to transfer the money to a new account, but he had already withdrawn most of their checking and savings, leaving her with a rent payment due on the first of the month and nothing to pay it with.

She was furious, and had called several numbers to tell him so, only to find he had disappeared. Even the Human Resources department at the job he supposedly had didn't know of him, and she had no idea how he had supported them over the last year and a half. After thinking about it, she decided she didn't want to know.

With no food in the cabinets or refrigerator, she took her last bus tokens and looked up the route to the Salvation Army, thinking of the kindly bell ringers every Christmas. She knew even if they couldn't help her, they would be nice about it and rejection was the last thing she needed right now. She bundled Stevie up and took along the last of her diapers hoping one would be enough today. The bus driver smiled when he saw her and helped lift the baby seat up the steps. She tried not to cry, but his gracious act meant more than he could know. At his questioning look, she just slightly shook her head and gently touched the back of his hand. He blushed furiously this time, though once again she didn't notice.

Soon the tears dried as Stevie started babbling at the bus sights and sounds. He loved the bus, and of course, all the grandmothers on their shopping trips loved him. A ham, he already knew that his outrageous two-tooth smile melted hearts and he could manipulate the ladies into entertaining him the entire ride. Before Cathy knew it, the bus arrived at the non-descript brown building with a cross above the front door. The building was small and simple, but neatly kept with bright marigolds planted alongside the walk and a freshly cut lawn.

Despite the welcome sight, Cathy almost stayed on the bus, pretending this wasn't her stop, but she was desperate and didn't know where else to go. She bundled up a protesting Stevie just starting to enjoy a new unsuspecting conquest, but a tickle kiss behind the ear had him laughing soon enough. If only she could laugh that easily without a care in the world.

The bus driver waved goodbye, his eyes questioning at this unusual stop. How could she explain her short marriage had failed and she was now penniless? She didn't even know how to get ahold of her absent parents to ask for help, and her brother was a poor college student working into the midnight hours himself to pay tuition and rent. She took a deep breath, stood up straight, walked up the narrow path and firmly opened the door. A pleasant bell sounded, announcing their arrival, along with Stevie's newfound skill at making razzing sounds and blowing bubbles. Once inside, Cathy looked around and was pleasantly surprised. The inviting bright yellow walls drew her in, and the building smelled clean, like freshly laundered sheets blowing in a summer breeze.

Stevie found his first victim easily and lifted his arms toward the elderly woman at the front desk. She was on the phone, but excused herself quickly and hung up as she exclaimed, "What a beautiful baby! Oh, may I hold him, please?" She looked toward Cathy with a pleading look in her soft blue eyes, and Cathy unbuckled Stevie from his car seat and handed him to the woman. He grabbed at her glasses, and she laughed and redirected his pudgy hands to a brightly colored beaded necklace instead. Cathy worried the baby would break the beaded string, but he was uncharacteristically careful and merrily played with the pretty beads before drooling all over the woman's blouse. She laughed again and got a tissue, softly wiping his chin and commenting on his lovely pearly white teeth, "Soon to be joined by two more, I see!"

The butterflies in Cathy's stomach lessened at the woman's friendliness, and she didn't feel quite so terrified about being here.

"I'm Mildred Washington, and this is the most delightful baby I've seen all week," she gushed.

"May I?" Mildred asked as she took Stevie over to a play area filled with large balls, beanbag chairs and big plastic trucks. A small gate opened into an enclosed circular area designed to keep younger children safe yet low enough they could see out if they pulled themselves up. She sat him down in the middle of the balls and proceeded to sit down herself in one of the big yellow beanbag chairs, easily within reach of the baby. Stevie was delighted and started batting around the balls and eyeing the big sturdy trucks. Mildred pointed to a bright orange beanbag chair next to hers and asked, "Will you please sit? It looks like you'll be here awhile," as she pointedly looked at Stevie playing contentedly by himself.

Cathy felt an overwhelming peace and security flow over her as Mildred Washington invited her to stay. She sunk into the chair and watched Stevie for a moment without speaking. Then she turned to Mildred with tears in her eyes and poured out the entire sad story, sobbing by the time she was done. Mildred clucked and shushed, shook her head slowly back and forth, and shed a tear or two herself while Cathy sniffled and wiped her tears on her sleeve, trying to get herself under control.

She patted Cathy on the back and miraculously found a box of tissues for them both. "Now, now, what do you think all those bell ringers are working for every Christmas, if not to help us show the love of Jesus to those who run into a bit of misfortune from time to time?"

"We share his abundant and sufficient love and it gets passed on, sure and simple as that. Why, after you get through this difficult time, it wouldn't surprise me to see you ringin' a bell yourself, along with that delightful little baby entertaining everyone who walks by dropping in those coins of love."

Mildred's face, though heavily lined from her many years, looked incredibly young as it lit up brightly like a Fourth of July firework celebration grand finale. A huge smile engulfed her whole face all the way up to her ears and eyebrows. Cathy stared in awe at this wonderful woman, knowing somehow she would leave today with more than just hope in her pocket, and it wasn't money or food she thought about. Love and acceptance, nurturing and caring, and a good friend, that's what she wanted to leave with and keep forever if she could.

CHAPTER 2
BOULDER, CO

TASHA DIDN'T know what to think. Her feelings were in such turmoil from seeing her photographs in Mr. Banks parlor. Her stomach was in knots and she felt like vomiting. She continued to walk, not knowing how long or caring where she went. The deluge of tears had finally stopped, but her eyes stung and felt swollen. Was she mad, hurt, grateful, relieved, hopeful or just dejected? Maybe a combination of all the above she thought as she reviewed the events of the morning in her mind.

She heard the squeal of brakes, a loud horn and a louder voice yelling, "Hey lady, watch where you're going!" Startled she looked up and found herself in the middle of a busy street, just inches from the bumper of a big truck. The tears returned and Tasha attempted to choke out a feeble sorry to the man as she scuttled back to the curb. Looking around, she saw a blurry park and rushed over to a vacant bench. She closed her eyes but the tears still ran down her face and she started sobbing again.

At least she thought the seat was vacant, for soon she heard a soothing soft voice telling her to breathe deeply and slowly. Tissues bunched up in a veined and wrinkled small hand gently wiped at her cheeks and the soothing sounds continued. Tasha dared not to look sideways to see who the caring person was. In spite of her turmoil, she felt embarrassed at her public display of raw emotions. Her sobs turned into hiccups and she repeatedly sniffled to control her red and runny nose. What would Stephen Banks think if he walked by and saw her? Finally, she gained the courage to look over at the person with a wrinkled hand and an unlimited supply of tissue.

The old woman's creased eyes were as kind as her voice. She had a small gray bun wrapped up on top of her head, a blue dress with pearl buttons closed all the way up the front and a creamy white cardigan sweater draped over her shoulders. From Tasha's earlier view of the ground, she knew the woman had on sensible shoes and support hose to complete the ensemble. It was her eyes that drew Tasha in. They were so kind.

"Now, that's better. Nothing like a good cry to clear the soul and help one to think more clearly. God gave us tears to use," she continued in her soft voice as she gently patted Tasha's knee. Tasha sniffled some more and nodded her head up and down in agreement. She was afraid if she tried talking that she would start crying again.

After years of being alone, she didn't know how to let someone take care of her. The woman's ministrations felt odd and uncomfortable. "Would you like to come to my apartment for a cup of tea?" The woman's question interrupted Tasha's negative thoughts. Tea again? What was it with tea today? Didn't anyone enjoy a good strong cup of coffee anymore?

Tasha took a deep breath, wondering if she could trust her voice. "Oh no, I couldn't possibly intrude." There, one small success, she talked without more tears.

"Nonsense! I live alone, and I would love your company. Actually, I hate tea, it just seemed like the right thing to offer after a cry like that. I do have some good strong coffee beans just waiting to be ground." Lifting her head and taking a deep breath into her nose, the old woman mused, "Imagine the air filled with a rich aroma and our anticipation waiting for the brew to be ready. Forget that awful skim milk my doctor wants me to use ... only real cream and sugar for me. What do you say? Would you care to join me for a delicious cup of coffee?"

Tasha's mouth watered at the thought. That was exactly what she wanted, actually needed right now. Some friendly companionship and a great cup of coffee just the way she liked it. How did this sweet elderly woman know?

Tasha looked down at her knees and shyly answered, "Yes, that would be very nice, thank you."

"Wonderful! Come on, I live right over there across from the park," she said pointing enthusiastically with her wobbly index finger.

She stood, grabbed Tasha's hand with an unexpected strength and tugged her up from the bench before Tasha knew what was happening.

"My name is Winnifred Gertrude Eleanor Schlesser. Can you imagine anyone naming a helpless baby such a thing? So my friends call me Winnie, and since you're my new friend, I would like you to do the same."

With her free hand, Winnie waved at many people who offered calls of greeting and big smiles in return. It seemed like everyone they passed knew her. She was certainly a friendly sort. Who was this woman, and why she was following a stranger to an apartment in an area of town she knew nothing about? She didn't even know how to get home. What a mess! And all because of Stephen Banks. Not completely true, she admitted. Dr. Guenther started this whole thing. She was so angry she could spit, though rationally she knew the kind professor was only trying to help her. Still, he had no right.

"My, what a scowl on your lovely face," Winnie commented as they stopped and she let go of Tasha's hand to dig around in her pocket book for the door key. Tasha looked up, completely surprised at their surroundings. She was at a garage. At least the outside looked like a garage. As they stepped inside her eyes moved across the lovely travertine tiled floors and smooth walls painted a warm, sandstone beige. Lush plants filled the room, their healthy green branches reaching toward huge picture windows on three sides of the large room. Thick oak wooden beams lined the high ceiling, framing several skylights that let the light filter in through massive redwood branches outdoors. A butter soft tan leather couch begged Tasha to come and sink into its comfortable depths. The other furniture was mismatched but inviting.

"Oh, Winnie, this is lovely," Tasha exclaimed and hiccupped again.

Winnie gave a small smile and poured water from a clay urn into the coffee pot. She carefully measured beans into the grinder and soon the fragrant aroma filled the air. Tasha sighed with pleasure at the simple things in life.

"My son and daughter-in-law live next door in the house. When they firmly suggested I sell my home and come live with them, I agreed on the stipulation that I could remake the detached garage into my own apartment. Young families don't need meddling mothers interfering in their lives. They're happy because I'm close by so they can keep an eye on me, and I'm happy with my independence. It works for both of us. I get to see just enough of my precious grandchildren, and the park is right across the street. I have made several new friends, including you." Winnie beamed at her newest friend.

Tasha nodded and wished for the millionth time that she had a grandmother who would spend time with her. What would it be like to have someone who loved her unconditionally and had time to go fishing, make valentine hearts out of paper doilies or fly a kite all day? Grandmothers were special people indeed.

"Ah, there's that melancholy look on your face again, and just when I was about to pour our coffee."

"I'm sorry, Winnie. I'm afraid I'm not very good company today," Tasha said, all the while thinking she hadn't been very good company for a long time. She forced a smile on her face and walked toward the small kitchen to help Winnie with the tray. The homemade mugs were big and bright, begging to be cradled in appreciative hands. A matching creamer and sugar bowl joined by two tiny silver spoons completed the display. The coffee smelled heavenly and Tasha waited in anticipation for the first sip.

"It's such a beautiful day. Why don't we go out to the garden?" Winnie stepped toward another door opening to a side yard. Tasha rushed over to help with the door and felt a soothing peace flow through her when she saw the tiny garden. A large Japanese maple tree gracefully spread her branches over a brick courtyard. A robin happily bathed in a small white fountain. There were two white wicker chairs with red pillows and a matching table. Clay pots of rosemary, mint, basil, thyme and other herbs sat in rows along the fence. Miniature azalea and rhododendron bushes graced one corner, their pretty flowers brightening the courtyard with pink, red and white splashes of color. Impressed, she saw in another corner there stood a small bookshelf, her shelves sturdy under the weight of assorted puzzles, checkers, coloring books and crayons and a few other games. Winnie knew what was important in life. Her grandchildren probably spent quite a bit of time here.

Winnie put the tray on the wicker table and sat in one of the cushioned chairs. She pointed to the other chair and motioned for Tasha to join her. Tasha sighed with pleasure and sat down. This truly was a haven, a refuge, even an oasis of sorts. Her mind started buzzing about having a home of her own with a little garden just like this one. Penelope would love it!

"There, this is better. How would you like your coffee, dear?"

"With cream until it's the color of a Jersey cow and a teaspoon of sugar, please."

Winnie looked up with surprise, "I know someone else who likes their coffee just like that, the color of a Jersey cow with a teaspoon of sugar, isn't that odd?"

Tasha felt a little tingle run up and down her spine, though for the life of her she didn't know why. That's always how she described how much cream and sugar to put in her coffee.

Shrugging her shoulders, she said smiling, "Your friend has good taste."

Winnie finished putting the perfect amount of cream and sugar in both cups and offered one to Tasha. She took the long anticipated sip, closing her eyes and enjoying the sensation.

"Oh, it's perfect. Thank you Winnie, I really needed this." Tasha's eyes stung from the morning of crying. She was sure they were swollen and her nose a bright shade of red. "Are you wondering why I was so distraught?"

"Of course, but you don't have to talk about it dear. This morning God prompted me to go over to the park. It was far too early for my normal stroll, but he just wouldn't leave me alone. I actually felt pushed out my door and right to that bench where you were sitting. I knew right then God wanted me to be your friend. That's all I need or want from you, just to be your friend."

"Oh Winnie, you truly are a gem. I do need a friend. I don't have very many, well I guess I don't have any good friends at all. I think you're an answer to my awkward prayer this morning. You must be."

Winnie smiled and reached over to squeeze Tasha's hand. Uncomfortable with the physical touch, Tasha gently pulled away, but smiled to let Winnie know it was okay.

"Winnie, I've never told anyone about my past, but for some reason I trust you. I think I need to say what happened, out loud. At least that's what my counselor keeps telling me. If you have time and want to listen, I hope when I'm finished you'll still be my friend. I've been alone and afraid so long, I don't want to live like this any longer."

Tasha tentatively looked over at the kind old woman, her delicate brows questioning if it was okay. Winnie returned her gaze with a small smile and slight nod of her head. Tasha received her love and acceptance, a soothing balm to her aching heart, and years of secret despair began to pour out of her troubled mind.

CHAPTER 3
LOVELAND, CO

"GOOD MORNING, sleepyhead. It's Christmas morning! Why are you still in bed?"

"Mom, I don't believe in Santa anymore," Tasha smiled under her covers. She had in fact been awake for over an hour waiting for her parents to get up, but she didn't want to let them know that. She knew if she went downstairs to the Christmas tree, she would be tempted to peek inside the wrapped gifts in the still, quiet morning, so she stayed in bed wondering what Santa brought her. It would be so cool if they got her a Walkman combination cd and radio player. She left enough hints around the house for the past three months; they couldn't have missed it.

Her dad ran into the room and jumped on her bed, tousling her hair and growling like a bear. "I've been asleep all winter, and I'm HUNGRY," the bear growled as he pretended to take bites out of her arms and legs through the covers, all the while tickling her mercilessly.

"Stop! Daddy stop it!" Tasha cried, squirming to get out of his ferocious grip.

"But I'm still HUNGRY!"

Her mom walked in laughing at the spectacle and asked the magic question Tasha heard every Christmas morning since she could remember, "Would homemade warm cinnamon rolls and freshly ground coffee satisfy the hungry bear?"

The bear stopped his pursuit and looked up, eyebrows lifted in consideration of which breakfast he would prefer.

"I suppose the rolls would be tastier and more filling than this skinny girl, yes I think I could be persuaded." He stood up, straightened his morning attire of sweat pants and an old t-shirt and meekly followed mama bear towards the door, inviting the skinny, obviously tasteless girl to come with them. "I'll be right down, Dad. Go ahead and save some for me. It seems you think I need to gain a little weight before I'm edible!" Tasha laughed as she watched her dad leave the room, eyebrows waggling.

Tasha sighed with contentment. Her parents were great. She was an only child and they lavished their love and attention upon her. Yet, she wasn't spoiled with the latest fashion or toy. Sometimes, she overheard their whisperings late into the night wondering how they would have enough money to make it until payday. Then there would be a lot of beans and rice for the next week or two for dinner. Tasha didn't care. She loved beans and rice. And going to garage sales. Often her mom would let her pick out a game or costume jewelry along with clothes if they found something worthwhile. After carefully choosing their items, they stopped at the Dairy Queen for a soft serve vanilla ice cream dipped in chocolate. Mother and daughter slowly savored their treat while talking about anything and everything.

The delicious aroma of cinnamon rolls filled the warm room and Tasha's mouth watered. She pushed aside the covers and stepped into the fuzzy yellow slippers she kept next to her bed. A quick stop in the bathroom and soon she was in the kitchen savoring the moment just before digging into a huge cinnamon roll. Her mother poured her a cup of coffee and added cream until it was the color of a Jersey cow and a heaping teaspoon of sugar. Just the way she liked it. Her friends didn't believe her when she told them she had coffee with breakfast on Saturday mornings, but she didn't care. Impressing her friends wasn't top on her priority list.

"Well, that was a perfect breakfast after a long winter's nap," Father Bear sighed with contentment. "I think I'll go back to bed now."

"NO, Dad!" Tasha exclaimed.

"Oh, someone *is* interested in what Santa brought for Christmas? Well, I guess I can wait until fall to resume my slumber," he sighed unconvincingly.

They left the empty cups and plates on the table while Tasha's mom got the camera and followed them into the small living room. The tree was bare except for a few handmade ornaments and decorations Tasha made through the years at school, but it was beautiful to her. The string of popcorn and tiny pinecones she had gathered and decorated with glue and blue glitter made the tree look festive. There were several presents under the tree, and she knew her parents must have scrimped and saved to buy them. One present in particular caught her eye. It was just the right size to be a Walkman. Could it be?

Dad handed her the family Bible and she turned to the gospel of Luke, her favorite version of the Christmas story, and bowed her head in prayer.

"Dear Lord Jesus, thank you for your birth. Thank you for these gifts, but help us to remember the real gift is you."

Tasha read the story about a young woman traveling far on a donkey to fulfill the words of the Old Testament prophets about Jesus' birth. She looked around at their small, but comfortable home and was grateful she wasn't born in a stable. Was Mary frightened? Did having a baby hurt? How did she clean him in a dirty stable? Was it cold? None of the details she was so concerned about were mentioned in any of the Gospels, so she was left to wonder. She read that the shepherds came to see the baby king and spread the word of his birth. Tasha sighed for too soon the story was finished, and she longed for more. She reminded herself to read the Bible more often. It's not like her life was that busy, just that other stuff got in the way. When she did read, even if she didn't understand some of the words, it felt good inside. "I'll try harder," Tasha said to herself, mentally making a note to set her alarm 15 minutes earlier so she could come downstairs and read in the quiet morning hours.

"Punkin', are you ready to see what Santa brought you?"

"No Dad, first I want you and mom to open the present I made you at my Wednesday night church club."

Tasha was excited for them to open the gift she worked so hard on. She spent a little bit of time every week for the last three months and a few Saturday afternoons working on her project. She hoped they liked it. Their teacher thought it was time they learned to sew, so she brought some simple cross-stitch samplers. Tasha picked her favorite Bible verse and with her teacher's help, carefully counted the little squares on the fabric and the letters to center it perfectly. She selected wild-flowers to decorate around the edges and framed it in a rough-hewn wood frame her teacher's husband made for each of the girls.

She handed the prettily wrapped gift to her dad, and grabbed the camera to capture the looks on their faces when they opened it. She hoped they believed that she made it. Tasha almost didn't believe herself that she created such a nice gift with her own hands.

Her dad handed the package to her mom who already had tears in her eyes. Tasha knew they loved her very much, though she didn't know the full details of just how precious she was to them. Her mom carefully opened the pretty paper so she could save it to wrap another similarly sized gift on a later date. Her dad wrapped his arm around her mother's shoulders as he waited to see what she made.

"Oh, Tasha," her mother exclaimed as the paper fell aside and she lifted the carefully framed cloth. "It's beautiful, honey. You did this all by yourself?"

Her father read, his voice choking,

> *"For I know the plans I have for you, declares*
> *the Lord, plans to prosper you and not to harm*
> *you, plans to give you hope and a future. Then*
> *you will call upon me and come and pray to*
> *me, and I will listen to you. You will seek*
> *me and find me when you seek me with all*
> *your heart."[2]*

"It's Jeremiah 29:11-13," Tasha said unnecessarily for it was also stitched into the lovely fabric. "We only need to seek God with all our hearts and we will find him. He listens to our prayers, see it says right there."

"Come here, baby," her dad lifted his arms toward her. He held her tight and she could feel the dampness on his cheek against hers. "You make your mom and I so happy and proud, Tasha. Always seek God's will for your life and you will be blessed, okay?"

Her mom was still gently touching the beautiful stitches Tasha had carefully made. "Thank you Tasha, I will treasure this always. The flowers are beautiful too. You chose some of my favorites. I really like the columbine. It's our state flower, did you know that?"

Tasha nodded, pleased that her parents liked her gift. Her dad handed her the larger package.

"This one first, punkin'. I think you'll find it appropriate considering the gift you just gave us."

It looked like a shoebox but the box was too heavy for shoes. They were always trying to trick her with odd package sizes and wrappings. She also carefully unwrapped the gift and handed her mother the paper. It was a shoebox, but one she recognized from last fall when she started school. She opened the lid and gently took out the book. It was a burgundy colored leather bound Bible with her name engraved on the front. Her very own Bible, God knew the desires of her heart! She remembered her mental note, and knew now she could read the Bible in her warm bed in the early morning hours.

"Open the front cover, Honey," her mom suggested.

Tasha read, "To our lovely Tasha. May you always love our Lord. May he bless and keep you safe from harm until we are reunited in his kingdom through all of eternity. We love you. Dad and Mom."

Now it was Tasha's turn to cry. "Thank you so much, Dad. Thank you, Mom. I will keep this forever!" She looked forward to showing her Wednesday night club teacher and classmates, but more importantly spending time with her new Bible, getting to know more about Jesus.

"Wait there's one more gift you still have to open."

"Dad, this was more than enough. You didn't have to."

"But we wanted to," he winked at her mom.

Tasha unwrapped the other gift, and sure enough, it was a portable Walkman cd and radio player. Not that they had any cds to play, but she could listen to her favorite Christian radio station while walking to school in the mornings until she got a job and bought her first Amy Grant cd.

"You'll have to use your allowance to buy batteries though, and you still have to talk to us sometimes," her dad warned.

"Thank you, thank you, thank you! You are such great parents. This is the best Christmas ever," Tasha exclaimed.

They all had one more big family hug before her dad went to find a hammer and nail to hang her gift. Tasha went to the kitchen to help her mom put the turkey in the oven and learn how to bake a real punkin' pie.

"Mom, why did you and dad only have me? Didn't you want other children?"

Her mother set the eggs for the pie down on the counter and turned to Tasha.

"Yes, honey. We did, do want more children, but the Lord hasn't blessed us with more. We are so grateful for you, though.

We thank God every day for you and the joy you've brought into our lives."

"It would be nice to have a brother or sister."

Her mom laughed, "You say that now, but if and when you get one, and they spill grape juice on your math book, spit toothpaste on your arm, or mark all over your wall paper with a permanent marker, you might not be so thrilled with the idea."

"No, I meant a brother or sister my age."

"Exactly!"

They both laughed and turned back to the Christmas dinner preparations.

Chapter 4
Spokane, Washington

STEVIE RAN back down the stairs, slightly out of breath. He almost knocked his mother over skidding around the corner. She laughed, knowing he was ready for the adventure of the day.

"Be right back, hon, just got to brush my teeth then we'll get going. Will you please feed the cat while you're waiting?"

Stevie obeyed even though he thought the cat food smelled terrible. He was careful not to spill or cut his hand on the sharp edges of the can. The old cat couldn't chew hard crunchy food anymore, and his mother was too kind to put him to sleep until it was absolutely necessary. The cat was a stray and they had no idea his age before it adopted their family five years ago. It didn't even have a name, just cat. He noticed the litter needed changed, but conveniently looked the other way. That was the worst job ever.

He looked around their home. His mom told him she bought this small two-bedroom house about a year after he was born. The nice sized kitchen and living room were downstairs, along with a small laundry area. The bedrooms and bath were upstairs. She painted the walls bright, fun colors and the furniture was the kind you sunk into after school or to read a good book.

There were lots of big windows to let in the bright spring sunshine, but it was still too cold to open them and enjoy the fresh air. He liked to lay on the sunny warm spots on the floor in front of the windows and sometimes the cat cuddled up next to him and purred.

The house was right around the corner from her work and only two blocks from his school. The yard was huge with a big maple tree along with some cedar and pine trees that reminded him of a small private forest. It was an older area of town, but that suited him just fine. He had friends close by and it was all he had ever known.

His mom came down with a huge bag that looked like an overstuffed pillow, "Ready?"

"Oh yeah." He had no idea how long they would be gone or where they would go. It didn't matter though, as long as he could spend time alone with just her.

Cathy grabbed a small cooler, which meant they would be gone at least long enough for lunch or a snack. He saw her struggle trying to open the door.

"Mom, I can help." She gave up the cooler, but definitely not the big bag, which is what he really wanted to help with, his curiosity piqued.

"Thanks Stevie, sometimes I would really like another arm or two."

They got in the old small Subaru sedan, perfect for just the two of them and the often snow-covered Spokane streets. The seats were chilly from the cold night, but the little car soon began blowing warm air on their feet and windshield.

"Let's pray for a great day, okay?"

"Can I pray today, Mom?" She was surprised, but tried not to make a big deal out of the question she'd been longing to hear for years.

"Sure, go ahead."

His voice came out not timid and meek, but like that of two good friends sharing conversation in the same room.

"Dear Jesus, thank you for my mom. I know it must be hard sometimes raising me by herself. Please tell her she's doing a great job, and that she's the best mom in the whole world. Help us have fun today. Show us some of the neat things you made. Please keep us safe. Thank you again. Oh, and I'm sorry I didn't change the cat litter this morning when I know I should've. Amen."

Cathy looked out the window so Stevie wouldn't see how choked up she was. Did he have any idea how special he made her feel? How loved? She swallowed a few times to try and remove the huge lump in her throat.

After a moment, she nonchalantly turned to him and said, "Thanks Stevie, that was very nice."

Soon they were traveling west on Highway I-90 out of Spokane and into the gently rolling plains. The earth was brown this time of year, unlike the golden blowing waves later in the summer when the wheat was ready for harvest. He knew there were some lakes out this way but not much more than that.

They drove for about 30 minutes, talking about his friends, soccer practice and how boring math was. Cathy thought he might have a slight crush on his teacher this year. She was young and pretty, a recent college graduate. Miss Zarling was very effective in her job and the children liked going to school every day just to be around her. She gave out a fair amount of homework and expected her students to do their best. Every A grade was earned, not given freely.

Soon they took an exit Stephen had never been on that rapidly turned into a dirt road. They drove a few miles over the hardened dips and bumps from many snow falls and melts over the winter. He was glad the Subaru had all wheel drive and sat a little higher off the ground than most cars. His mom drove right through the mud holes, making big splashes. She was definitely a cool mom. Up ahead he saw an old farmhouse with a very big barn. The barn was at least three times the size of the house. He wasn't really surprised when she pulled into the driveway, for he had learned to expect almost anything from her over the years.

Cathy pulled right up to the gravel area in front of the house and turned off the car.

"Okay, here we are," she enthused and got out of the car with a look of anticipation on her face. Stephen got out too, not having the slightest idea what they were doing here.

"Hello, anybody home?" Cathy called out as they crunched across the gravel and across the swept walk. Still spry as ever, Mildred Washington opened the front door and gathered her wrinkled face into one of her familiar huge smiles. Stevie ran the rest of the way up the walk to give her a big hug, careful not to knock the old woman down as his mother constantly reminded him.

"Mrs. Washington, what are you doing here? I thought you lived in town."

"I do, my precious boy, I do. But my son and daughter-in-law live here, so when I found out you were going to be out today to visit, I asked to tag along, though I certainly won't be joining in the adventure." Mildred looked up over Stevie's head and caught Cathy's mischievous smile.

"Thanks for the cool sneakers, Mrs. Washington." Stevie looked down at the Nike high-tops. He wore them every day, not wanting to take them off even at night for bed. They were so awesome.

"I'm glad you like them, Stevie. It was fun shopping for a pair I thought you would like. Your mom told me your size. My, your feet are already bigger than mine! I think your mom wants you to wear boots today though," she teased, looking over his shoulder at Cathy with a secretive grin.

Mildred remembered the fateful day when Cathy and the baby walked into her office. They were both an answer to a desperate prayer just that morning. God's timing never ceased to amaze her. Cathy was the best counselor for high-risk teen-agers she had ever worked with, and Stevie was the grandchild she never had from her own son. Not that her son and daughter-in-law hadn't tried, they had for years, but nothing worked, and they hadn't wanted to adopt. So, Stevie was her only grandchild and she couldn't have loved him any more than if he were her own flesh and blood. She loved his mother like her own daughter as well.

"Stevie, this is my son, Mr. Washington. He's a wheat farmer and today he's going to prepare the earth for planting this summer's crop. He wants to know if you would like to help him drive the big machine that overturns the soil.

"How about it Stevie, think that would be interesting for you?"

"Sure! I've never done anything like that before, but I've seen it from the highway and it looks fun."

Mr. Washington laughed, "We'll see how much fun it is in about three hours when we break for lunch. Come on, the soil is thawed enough to turn but not wet and muddy."

Stevie quickly changed his shoes and followed the big man out, giving his mom a thumbs up sign on the way out the door.

Cathy relished the thought of three hours catching up with Mildred and Sara. She also thought about the surprise they would take home after Stevie's big day on the farm.

"Would you like some coffee, Cathy? I have some fresh brewed and ready to pour," Sara offered.

"Sure, I already had one cup with Stevie, but another sounds just fine."

Sara ran off to the kitchen, and Cathy reached over to give Mildred a big hug now that Stevie finished monopolizing her. What a great idea, Mildred. Thanks for asking Carl if Stevie could come out today.

Mildred sighed, and wondered at the heartache her son might go through doing the simple chore with a delightful boy, perhaps wishing for one of his own.

"Maybe if Stevie has fun today he could come out more often. I know Carl and Sara would love to have him visit sometimes. I'm sure you could use the break as well."

Cathy disagreed with the break. It seemed between school, work and sports, she didn't see enough of Stevie as it was, but agreed it would be good for everyone involved if Stevie liked coming out here.

The three women looked at the country oak table piled high with homemade deli sandwiches, sliced oranges, a bowl of chips and salsa and an apple pie warm from the oven. Cathy contributed a potato salad from her small cooler, to help with the meal and also to throw Stevie off when they left this morning about their surprise destination.

They wondered where the men were. They left four hours ago to turn the fields, and the lady's tummies were growling despite the earlier coffee break. The hours had flown by as they talked about upcoming summer plans for the Salvation Army's new outreach programs and the vacation Cathy and Stevie had planned together.

"Let's give them fifteen more minutes before we start eating or start worrying," Mildred frowned.

"Mom, they're fine, they probably just got involved and lost track of time."

"What about that new-fangled cell phone you got him for Christmas? Couldn't he use that?"

"If he remembered yes, but you know how Carl gets when he sees and smells the freshly turned earth. It's intoxicating to him and every row is a work of art."

Cathy knew Stevie was probably fine, but he meant the world to her. She sighed with relief at the sound of gravel crunching under heavy truck tires a moment later.

"Mom, mom, where are you?" Stevie hollered and ran into the house like an out-of-control puppy. She laughed at his excitement, and said "Hold on buddy, take off your dirty boots and coat, then you can tell me all about it."

Out of breath, cheeks flushed and smelling of the outdoors, the boy was irresistible. She tried to give him a hug. Her heart overflowed with gratitude that he was okay. The wiggling boy would have none of it as he tried to recapture the adventure of it all.

"Mom, the tractor was HUGE, and Mr. Washington let me drive it all by myself! You should see how much we got done. The entire north quad, um, quad, uh, corner, is done and ready for planting, and I did part of it. Mr. Washington said I could come back any time and help plow, plant and harvest if I was interested. Can I Mom, can I please?"

Cathy laughed and gave Mildred and Sara a helpless look, her lifted eyebrows and parted lips conveying the unspoken words that she had just lost her son to farming.

"Well, if Mr. and Mrs. Washington don't mind and you listen and obey their instructions, I suppose that would be okay."

Carl boomed out as he came in the door stomping his feet and shaking off the old flannel shirt, "The boy's welcome anytime Cathy. He was a pleasure to work with and even a bit of help. You've done a good job with him." Carl's ruddy cheeks and bright eyes conveyed his pleasure at Stephen's company that morning.

The men washed up and came to the table. Cathy wasn't surprised at the number of sandwiches Stevie put down before digging into a big piece of the delicious apple pie. He was definitely growing again and soon she would have to take him shopping for more shoes and clothes. It was an expense she didn't mind, unlike car repairs, unexpected visits to the dentist for a lost filling or outrageously high utility bills. Watching Stevie grow was a good thing, but it also meant her time with him as a child was going fast. She dreaded the day he graduated from high school and left for college.

They both decided he would go to college. He knew it was very important to her so he would have more choices in life. She put aside a set amount every month for his college education that they never touched, even when times were rough. So far, school was interesting and fun and college was just an extension of that which he already enjoyed. He wasn't sure what he wanted to do yet, though art and science were his favorite subjects, along with P.E. and recess, of course.

"That was an awesome lunch, Sara. Thank you. Now, if you'll excuse us, Stephen and I have one more thing to do before you go back to the city." Stephen checked with his mom, who smiled and nodded her permission.

Lately, Cathy had been considering getting a dog for Stevie. She knew every boy should have a dog and Stevie had proven himself to be responsible and worthy of having a dog he could call his own. He did his chores and homework without being asked and she often found him helping the neighbors just to be friendly. She remembered this morning's conversation and admitted to herself that he *usually* did his homework.

Mildred called Cathy the night the golden retriever pups were born and asked if Cathy would like one saved for Stevie.

Thinking just for a moment, "Oh, I think the timing is perfect, Mildred! When will they be ready?"

"In about eight weeks once their mother weans them onto solid food." That gave Cathy time to save and plan for another newest family member, along with hurt birds, small reptiles and the goldfish Stevie won at the fair last year.

She bought some lumber and the unsuspecting boy helped her fix the fence and gate. She purchased a used doghouse from the neighbor, a second hand rug and a big bag of puppy chow. She shoved everything in the doghouse and hid it in an unused corner of the garage to wait for the big day.

The three women waited a moment, then quietly took the path to the barn, seeing Carl and Stephen's backs as they stepped through the large double doors.

"He's going to be so excited when he finds out he actually gets to take a puppy home today. It will be the first one to go. We've been waiting to give Stephen the pick of the litter," Sara beamed.

"Thank you so much for giving us a puppy for free. I know they are pedigreed and you can sell them for much more than I can afford."

"Phooey, knowing the puppy will go to a good home is worth more than making money. The pup's mother and father are devoted and gentle dogs and are a part of our family. To keep one of their offspring close by with a good friend guarantees we will get visitation rights. It's purely selfish on our part."

They reached the barn door, and Cathy's heart filled when she saw her beloved son sitting in the middle of eight adorable golden retriever puppies. They were jumping all over him, licking his face, biting his fingers and pulling on his shoelaces. Stevie giggled and laughed.

"Hey, that's my shoe," he said to one, while wiping dog slobber off his nose from the wet kisses of another.

He looked up, grinning at his audience and saw his mom smiling down at him.

"Aren't they cute, Mom? Can we visit them sometimes while they grow up? I can help Mr. Washington train them to be good dogs if you agree!"

Carl looked over to Cathy and she gave him a big smile and nod.

He swallowed and cleared his throat a couple of times while watching Stephen play with the puppies.

Finally, he said, "Stephen, would you like to take one of these puppies home with you for it to be yours forever?"

Stephen gasped, jumped up, puppies falling all over the place and ran to Carl. Giving him a big hug around the waist, he cried, "Really, Mr. Washington, can I?" He jumped up and down, and spun around and around. Then all of the sudden he stopped, and looked down at the ground, very quiet. One of the puppies nibbled at his shoe again, and Stephen picked him up, hugging the little guy tightly and burying his face in the soft fur. He wanted one so bad, but he was afraid to ask his mom. He knew she already had a lot taking care of him by herself and having to buy food for the old cat.

He turned to Mr. Washington and swallowing hard said, "Um, thank you sir, but it's very hard for me and my mom right now, and I think we should wait until I get a job to help pay for the puppy's food, and what if he has to go to the vet? I don't want to make it any harder for my mom."

Cathy was never more proud of her son than at that moment. She took the puppy Stephen had just given back to Carl, and offered it back to her son. "Stevie, I can't begin to tell you how much I love you, and I am so proud of you. God provides Stevie, and I spent much time in prayer about this puppy. I know this is the right decision now for our family. Carl and Sara generously offered the puppy to us for free. You may pick whichever one you want and he or she will go home with us today."

Stephen put the puppy back down and hugged him fiercely, his eyes tightly squeezed shut to keep the tears of joy and excitement from showing. "You are the best mom in the whole world. Thank you, thank you, thank you!" The puppy Stephen put down was still nibbling on his shoelaces, and Stephen said, "I don't think I need to pick one, Mom. This one picked me!" Grabbing the little troublemaker, the puppy licked Stephen's cheeks, nose and chin, making little excited whimpering noises before settling down into Stephen's warm neck for a nap. "I'm going to name you Nate," Stephen said and buried his face in the puppy's soft fur.

All four adults knew they would never forget this day or the special boy that had wrapped himself around their hearts. Cathy quietly left the barn to pull an old blanket out of the large bag she had brought. She laid it over the worn but clean car seat, her heart filled with gratitude. As full as her heart was, she knew something was still missing, but brushed the thought away on this memorable day.

CHAPTER 5
LOVELAND, CO

"OH, THIS math homework is killing me," Tasha groaned. "Why did I sign up for Algebra? Business math would have been fine. A simple percentage problem to determine if I should buy one 24-ounce can or two 12-ounce cans of beans. Who cares about all these x, y's and z's?"

Tasha's mom smiled at the dough she was kneading for dinner rolls. The dough felt good in her hands. Each batch took on a life of its own as the simple ingredients transformed into a pliable and smooth mound, offering comfort in the repetitive task. She looked over at Tasha sitting at the worn kitchen table, her daughter's head all scrunched up in concentration.

"Stop your complaining, Tasha. You know this stuff is easy for you. Perhaps you're just bored with the homework problems, but you know your teacher says it's important to practice until the steps become second nature. That's why the tests are so easy for you. If you really do need help though, you're going to have to go to after school tutoring because neither your father nor I know a thing about Algebra."

"Why am I so good at math, Mom? Is there someone in our family who likes math? You're an amazing artist and dad is a really good mechanic, but neither of you like math. Or science. I love science too, just not the homework part."

Joan stopped kneading the bread, and her face paled as the familiar gut-wrenching fear gripped her belly and threatened to make her run for the bathroom. She forced the words out and hoped her voice didn't quiver. "Why would you say that, honey? I'm sure there's someone in our family who's good at math. In fact, your grandfather loved math, though he never had the opportunity to finish school."

"I guess you're right, maybe I did get math genes from Grandpa. He's very good at figuring out the prices he'll get for his corn crops every year, and he budgets wisely to have enough to replant and for their living expenses. Their life is so hard, Mom. Why does Grandpa continue to farm?"

Joan breathed a sigh of relief that the subject had changed. "It's the only way of life they know, honey. If you took Grandpa's farm away from him and forced him to move into the city, he would be lost. Grandma too. They love wide, open spaces, their old farmhouse, the feel of fresh turned soil in their hands and the summer rains that nourish their crops. I don't know what we'll do if their health fails and they can't farm anymore."

"I'll help them when I'm done with school, Mom. Don't worry."

Joan knew Tasha would have her own life with college and a career, but she didn't disagree with her daughter. Let her have her dreams and ideology. Youth is fleeting and lasts only for a short while.

"Thank you Tasha, but we want you to go to college first, then you can save the world. Okay?"

"Sure Mom, unless I'm needed sooner." She turned back to the math homework she both loved and hated. She wanted to finish it so she could read before dinner. Last night it was hard to turn the light off after finishing a chapter in her latest novel, but she knew it would be hard to get up, let alone pay attention in class if she didn't get enough sleep.

The tree house and beanbag chair were patiently waiting for her to finish her homework before she could sink into their secluded comfort. Sometimes her parents worried she didn't get out enough, spend time with friends or at least talk for hours on the telephone as other girls her age did, but Tasha was content with her family, music, photography and books. Other girls her age seemed so immature and only interested in boys, especially popular boys. She would love to tape their conversations and play them back so they could hear how silly they sounded. She didn't want to hurt their feelings, so she kept her thoughts to herself.

A few boys had asked her out, and while Tasha was flattered they asked, she wasn't interested. What she didn't know, was that her elusiveness made them even more attracted to her. It was almost like a conquest they had to have. Her innocence and purity were like a moth to flame. The boys wanted what they could not have, and Tasha wasn't even aware of their interest or the whispered comments in the hall as she walked by. Last year when she ran for Student Body Treasurer, she won by a landslide. She had no idea that many people even knew her, much less trusted her with their hard-earned fundraising dollars. So, she just kept on being herself, enjoying the friendliness of her classmates and teachers, but mostly keeping to herself.

She closed the book with a snap. "Finally, that's done for today," she thought. Grabbing her backpack, Tasha carefully placed the book and folder inside before heading to her room. Continuing the conversation with herself, "Hmmm, do I want to read or take some photos before dinner?" It was such a pretty day and very mild for March. They hadn't had much snow this year, and already the little crocuses were blooming in her mom's garden. She grabbed the camera, checked for film and called out, "I'll be at the park across the street for an hour or so, okay Mom?"

"Don't be late. Dinner's early tonight since we have a meeting at church."

"Okay, thanks."

"And, be careful!" Joan called to the already shut door. She frowned. No one told her how much she would worry over this precious person in her life. There were so many reports on the news about abducted children, runaway children, children hurt by drunk drivers and children molested by relatives or teachers. How could she not worry?

"Do not be anxious about anything, but in everything, by prayer and petition, with thanksgiving, present your requests to God. And the peace of God, which transcends all understanding, will guard your hearts and minds in Christ Jesus."[3]

The familiar verse gently eased its way into her thoughts and Joan turned her worry over into prayer.

"Thank you God for helping me to remember. Over and over again. I am weak and you are strong. Please help me not to worry. Protect her God, you know how much she means to me. I love her so much. Help me to remember you love her even more."

Joan turned back to her dinner preparations, humming the familiar and comforting hymn, "Blessed Assurance." The fear that gripped her gut slowly faded, replaced with an assurance that God was in control. She thought about the many mistakes she made in her life and was grateful for a God who loved her anyway.

"Should we tell her Lord? When? I don't know what to do. But you do, God give us guidance. What should we do? You tell me that I should present my requests to you. Well this is a biggie God. You gave her to us, do we get to keep her? Should she know the truth? I'm so scared God. Will she still love me?"

The door slammed and Joan jumped, dropping the bowl of green beans she was snapping for dinner. They flew everywhere, under the table and across the counter, in the open silverware drawer and finally into the sink full of dirty dishes.

"It's just me, Joan. Why are you so jumpy, Hon?" Tom leaned down to help her pick up the beans off the floor, thinking that during their 17 years of marriage, this was a first.

They were both on their hands and knees under the table when he saw the tears in her eyes. He reached over and gently touched her arm, his fingers stroking little circles around and around on her soft flesh.

"Want to talk about it?" He loved this woman so much. Any hurt Joan was going through was his hurt too.

She nodded, "Tom, I think it's time."

"Time for what Joan? What are you talking about?"

She looked up into his concerned eyes. He looked blurry from her tears and his face wavered in front of her. She replied, "I think it's time to tell Tasha before she finds out from somewhere else."

"How would she find out? She's still a kid!"

"Have you looked at her lately, Tom? She's a young woman. Before we know it, she'll be leaving for college. What if some unknown stranger comes knocking on the door and tells her we're not her real parents? She deserves to know, but it scares me to death."

"Why does she ever have to know? We're her parents, Joan. We might not have blood ties to her, but who sat up with her every night when she was sick? Who went to all of her piano recitals and cheered the loudest at her swimming meets? Joan, I pulled Tasha's first tooth and you slipped the dollar under her pillow after she fell asleep that night. Do you remember how excited she was that morning when she found out the tooth fairy was real? Who loves her with all of our hearts, so much that we would do anything for her? Even lie if I have to! I will not tell her that you did not birth her and I am not her real father, for I am. I will walk Tasha down the aisle on her wedding day, proud to be her daddy. No one else deserves that honor. And no one else will feel as lost as I will that day when she gives her heart to another man."

"Maybe you're right, Tom. We don't even know who her birth parents are. If they haven't tried to find her yet, maybe they never will. Why borrow trouble?" Joan wiped the back of her hand against her cheeks to wipe the tears away as best she could without a tissue.

At that moment the door quietly closed and they both scrambled out from under the table and looked up at Tasha's questioning gaze.

"I came back for more film."

The silence was deafening as daughter and parents looked at each other. Tasha awkwardly rocked back and forth, her camera grasped tightly in her hand, the empty canister of film in the other. The short minute seemed more like ten. Tasha wasn't sure if she heard correctly and didn't know if she wanted to know the horrible truth that her parents weren't really her parents.

"Oh, God, not this way, please," Joan pleaded. Her wet hand grabbed onto Tom's for dear life.

Tasha turned around and walked out the door without a new roll of film.

Tom and Joan turned to each other, wrapping their arms around one another for a quick but desperate hug.

"She heard, Joan."

"I know she did. I'm so sorry Tom. We've never talked about it at home before, I broke our rule. Please go after her."

"No, she'll be back soon. Let her absorb the news, and when she returns we'll sit down and pray as a family first, and then we'll tell her everything. Maybe it is for the best. Don't blame yourself, Joan." He unwrapped his arms and tipped her chin up gently to face him.

"I love you Joan. Never forget that. No matter what, for forever. Okay?"

Tom attempted a weak smile. "Let's get these green beans picked up so we'll have dinner sometime tonight. I'll call Mike at the church and tell him we can't make it to the meeting."

She nodded at him and went to the sink. It was good to have a task to keep her busy. Her feet longed to run out the door after Tasha, but perhaps Tom was right. This was huge, especially for a 15-year-old girl who had been protected all her life. Joan gathered the beans and washed them along with those Tom had collected. She put them on the stove to simmer and put the dirty dishes into the dishwasher. She set the table, scrubbed the sink, swept and mopped the floor and still Tasha had not returned. Checking the lasagna, she saw it was bubbling nicely, but not yet overdone, so she turned the heat down to warm, wishing she could turn the heat up to warm her cold heart as easily.

Wandering into the living room, she saw Tom on the couch, leaned over in prayer. His open Bible was next to him.

"God, thank you for a husband who believes in you."

She could never imagine trying to live life without this good Christian man. He was a rock, his belief so strong she often wondered if her own was enough compared with his. Yet the Bible talked about faith the size of a mustard seed, and that was mighty small.

Joan walked upstairs to Tasha's room. It was still decorated with tiny pink rosebud wallpaper, white eyelet curtains and a matching bedspread. She offered to update it last year, but Tasha didn't like change and was still happy with the décor. Joan paused at the door as she heard sniffling. She walked into the room and the sound grew louder, but she didn't see Tasha anywhere.

"Tasha? Honey are you in here?"

The sniffling stopped, and she heard hiccups in their place. Joan followed the sound over to the closet door.

"It's me Tasha, may I open the door?"

The hiccups continued, but her daughter didn't answer. Maybe she didn't think she could be heard. Or more likely, she just wasn't ready to talk yet.

Joan felt Tom's arm reach around her waist, and he gently pulled her away from the door.

41

Tom's rich deep voice filled the room, "Tasha, your mom and I want to explain the conversation you overhead in the kitchen a little while ago. When you're ready to come out, we'll be downstairs. We both love you very much, honey. God does too. If you don't want to talk tonight, that's okay, we'll talk about this tomorrow."

Tom led her out of the room, both of them shaking with fear and uncertainty about their daughter's reaction and even more so, what she would do once she knew the truth about her birth parents. They both believed there were no coincidences in this world, and God could use even this for good. At the moment, however, their precious daughter was hurt. She only knew they weren't her birth parents, but not the circumstances of how it came to be. Tasha was mature for her age, yet this would be difficult news for anyone.

Tom squeezed Joan's waist and pulled her into a tight hug once they reached the living room. He could feel her tremors and wished his own weren't so obvious. It was hard being the strong one.

"Shhhh, Joan, shhhh." It reminded him of when he used to make the comforting sound for Tasha when she was tiny and had scraped her knee. It came so naturally for him. He wished God talked audibly to him because right now, he was sure that was the exact sound that God would be making for him.

"Shhhh, Tom. It's okay. I've got everything under control."

He could imagine the words, but what would God's voice sound like? A gentle breeze or roaring thunder? Tom thought tonight it would be a gentle breeze.

"I know you're right here with me God. Please keep our family together and give us all your amazing peace. I'm scared God. I don't want Tasha to leave us."

"She's mine, and I love her even more than you do."

"I know God, but you can see into the future and I can't."

"Trust me."

Tom pulled Joan even closer.

"It's going to be okay, my love. Our hearts are broken for the moment, yet God is in control and he will work this for good."

"What will we tell her?"

Tom paused, looking deep into her eyes, and replied, "The truth."

CHAPTER 6
CHENEY, WASHINGTON

"RUN, STEPHEN, run!" Cathy screamed along with 500 other dedicated Cheney High School Blackhawk football fans. It was very cold outside, and the weather forecast warned the temperature would drop down to the 20's tonight. The gardeners who hadn't put their roses to sleep for the winter might lose them. There had already been several snowstorms, so it was probably too late anyway.

Cathy didn't feel the cold as she jumped up and down watching her son running as fast as his long legs would carry him towards the Blackhawk goal. He caught a perfect pass and the closest defensive player was a good five yards behind him. She saw the white puffs of his breath in the cold air and knew he was giving it his all.

Carl and Sara screamed along with her. They never missed Stephen's activities. The day Cathy took him to their house five years ago was the best day of their lives. They gained a good friend and treated Stephen as their own son. Carl whooped and hollered as Stephen crossed the goal with just 15 seconds left in the game to help the Blackhawks take the lead by four points. The whole crowd cheered wildly, thrilled that the Blackhawks won their homecoming game.

The game ended and someone lit off a few fireworks saved from the Fourth of July to celebrate. Cathy turned to Carl and Sara and invited them over for hot cocoa. She was not quite ready for the evening to end, her heart so full of joy to share. Marcie, the sweet young woman seated on the other side of Cathy was Stephen's good friend from church. Cathy liked her, but had to admit she was relieved they were just friends. Someday, she hoped to have a daughter-in-law just like Marcie, maybe even the young woman herself if the relationship blossomed into more than friendship, just not yet.

Stephen wouldn't be going home after the game; he brought his clothes with him. The dance was informal and located in the gym right here at the high school.

Carl glanced at Sara who nodded yes. They were tired, but knew how much Cathy needed them. In just one more year, Stephen would leave for college and she would be alone. Stephen spent a lot of time at their house since the day he took the adorable puppy home. Nate had grown into a big beautiful dog, completely devoted to the young man.

Three years ago when Cathy took the job as a counselor at Cheney High School, she and Stephen moved in next door. Carl and Sara never used the guesthouse and figured since the small family was over at their house several days a week anyway, it would be nice to have them so close. Leaving the Salvation Army was a difficult decision, but when the job offer came, Cathy's life-long dream to be a high school counselor to help kids like her friend Jenny inspired her to accept it. The opportunity to be near their dear friends clinched the decision.

Cathy just needed to look out her front kitchen window to see Stephen and Carl fixing a tractor or mending a fence to know her beloved son was close by. Nate loved the country setting and ran to his heart's content chasing rabbits and squirrels. Cathy and Sara had quickly become best friends and leaned heavily on each other when Mildred passed on quietly in her sleep last year.

Mildred's passing had finally shown Cathy what she was missing. She now understood the emptiness that never filled regardless of how happy she was. Mildred resonated a peace and serenity that went beyond anything Cathy had ever experienced. Even during poor health and her desire for grandchildren, the peace never wavered and Mildred certainly didn't waste time worrying about things she couldn't change. Mildred tried to explain the love of Jesus Christ, but Cathy never fully understood.

The night Mildred died, Cathy tried again to pray to an unknown and unseen God. The words didn't come and in her anger, she sobbed and shook her fist up at the heavens, staring at the vast expanse of stars, crying out that it wasn't fair.

God responded. It was as real to Cathy as if he was standing right next to her in the cemetery that night.

"No Cathy, life is not fair, yet I still gave up my son for you. I turned away as my son died on the cross for you, so you would know peace, love and forgiveness. Mildred is with me, and she is so very happy, Cathy. Would you deny her that happiness? Will you join her someday when it is time? Or will you turn away from my gift to you and continue to suffer the emptiness?"

Cathy lowered her raised fist, all anger drained from her body as it filled with the indescribable peace that Mildred knew so well.

"Oh God, she cried, I knew of you, but I did not know you. I want to know you more and more. I want the kind of life Mildred had, please show me."

Cathy joined Carl and Sara's church and soon afterward Stephen also accepted Christ after seeing the changes in his mom's life.

Cathy had her church family and her co-workers from the high school, but it wouldn't be the same when Stephen left for college. Eastern Washington State didn't have the photography program he was interested in, and Stephen had set his heart on studying under Professor William Guenther at the University of Colorado.

In time, Cathy would learn how to be comfortable with the quiet, for now however, she needed good friends to keep her company on this exciting night. Carl boisterously reached out and put his massive arms around both women. "Let's go. I'm chilled to the bone and could use a good hot cup of cocoa."

Cathy turned her head and called, "Marcie, have a good time with that son of mine. You're welcome to sleep on our sofa if it gets too late or the roads get icy. I'll call your parents so they know it was my suggestion." She would have given Marcie a gentle hug, but Carl was leading both women away with his firm hold and she had no choice but to follow, laughing at his urgent quest for the hot cocoa with *lots* of marshmallows.

Stephen woke to an icy cold house and moved his curtain aside to peer out the frosty window. Sighing, he knew he would spend part of his Saturday shoveling the walks and driveway … again. Saturdays were still special, but neither one of them felt they had to go somewhere every weekend to have a good time. They liked playing a game of Scrabble or going through old picture albums, after he finished his homework. She never let up on him about that.

Stephen didn't remember a winter with this much snow in a long time. It was really cold this morning. His mom was an early riser and usually had the house warm by the time he got up. Glancing at the clock on his nightstand, Stephen saw it was only 8:00. Maybe she stayed up late after the game last night and was sleeping in today.

He got out of bed, dressing quickly in flannel-lined jeans, a turtle neck and a wool sweater Sara had knitted him last Christmas. His feet were still freezing, even on the rug covering the hardwood floors next to his bed. He braved the bare floor, pulled thick socks out of his dresser and put them on. He wasn't ready for the heavy boots yet, choosing to delay the shoveling until after breakfast.

He had fun with Marcie last night, glowing in the recognition from his friends about the winning touchdown. Everyone liked him, though he chose not to hang out with any one crowd. The jocks thought too much of themselves, the nerds played chess *every* day at lunch, and he definitely didn't want to be part of the heads who hung out in the smoking area and ruined their bodies.

Stephen remembered the way Marcie felt in his arms during the slow dance. She was so soft and willowy, her hair smelled of spring flowers and sunshine. He could easily ask her to go steady with him. Did he want that right now? What if she chose someone else while he waited?

No, he saw too many of his friends get involved with a girl, then the relationship turned to sex and then neither of them were happy once the excitement wore off.

A few years ago both Stephen and Marcie had promised along with their peers during a Saturday night small group that they would remain pure until marriage. They knew the risks of dating and chose not to put themselves in tempting situations. Group dating was fine, but to be alone with one another was just asking for trouble.

So, last night he showed Marcie to the sofa, softly said good night and thanked her for a wonderful evening. She looked so cozy cuddled under the down comforter his mom left there. He firmly turned away and uttered a prayer to God asking him to give them the strength necessary to resist the temptation he knew they both were feeling.

The phone startled him and brought Stephen back to the reality of a cold morning and work to do. He quickly walked to the kitchen and picked it up.

"Hello?"

"Stephen?" a deep and serious voice questioned on the other end of the line.

"Yes, who is this?"

"Stephen, I want you to go over to Carl's house right now, and I'll call you back, okay? Just do as I say, Son."

"Who is this, and why am I supposed to go to Carl's house. I'll go get my mom, just a sec."

"No, Stephen, hang up the phone and go right over to Carl and Sara's then I'll call you back in five minutes. Now, Stephen."

The slightly familiar but still unknown voice on the other end of the phone gave Stephen no choice. For some reason, he felt compelled to obey the unusual instructions just as the man ordered him to do.

"Okay, I'll go right now sir."

The voice gently said, "Stephen, I'll call you in five minutes." The line went dead.

Stephen felt a deep consuming pit in his stomach indicating something was seriously wrong. He glanced at the couch and noticed Marcie was gone. His mom's bedroom door was open and her bed was empty as well. The gnawing feeling grew deeper and he knew something terrible must have happened. As he rushed to grab his coat and boots from the hall closet, he saw a note on the coffee table.

Stephen,

Marcie asked me to take her home early this morning. She's doing some Christmas shopping today. I think she wants to be alone with me so she can find out what you want. I'll probably be back before you wake up. That was a great game last night Stevie, congrats!!!

I love you to the moon and back!

Stephen opened the front door and was surprised at how much snow had actually fallen during the night. They had a new all-wheel drive Subaru Outback with studded snow tires, but he still worried about his mom on the road with Marcie. He was sure that was what the phone call was about.

Was his mom stuck somewhere? Did something happen? He started running to Carl and Sara's house, not 50 yards away, less than the distance he ran last night for the winning touchdown. Frustrated because the snow was so deep, he had to work hard to plow through it, stumbling every few steps. He couldn't miss that phone call. Tears came to his eyes and stung his cheeks, not entirely just from the cold. His lungs burned from the frigid air, and his legs ached. Finally, he was at Sara's door. She opened it and gave him a hug, tears in her own eyes and he could tell she was trying not to cry.

What was wrong? Carl was on the phone, his face gray and drawn. His back and shoulders, normally so strong, stooped over as if a heavy weight were upon them. He heard Carl say, "Yes, Officer, we'll be here. No, we won't go anywhere."

Carl hung up the phone, but didn't immediately turn toward Sara and Stephen. He softly said, "Close the door Sara. It's awfully cold outside."

Sara let go of Stephen and turned to close the door. Neither of them noticed it was open as they listened to Carl on the phone.

"Carl?" Stephen's voice wavered. He had never seen Carl look so haggard. He had aged into an old man since last night.

Carl turned to Stephen, took a big breath and held out his arms.

Stephen couldn't move. His mind and feet refused to obey.

"Carl? Who was that on the phone? Someone called me and told me to come over here. Who was it Carl? Does it have something to do with my mom and Marcie? Marcie spent the night at my house because of the snow, and Mom took her home this morning. Carl?"

Sara was now sobbing openly, her hand resting on Stephen's shoulder whether to give support or receive it he couldn't tell.

"Let's go sit down, Stephen and I'll tell you about the phone call."

"No! Tell me."

Carl took a deep breath, and dropped into the old rocking chair next to the phone.

Anguished eyes glistening with unshed tears, he looked up at Stephen and began, "Your mother and Marcie were in a car accident about two hours ago. They found the car half buried in a ditch off Highway 90."

His voice trembled as he went on with the inconceivable news, "I'm so terribly sorry Stephen. Neither your mom nor Marcie made it." Carl choked as he tried to continue. "The police think they were hit by a drunk driver." The words tasted bitter on his tongue, and he forced them out.

"They found a man asleep in his car at the Shell station at the next exit. The whole front of his car is smashed and there are several empty bottles of booze in the passenger seat. He has cuts and abrasions on his forehead from when he apparently hit the windshield. A preliminary investigation shows maroon paint from your mom's car on his front bumper."

Carl shakily stood up and slowly walked over to Stephen. He reached out to hold him tight, to support and show his love. This young man meant the world to him, and he would have gladly exchanged places with Cathy. Stephen would still have his mom with him right now, enjoying a cup of coffee over breakfast and recounting the game last night.

Stephen felt the big strong arms wrap around him from the front. A second pair of smaller softer arms embraced him from behind. He felt empty and void, and so very cold. The voices were distant and he knew the words were reassuring but his brain could not comprehend what they were saying.

His mom and Marcie, surely they were still asleep, warm and snuggled in their beds. He wanted to run home with a fist full of snow and sprinkle it on their faces to wake them up, laughing at their reaction and teasing about what sleepyheads they were. They would share a cup of coffee and warm fragrant cinnamon rolls, his mom's favorite Saturday morning breakfast. Marcie would look beautiful with her tousled hair and flushed cheeks.

A rush of cold air, and another voice penetrated his daydream.

"I'm Officer Perry of the Washington State Highway Patrol. Thank you for agreeing to have Stephen come to your home. I got your number from an emergency phone list from Cathy's glove box, along with her home phone number and son's name."

In a distant fog, Stephen heard Carl reply, "Yes Officer, this is Stephen, Cathy's son. Thank you for asking him to come over ...."

Stephen broke free of the embrace and struggled to bring himself into the present. He stepped toward the police officer and the words came out in a rush.

"You've just come from the car? Are you sure my mom's gone? Are you sure? Is she at the hospital? I need to go to the hospital now, to see her. Marcie too, she was with my mom." He grabbed the police officer's arm and started pulling him towards the door.

"Stephen, stop! We are not going to the hospital, not right now anyway." Officer Perry commanded and shook his arm free of the young man's strong grip and forced himself to use a calm voice.

"I'm sorry, son. She was dead when I arrived at the scene. The young woman with her died too. The car is a mess, and it's extremely cold outside. They didn't have a chance." The officer recalled the gruesome scene and tried to force it from his mind.

"Where is she then? Is she still in the car?" Stephen cried, thinking of how cold it was outside. He didn't want his mom to be cold.

"No, Son, she's not in the car anymore. An ambulance took her and your friend to the hospital, but they are downstairs, in the uh, the morgue."

Carl gave the officer an angry glare, knowing Stephen didn't need to hear that terrible word right now, but he was surprised at the youth's strength.

"I want to see her, I want to see Marcie. Right now. I need to see them."

Officer Perry looked over Stephen's shoulder at Carl, who sighed and nodded his approval.

"Okay, Stephen, I'll take you there. Would you like Carl and Sara to go with us?"

Stephen turned around and looked at his dear friends, more like a beloved aunt and uncle.

The young man's face was drawn and pale, though no tears fell from his vacant eyes, "Yes, please, I need them to be with me."

The ride to the hospital was filled with silence, except for the crunching of chains on snow-covered roads. It took almost an hour to get there, though no one noticed the time. Snow was falling again, soft and quiet, gray and cold, just like Stephen's heart. His heart didn't feel soft. It felt hard as stone and impenetrable, incredible pain locked inside, ironically similar to the steel separating them from Officer Perry in the front seat of the patrol car. Carl and Sara were on either side of him, gripping his hands, but his own lay on the seat, refusing to return their comforting hold.

When the car finally stopped, they all sat for a moment. Officer Perry watched them in his rearview mirror. Carl and Sara sat with their heads bowed, lips moving silently and he knew they were praying. He hoped it did them some good. He'd seen too many horrible things to believe in a God who could let innocent people suffer like this. Let them have their faith if that is what they needed. Just don't expect him to buy into the whole delusion.

Stephen on the other hand, looked straight ahead, seeing nothing, yet everything. He could tell the young man knew exactly what he would find in a few minutes as he gazed upon his mangled mother and girlfriend. Once again, the officer shook his head at the unseen God so many believed in. Maybe it was time for a new career. He announced the sporting events for the local high schools. In fact, he announced the football game last night when Stephen scored the winning touchdown. Perhaps coaching, it would be worth the pay cut.

He felt the young man's eyes upon him, questioning.

"Are you ready?" he replied in answer to the unspoken question.

"No, but I never will be. Let's go in," Stephen replied resolutely.

Carl and Sara raised their heads and let go of Stephen's hands. They zipped their coats and drew on gloves before stepping out into the frigid, dismal day. The walk to the hospital was shoveled earlier, but it was already covered with more than an inch of new snow. Officer Perry moved quickly ahead to open the doors for them. The antiseptic smell almost choked Stephen but he continued to follow the others. When they got to the elevator, the officer pushed the down arrow. Stephen had never been down, only up to visit friends recovering from a broken bone or with his mom to visit a family with a new baby. Down was bad, he could feel it.

When the elevator doors opened, Stephen was relieved he had his coat on. It was cold in the basement. He thought again of his mom and how cold she must be. Did she remember to put on her coat and gloves before leaving the house?

The officer and receptionist talked in hushed voices as he signed a log to record their visit. B13 and B14 please, the receptionist softly called to the medical attendant inside the morgue.

He pulled out two long drawers with white sheets covering the bodies. It reminded Stephen of when he was younger and wanted to hide from his mom at bedtime.

He would stuff his bears and other animals under the covers, then when she came to tuck him in he would jump out from the closet door and grab her from behind. She always acted shocked and surprised, but looking back, he knew she played along with his trickery.

His attention was drawn back to the white sheets. The attendant drew down the sheets to uncover their faces. His feet moved of their own accord toward the bodies. That's what they were, just bodies. His mom and Marcie weren't in there. It was too cold and they were still and lifeless. He felt separate from his body, as if he was floating and could not turn back because he had no control over his feet.

Looking down first at Marcie, there was just a small cut above her right eyebrow. The rest of her looked perfect. He leaned down and kissed the cut, as if to make it all better. Her hair was tumbled just as he pictured it in his daydream. But her cheeks were not flushed. They were white and somewhat translucent. The kiss was cold and her skin didn't feel like Marcie should feel at all. He thought it ironic that was the first time he kissed her. He wished he had told her how he really felt while he still could. To kiss her warm soft lips and have hers respond to his. He knew it was too soon though. Neither of them were ready, and the temptation would have been too great. He was glad she had gone to heaven with no regrets as a result of their impetuousness, but angry at the same time at what they lost.

Stepping back, he took one last look at what was to never be, his heart filled with an anger and ache that hurt so bad, he thought it might break in half. "Do people die from a broken heart," he wondered? Surely if it was possible, his life would soon be over. The pain was excruciating.

Stephen turned and walked over to the other drawer. His mom didn't look so good. She had abrasions all over the left side of her face and her cheekbone looked too flat. He could tell she hadn't showered that morning because her hair wasn't styled. He figured she left to take Marcie home right after she got out of bed, stuffing her hair into a stocking cap before rushing out the door.

He sunk to his knees on the cold hard floor and laid his head on her chest. The tears finally came and he knew she was gone to him forever. She was his life and he hers. They were a team. His mom was his best friend and confidant. There was nothing he couldn't tell her, and she never judged, just listened and gave advice when he asked.

Stephen groaned, "Oh Mom, how will I live without you?" At that moment he didn't want to go on living. Why? What was there to live for? He sobbed, soaking the sheet with grief from the depths of his soul. She couldn't hold him ever again. Her arms laid still beside her body, cold and lifeless. He regretted every time she tried to hug him and he shrugged it off, thinking he was too big for her hugs anymore. He ached for one more hug. Just one. "Please God, one more hug, one more smile." She was so very cold, and there was no answer.

He didn't know how long he lay there, but eventually he felt the warmth of Carl and Sara sitting on the floor beside him. They were sobbing too, and he tore his arms away from his mom and held them close as they held him. He laid his head on Sara's warm chest, hearing her sobs and the strong beat of her living heart. It felt good to lean on Carl's strength for without it, surely he would collapse. There were no words, only three grieving people holding onto one another for dear life. A fourth pair of unseen arms circled them all, willing them to turn to him for their strength and comfort.

CHAPTER 7
LOVELAND, CO

TASHA WOKE up cold and with a stiff neck. It was very dark. Where was she? She felt around her and found shoes. The memories came rushing back. She was adopted. She was in her closet. What time was it? Reaching for the doorknob, she opened the door and found her bedroom dark as well. Her clock showed it was 3:03 a.m. Tasha's eyes burned and her throat hurt from crying. She had to go to the bathroom and her stomach growled from missing dinner. Well, at least she was still hungry. That was a positive sign. From her Psychology class, she learned that lack of hunger was a sign of depression. Tasha stretched her legs and waited a moment for the stiffness to ease before standing up and walking over to turn on the small light next to her bed. Despite her need to go to the bathroom, she sat down on the edge of her bed and lowered her head into her hands. *"Why, God? Why this? Why me?"*

"Amy, Sarah, Justin, Mark."

The names of her friends from school and church filled her mind. Tasha thought for a moment. It dawned on her that all four were adopted. And all four were happy and loved their parents. Amy and Justin actually had relationships with their birth parents, though Sarah and Mark didn't know who their birth parents were. Tasha hadn't given it much thought before that they were adopted. They were just normal kids that she did stuff with. They didn't make a big deal about it. So why did it bother her so much now that she was adopted?

"Give it time."

The gentle words came to her again. She wasn't used to hearing God's voice, and she wasn't even sure the words came from God. Who else would be putting thoughts in her head at 3:03 in the morning? Sounds of running water came from down the hall and Tasha longed to be held by her dad and mom. It was a strange mixture of anger, disappointment, curiosity and love that drove her down the hall to find them. She used the bathroom and then wandered into their room. The light was on, but neither her mom nor dad were in bed, so she went downstairs. They were sitting very close to one another, their heads bowed in prayer. She could hear her dad's gentle voice and knew that no matter the circumstances of her birth, these were her "real" parents.

"God, help me to keep an open mind and listen to what they have to say."

Tasha quietly walked over to where her parents were praying. They were so intent in the prayer, they didn't notice she stood right next to them. Tasha dropped to her knees and gently touched them. They both reached over and encircled her in their arms, but the prayer continued. God always came first in their family, no matter what the circumstances, and her father would finish his conversation with God before it was time to talk to her.

"Finally Father, I thank you for my family. I place them in your loving hands. Your will be done, please help me to accept that, Lord."

Not quite ready to talk about ... the adoption ... Tasha gave both her parents a hug and before anyone could speak, she stated in her most matter of fact voice, "I'm hungry."

It was just what they all needed. Everyone laughed, and Tasha's mom asked, "Well, what sounds good? I don't know that I've ever cooked a meal in the middle of the night, so I guess we can have breakfast, lunch or dinner!"

"Pancakes." Tasha and her dad both replied at the same time.

They all started laughing again.

"Okay, pancakes it is, coming right up. That was an easy request."

"Joan, we'll help, come on Tasha." Her dad pulled her up and playfully shoved her into the kitchen. They worked on the meal together, laughing and recalling special memories. The simple task was soothing and comforting for all three of them and a sweet peace filled their souls. It was just what they needed, all the while knowing an enormous white elephant sat in the corner. Eventually it would have to be acknowledged and discussed.

When the small family finally sat down to eat, it was to a feast. Each had to have their favorite toppings for the tall stack of golden brown pancakes. Tasha cut up fresh strawberries she found in the fridge and made a sweet cream cheese sauce with lemon, milk and powdered sugar. Her dad had to have roasted chopped pecans to sprinkle over his with real butter, pecan syrup and whipped cream. Tasha's mom added a bowl of sliced bananas, vanilla yogurt and brown sugar. They made big steaming mugs of hot chocolate using cocoa, sugar, whole milk, vanilla and a hint of cinnamon. Tasha made quite a production out of putting just the right amount of whipped cream on the cups of cocoa, and just the right amount on each of her parent's noses.

"You'll pay for that young lady," her dad growled in his best bear voice.

Anticipating the worst, Tasha squealed and ran to hide behind her mom, knowing from years of experience, it wouldn't do any good. In fact, sometimes her mom would actually help with the tickle torture, tying her shoes together, or another silly game they made up. Of course, Tasha would never admit these were some of the best times of her life.

She was getting too big for the tickle torture, but definitely not for a good dose of whipped cream on her own nose, cheeks and forehead.

The bear laughed, "There, now we're even, let's sit down and pray for this feast."

When they sat down and looked at each other, all with whipped cream on their faces, they burst out laughing again.

"Ok family, let's get serious. Let's do the easy one, all together."

"God is great, God is good, let us thank Hi …"

"Joan! Stop giggling. How can we praise God if you are giggling?" Tom said in his most stern voice while chuckling himself. "Try again."

"God is great, God is good, let us thank him for our whipped cream…"

"Tasha! You're worse than your mother. This is serious business." His chuckling was dangerously close to becoming a full out belly laugh. "Okay, let's get it right this time."

"God is great, God is good, let us thank him for our food. Amen."

"Finally. Now let's eat, and please try to not mess up your masterfully decorated noses."

"Tom, I don't think I can eat with this big blob of white in front of me," Joan whined. "What if it falls into my pancake bite? It would ruin the whole yogurt, banana, and brown sugar flavor."

"Okay, fine, let me help you. He leaned over and licked the whipped cream off the tip of her nose, and she happily returned the favor for him."

"Oh, no you don't," Tasha yelled as they both leaned over toward her. "That's disgusting!" She quickly swiped the whipped cream from her face and licked her own fingers with the treat.

They laughed again, and then hungrily tackled their middle of the night pancake feast. This would definitely be a night to remember and someday tell the grandchildren. After the dishes were loaded in the dishwasher, Tasha gave her parents a big hug, and asked, "We'll talk in the morning, okay?"

"Hon, it is morning now. Are you sure you want to wait?" Tasha's mom asked.

"I'm sure, let's just be like we are now for one more day, okay?"

Her parents nodded and pulled her into a fierce family hug. Reluctant to let go of one another, they all held hands and made choo-choo train noises while going up the stairs, remembering how the activity helped Tasha go to bed when she was five and afraid of the dark. Tasha climbed into bed, and her parents tucked her in saying one last prayer of the day before tiredly going to their own room, hoping for some restful sleep. Tomorrow would be one of the most difficult days of their lives.

By the time Tasha awoke, the sun was high in the sky and her stomach was telling her it was time to eat again. She smiled as she remembered the middle of the night pancake breakfast, but flutters soon filled her stomach as she knew today would forever change her life. She was tempted to roll over, cover her head with a pillow and stay in bed, except she knew that wouldn't solve anything. Her parents had taught her from the time she was very young to face her conflicts head on and to resolve them as soon as possible. Groaning, she rolled out of bed, pulled on a pair of sweat pants and an old t-shirt before tearing a brush through her hair and gathering the thick mane into a ponytail.

Her parents were waiting at the kitchen table, their expressions hopeful and anxious at the same time.

"It's okay, I promise to love you no matter what you say. I just want to know how I came to be adopted and anything you know about my birth parents," Tasha stated in a no-nonsense voice. She walked over to the coffee pot to pour a steaming, fragrant cup of the brew and grabbed a piece of sourdough bread, dropping it into the toaster. While she waited, no one said a word and Tasha hated it. The silence was deafening and uncomfortable. After an eternity, the toast popped up, not quite brown of course, so she pushed it down again for another long minute. She popped it up, noticing it was a little too brown this time, but not bad enough to start over. After a quick smear of crunchy peanut butter, Tasha sat down at the table, took a bite, and looked up expectantly at her parents.

"Shoot."

"God give me strength, please," her mom whispered.

"I'll tell her Joan. Please continue to pray?" Tom asked his dear wife.

She nodded and grabbed a tissue from the box Tasha just now noticed on the table.

"When your mom and I first got married, we desperately wanted a baby. We didn't wait like most couples do nowadays. Right away we started trying. After six months, your mom was pregnant with our first child."

"I have a brother or sister?" Tasha exclaimed.

"Let me finish before you ask questions. Okay honey?"

Tasha nodded in affirmation, but her dad could see the questions in her eyes.

"When your mom was four months pregnant, she had a miscarriage. We were devastated. Folks told us it wasn't really a baby yet, but we knew different. He was very small, but the baby was a complete person, a little boy ...." Her dad stopped at the memory as he struggled to regain control of his emotions.

"We named him Michael and buried him in a tiny casket the next day in the town cemetery. Someday we'll be buried next to him. We grieved deeply for our lost baby and were scared to try again. It took about a year, but we were ready to ask God for another baby. The doctor said the chances of us having another miscarriage were slim, but of course we still worried."

Joan grabbed another tissue as the silent tears coursed down her cheeks. Tasha could see this was very difficult for them to talk about. She reached over, held her mom's hand and waited patiently for her dad to continue.

"This time it only took two months before we realized your mom was pregnant again. She took it easy, not lifting anything heavy and taking a nap every day along with a good night's sleep and a healthy diet. Before we knew it, we could feel the baby kicking and doing somersaults in her womb. Sometimes the baby even got hiccups. The heartbeat was strong and we were encouraged as the months went by, each meaning the baby was growing bigger and stronger. We had so many plans. After six months we felt confident enough to set up a nursery and buy all the things a baby needs."

He paused again, and Tasha could see the pain in her father's eyes, but he continued.

"Your mom was very concerned because just a few weeks before our due date she couldn't feel the baby move. We went to the doctor, and they couldn't find a heartbeat, so they induced labor. Your sister Michelle was born, after your mom labored for fourteen hours, but she never took a first breath. Michelle was perfect in every way, and your mom and I rejoice that Michelle is with Jesus today. We held her sweet little body and said goodbye. Yet our arms ached with the emptiness of having a baby but not ever being able to hold her. We never got to see what color her eyes were, but she had beautiful brown curly hair, just like your mom."

Tom looked over at Joan and her heart broke when she saw the anguished look on his face.

"Do you want me to continue?" She asked. He gave her hand a squeeze and nodded yes.

"Your father and I were both so distressed. How could God take another baby from us? We didn't understand then and we still don't understand today. He healed people in the Bible, why couldn't he make our baby live? We questioned and questioned, and finally accepted God's plan in our lives."

"Remember, Tasha, that God always has a plan. We might not know it immediately, but He always has a plan. That night in the hospital, my breasts hurt and my womb was still contracting, trying to cleanse itself of little Michelle's home for the past eight months. I was in so much pain, both physically and emotionally. My heart was crushed, and it felt like it was broken in thousands of jagged fragments. I didn't know how I would survive."

"Yet, in spite of my grief, I could hear the screams of a woman in labor in the room next to me. The nurse encouraged the woman to push, but she continued to scream and begged the doctor to give her more drugs. He refused, saying it was too late. It seemed like her labor went on forever, and soon the screams stopped and I heard only her whimpers. As the hours went on, the nurse became more urgent and desperately urged the woman to push. The doctor came back in, there was more yelling, and finally complete silence. It was torture not knowing if the mother or baby survived the ordeal."

Joan looked over and found Tasha totally engrossed in their story. She noticed Tom had his emotions back in control and she motioned for him to continue.

"The next day I got a call from the hospital. I was so scared something had happened to your mother, but the kind voice on the other end of the phone said she was fine, and that I needed to come immediately. I was just on my way to visit your mom, of course wondering what was going on. When I reached the maternity ward, the doctor and an administrator were waiting for me. 'Follow me' they said, so I went to a small quiet room with them, wondering what this was all about. The walls were painted sky blue and there were tropical fish pictures. It had a floral scent, gardenias perhaps. The aroma was definitely unlike the medical smells in the rooms and hallways. I will always remember what that room looked and smelled like."

The doctor looked at me with great compassion and said, "I am so sorry about your baby. We don't know why she died, and if you like, we can perform an autopsy. When you are ready, if you want to try again, we'll monitor your wife even more carefully. We can sew her cervix shut until it is time for the baby to be born. We've had great success with that procedure. We can talk about options later, but that's not why I called you here today."

"I waited while he gathered his thoughts and continued."

"Perhaps you recall the woman laboring in the room next to yours yesterday? She had a rather long and difficult labor. Her great effort produced a beautiful little girl. Both mother and daughter are fine, however, the baby's head had already come out, but her body refused to follow, and the woman was too weak to continue pushing. I did what I had to do to save them. I reached inside her and broke the baby's collarbone. It will take a few weeks for the baby's collarbone to heal, but other than that she's completely healthy."

Tasha's dad looked up at her, "I couldn't figure out what this had to do with us. Why was the doctor telling us about another baby who had lived when ours had died?"

The doctor gravely continued, "The woman doesn't want her baby. She overheard that your baby was stillborn, and she wants to give you her baby. In fact, she wants nothing to do with her baby. The woman refuses to even look at the child. She said if you don't want her, to call the closest adoption agency and get rid of it. The mother leaves the hospital this afternoon and doesn't want to be contacted again, and she's not taking her baby with her. She's already signed the necessary papers releasing her custodial rights for the child."

Tasha felt the slight bump in her collarbone and whispered, "Am I the child?"

Her dad paused, then looked deep into Tasha's eyes and said, "Yes, Tasha, you are that child."

"I left the tropical fish room and went to talk with your mother. As soon as she heard about you, she rang the buzzer next to her bed, not even asking my opinion or what I thought we should do. The doctor entered the room, and your mom said, 'Please bring us our baby.' I've never seen our doctor's face light up so brightly since that moment. In this case, bad plus bad turned out to be good."

"Tasha, if we haven't said it enough before, please know now, that was the best day of our lives. Daughter, you have brought only joy to us. We love you as much or more than if you were of our own flesh and blood. We are family at home, family in law and family in Christ. You are first and foremost Christ's Tasha and then ours. We love you with our entire beings. Please always remember that."

Tom looked over at his precious daughter and saw nothing. No acceptance, no grieving or anger. Nothing. What was she thinking?

"Oh Lord, should we have told her the truth?"

Tom continued, "I sat down in a chair in the corner, and a nurse brought you to us, Tasha. Your mom reached out her empty arms and you filled them. I looked at her and saw a love so big and so bright it could only have been from God. She immediately offered you her full and swollen breast and you eagerly sucked the life-giving nutrients. Your soft downy golden curls brushed against her arm and I longed to reach out to you, but I was afraid, and you had a broken bone. You were so tiny. Then I noticed how your little body snuggled into my beautiful wife, flesh-to-flesh, heart-to-heart, and at that moment you became ours. Of course, we miss Michael and Michelle, but we never got to know them like we know you. You are the love of our lives Tasha. God gave you to us and us to you. We are a family. It doesn't matter that we don't share the same DNA. You are ours, forever."

Joan sniffed, and Tom reached over to grab her hand. "We only have a little bit more to tell you baby." Joan said.

"While I was nursing you, your birth mother came to our doorway. I invited her in, but she refused to enter. She was rough looking. There were tattoos on her neck and upper arms and her dirty hair was bleached an unnaturally bright shade of blond. She had a nice smile, but I couldn't help but notice she was missing a few teeth on the right side of her face, and she had a dark purple bruise on her cheekbone. She lifted a shaking hand to her forehead and brushed her hair aside. Tears welled up in her eyes, and then all she said was, 'Thanks for taking the kid. Name her Tasha, will you?' Then she turned and left. That was the last we have ever seen of her. There's been no contact since on either of our parts. We were afraid at first that she would come back to get you. Your first birthday was the hardest, we were so afraid. She never came for you, and to be honest, both your father and I are grateful. The signed adoption papers in our safe are legal proof that you are our daughter."

Tasha still sat unmoving and her father and mother anxiously waited for a reaction, any kind of reaction from her. Did she still love them? Would she try to find her birth mother?

In a very small, unsure voice, Tasha asked, "What about my birth father? Do you know who he is?"

Both Tom and Joan shook their heads no. "I'm sorry baby, that's all we know. We were never told the father's name."

Tasha slid her chair back from the table and stood, "Will one of you take me to church, please?" She ran out the kitchen door to the garage, not even noticing that she was barefoot.

Tom jumped up, "I'll take her, sweetheart."

"No, we'll go as a family," Joan replied. "While you get the car keys, I'll quickly call the pastor to let him know we're coming."

"Actually Joan, I think perhaps the new youth pastor would be better for Tasha to talk to if she feels like it."

"Okay, I'll tell the pastor what happened and ask him what he thinks is best," she said while walking quickly to the kitchen to make the call.

Tasha was already sitting in the back seat of the car when her parents joined her. They considered it a good sign that she wanted to go to the church. Tom and Joan's prayer for years was that Tasha would come to the realization that her strength came from God, not the world. Maybe this horrible day would bring their daughter closer to the Almighty. If that were the case, then all this pain would be worth it.

Chapter 8
Boulder, CO

"**OH MY,** what a way to find out you were adopted." Winnie whispered.

Winnie was a zealous advocate for adoption, especially for young unwed mothers who found themselves in a difficult situation. She spent a fair amount of time at the local pregnancy crisis-counseling center, and adoption was a great option for some of these cases. Winnie thought of the many loving couples who could not have children of their own. Their tears of joy when their son or daughter was placed in their arms for the first time filled her own heart with happiness every time. Of course, it devastated most young mothers who gave their babies away. Their breasts were full and tender and their arms devoid of a new little life. They desperately clutched a pillow or resolutely stared out the window to keep from running after the baby most would never see again.

"God forgives sin, but that doesn't mean there won't be consequences for the wrongdoing," Winnie thought. She remembered the many times she experienced pain and heartache for her own moments of weakness.

Winnie reached over and gently placed her hand on top of Tasha's. Her hand looked wrinkled and veined over the younger woman's smooth skin. However, Winnie wouldn't trade places with Tasha for a minute. She was ready to meet her Savior, but it was obvious he wasn't done with her yet on this earth.

"Is Tasha why you haven't taken me home yet, Lord?"

Tasha had grown quiet. Winnie didn't mind quiet. Far too much noise filled the world in her opinion. How was one to pray and listen to God, much less just daydream with constant racket filling homes, businesses and even churches? Winnie felt a warm breeze on her skin and enjoyed the delicate fragrance of roses it brought to her senses. Birds chirped to one another and the children next door laughed over some silly game they made up. Yes, Winnie was content in her mature years. If God wasn't ready for her to go home yet, at least he made her life here very pleasant and fulfilling.

She squeezed Tasha's hand and got up with more energy than most women half her age.

"I'm going to get us another cup of coffee, dear. I'll be right back."

Tasha smiled up at her hostess in appreciation, ready for a break before she got to the most difficult part of her story. She wasn't sure she could get the words out today. Yet deep inside, Tasha knew this was part of her healing process. She needed to do it. A wave of comfort settled over her and Tasha once again felt God's presence.

"I'm sorry I've been absent for so long, Father. I've missed you."

Tasha vowed to herself that she would make time to read her Bible and pray regularly. She remembered the little church around the corner from her apartment and wondered if she should try it. The people seemed friendly enough. At least she saw them laughing and smiling before and after church every Sunday. She often saw the pastor sitting on the front steps talking with people passing by or tossing a ball with the local neighborhood children. It would be nice to have some friends. Maybe she would meet a girlfriend to go shopping with or have over to watch a good movie and indulge in buttered popcorn and ice cream.

"Here we go. I also found a ripe mango, a wedge of gouda cheese and some lemon bars I had stashed away." Winnie put the tray down and Tasha realized she was hungry. The rich aroma from the coffee made Tasha's mouth water.

"Thank you, Winnie. I didn't realize I was so hungry. That looks wonderful."

"It's way after lunch, dear. You probably haven't eaten since early this morning." Winnie scrunched up her face, "You did eat this morning didn't you?"

"Just a banana. I was in a hurry to get to my appointment."

"You had an appointment this morning?"

"Yes, that's what started this whole deluge of tears, though to be fair, it wasn't his fault."

"Well, eat first, then if you want to talk some more, I would love to listen."

"I've never had mango or gouda cheese before. They're delicious, especially together. Did you make the lemon bars? They're really good too," Tasha raved.

"Mango is a tropical fruit and now that you've had it once, you'll be hooked for life. Gouda cheese is from Holland. It's creamy and has a rich buttery taste, probably because it's so rich and buttery! Don't tell my children. They are way too concerned about my diet. I figure a little bit every once in a while isn't too bad. The lemon bars are from the bake sale yesterday at this little church I attend. Mrs. Rollins made them and she snuck an extra plate in my bag."

"I think I like Mrs. Rollins' cooking. Perhaps I can go to church with you sometime," Tasha grinned. "Let me know when the next bake sale is."

Winnie felt a little tremor of hope flutter in her chest. She would enjoy taking this delightful young woman to church with her. The people were so friendly, and while she wouldn't *intentionally* play matchmaker, there was this incredible young man to whom she would love to introduce Tasha. God could do the rest if he saw fit.

Trying for a relaxed, no pressure voice, Winnie replied, "That would be lovely, Tasha. Just let me know when you're ready and I'll have my son stop by to pick you up on the way. Now, where were we?"

Tasha sobered as the memories came back. Winnie gave her an encouraging smile and a slight nod of her head, and Tasha began the most difficult part of her story.

CHAPTER 9
CHENEY, WASHINGTON

STEPHEN LOOKED around the small home he and his mom shared for the last three years after moving to Cheney. It was home and hard to leave. Sure, he had spent the last six months with Carl and Sara after the accident, but until today he hadn't done anything with their home.

He was grateful for the couple who loved him as their own. Without them, he didn't know how he could have survived the loss of his mom and Marcie. It was still difficult and every day he woke up expecting to hear her cheerful voice.

Prints covered the walls. His mom was his greatest fan, enlarging and framing his photographs from the time he got his first camera. He smiled as he remembered how she gushed over the first roll of film developed soon after a visit to the zoo. "Look Stevie, you captured the elephant cooling off his mate. The stream of water is spraying out of his large trunk like a garden hose gone wild!" That one was on the living room wall along with several photos of Nate, Carl and Sara, and scenic shots from hikes they had taken over the years.

Sara offered to go through his mom's things and give everything without sentimental value to the Salvation Army. That's what she would have wanted. Today Stephen faced the tough task of deciding what he wanted to keep from the house before leaving for college. He had been dreading it for months, and Carl and Sara said it was no rush, he could wait as long as he needed. Stephen knew he needed to do it for himself, and to wait would just postpone the inevitable.

Nate leaned heavily against his leg and whined. Stephen reached down and absentmindedly caressed the silky fur. The dog's tail thumped softly against him in gratitude for the attention. Nate looked up at him with complete devotion in his eyes.

"Oh Nate, what am I going to do without you when I leave?" The dog continued wagging his tail and his ears perked up at his name.

Stephen felt the now familiar deep ache in his chest as one more painful thought entered his mind. He knew Carl and Sara would take good care of the dog. That wasn't the point. He needed Nate and Nate needed him.

Nate was such a comfort since his mom's death. Late at night when he couldn't sleep, the dog would gently climb up on the bed with him, nudging his hands and face until the heart wrenching sobs subsided. Stephen would bury his face in Nate's soft fur and whisper, "Why boy, why would God take them away from me?"

Stephen hadn't been to church or prayed to God since the accident. Would a loving God take his mother and Marcie away from him? He wasn't a toy to play with, to see what happened to the little person's feelings when you take away the loves of his life. No, he had no need for a God like that.

Carl and Sara pleaded with him to pray with them, to go to church, at least acknowledge God's existence. Stephen didn't mean to be disrespectful, but the last time they brought it up several weeks ago, he yelled "Leave it be, I'm not interested," and ran from the room. They hadn't talked to him about God since, and he was relieved. They treated him the same, with love and kindness, yet there was a sadness in them too. He remembered as a young child when his mom wanted to give him medicine for a tummy ache, but he refused because it was too hard to swallow. She knew what was best, but his stubbornness kept him from feeling better.

Stephen sighed and said, "Nate, let's get this over, maybe there's something in here for you too." The dog once again wagged his tail and followed Stephen into his mother's bedroom.

It smelled musty, so Stephen opened the windows letting the fresh spring breeze caress his skin and gently flutter the ecru lace curtains his mom ordered from the Sears catalog. He sat down on the bed, remembering the nights he climbed in after a bad dream, sometimes several nights in a row. Her hugs made him feel so safe, and her soft warmth lulled him back to a dreamless sleep. She always welcomed him with open arms. When he felt too old to climb into her bed, he would bring his comforter and sleep on the floor to be next to her. She hugged him and prayed to God to fill her son's mind with good thoughts of the things he had made and done.

"Like what, drunk drivers? Snowstorms?"

The *driver* of the car was doing 10 to 15 years in a minimum security prison, while he was left forever without his favorite person in the whole world. It left a bitter taste in Stephen's mouth, the taste of hatred and a desire for revenge. He knew it was wrong, but it felt so good. It was incomprehensible who the driver had turned out to be.

Stephen remembered that night as if it was yesterday. When the investigator came to share the police report a few days after the accident, his face was grim, and Stephen knew the news was not good. Carl and Sara sat on either side of him, grasping his hands tightly, though he didn't notice.

"I'm afraid I don't have very good news," the investigator began.

"Would you happen to know a man named Rich Banks?"

Sara gasped and Carl turned white. The grip on Stephen's hands tightened even further.

Stephen had never heard the angry and livid voice from Carl before, cringing at the words spewing from his mouth.

"What does that disgusting man have to do with this? He will NEVER take Stephen from us, he belongs here, not with someone who ran out on his family and hasn't been heard from since. Not over my dead body!" he raged.

"Sir, I agree completely with you. That's not the problem. When we determined who the driver of the car was, I thought this could never happen in a million years. It's just too small of a chance."

"Chance?" Carl growled. "Spit it out man, what are you trying to tell us?"

The officer ignored the obvious disrespect in the unusual circumstances and replied so softly they had to strain to hear him.

"The driver of the car was Cathy's ex-husband and Stephen's birth father."

"No," Stephen moaned. Suddenly he felt sick and tearing himself from Carl and Sara's hands, he ran to the bathroom and threw up. He silently wept and remembered his mother gently wiping his face and helping him brush his teeth when he was sick. Could it get any worse?

Later, Carl filled him in on the details. Rich had celebrated that night after hearing of Stephen's winning touchdown. For the first time in Stephen's life, his father had been on his way to meet the son he never knew but secretly followed as he grew into a man.

"He probably didn't want to pay the child support. I obviously wasn't worth it."

Stephen couldn't help the bitter thoughts that flooded his mind and the anger grew.

His father was still drunk from a late night partying with his friends and fell asleep at the wheel. He didn't *even know* that he had hit another car, much less the woman he married and deserted a lifetime ago.

What did he do to deserve a father who not only didn't want him, but carelessly killed his mother through thoughtless and stupid actions?

Oh, his father, no, the man didn't deserve the title, *Rich Banks*, tried to make amends by offering to take him to the Spokane Chiefs hockey game and lunch downtown when he got out of prison. This Mr. Banks wanted to get *reacquainted*, to make up for lost time and be a *real* father so he said. He was *sorry* for what he had done.

Where was he all the years when his mom struggled to make the mortgage payment, help him with his math home-work or fix a flat bicycle tire? He had no need of a father now, especially one that killed his mother.

Images of Carl flooded Stephen's mind. Carl giving him the puppy, love filling his heart at the young boy's delight. The big man's hands helping his smaller ones fix a tractor together. Carl laughing in the perfume section of the Bon Marche department store while helping him shop for his mom's birthday present. And Carl cheering him on at football games. If anyone deserved the title of father, it would be Carl. Stephen briefly considered asking Carl to adopt him, but he wanted to keep his mother's last name, even if it came from the scumbag who provided half of his genetic makeup.

Stephen got up and stomped out of the house, Nate fol-lowing closely behind. He couldn't go through their treasured possessions today, and he didn't know if he would ever have the courage. It was unfair to ask Sara to try to figure out what was sentimental and what could be donated, but at this point Stephen couldn't stand the memories.

He wanted to kill Rich Banks, rip him apart with his bare hands, and enjoy doing it. He knew it was wrong to feel such things, his upbringing in the church taught him that. His mouth drew into a grimace as he thought of what the pastor would think if he told him what he wanted to do. Complete and utter raw honesty, could the pastor handle it? Intrigued and still filled with anger, Stephen wanted to know.

With determination, Stephen strode over to his Jeep Wrangler, climbed in and started the engine. Nate whined, giving Stephen the questioning look if he could go too. Stephen didn't even notice, pulling out in a rush and spraying gravel on the dog as he left. Nate whimpered and slunk back to the porch.

Sara, tears streaming down her cheeks, opened the kitchen door and sunk down next to the dog. Always forgiving he pressed his wet nose against her cheek and risked a small lick, taking her tears as his own. Sara leaned down to wrap her arms around his solid chest and back. The dog rewarded her with a slow wag of his tail, though Sara could tell he was still hurt by Stephen's rejection and cruel behavior.

"I know it won't make it all better, but perhaps a juicy bone from last night's dinner will help?"

Sara released the dog to retrieve the treat. On her way to the kitchen, she called up yet another prayer to God to help Stephen with his anger and to help him forgive the man who killed his mother and Marcie before it destroyed him.

Stephen didn't notice the new plants poking their heads up through the fertile soil reaching their tender shoots up to the sun as he drove to the church. He didn't notice the flocks of geese migrating north or his gas gauge almost on empty. He only thought of one thing. What kind of answers would Pastor Mark have to say about him wanting to kill *Rich Banks*?

He pulled into the church parking lot, spraying more gravel, and rushed into the office. Mrs. Collins was on the phone, so she smiled and waved him on through to the pastor's office, not noticing the black cloud covering the young man.

Stephen stopped at the pastor's door, his mom's upbringing still ingrained enough that he knew to wait until he was invited in, despite his anger and turbulent emotions. When Pastor Mark saw Stephen, his smile of greeting slowly disintegrated when he saw the angry face and defensive stance.

"Come on in Stephen, have a seat." Mark closed the book he was reading, got up and quietly closed the door as Stephen entered.

The young man did not take a seat, rather he paced back and forth in the small office for several long minutes. Mark watched him closely, praying to God for wisdom and guidance for the right words when Stephen was finally ready to release the words that burned inside him.

Mark had been praying for God to open an opportunity to talk with Stephen since the accident, and he finally opened the door. Mark didn't know what event finally happened to bring Stephen to talk to him, but he was grateful for the answered prayer.

Finally, Stephen stopped pacing and tightly gripping the window ledge, spoke in a cold and calculated voice, enunciating each word slowly and clearly.

"I want to kill him. He doesn't deserve to live. I don't know how or when, but I want him dead and to burn in Hell forever."

"Oh Father, please help me," Mark silently prayed.

"He *killed* my mother. Does he have any idea what he took from me and everyone else who loved her? Does he? *If* there is a God, he would help me murder the criminal in his cushy cell, slowly and painfully, and my *father* would know it was his *own son* who enjoyed taking his life and watch him draw a last agonizing breath on this horrible earth."

Mark dropped to his knees. He could feel the oppression all around him. There were no words, no offers of assurance coming to his lips. How could a pastor not be able to comfort his own flock? Mark had never been confronted with such deep pain and anger. His prayer had no words either, but God knew Mark's frustration and completed the prayer for him.

He understood better than anyone what Stephen felt and what he needed. A peace flooded over Mark and he could feel the oppression lifting.

Stephen dropped to the floor, spent of his anger for now. The terrible words were finally out. Six months of thinking them, wishing them. They were a cancer spreading throughout his soul. Pastor Mark was the last person he would have thought of coming to with the terrifying confession, especially since it was how he truthfully felt.

Mark crawled over to Stephen and gripped the young man's arm. He could feel Stephen tense, but at least he didn't pull away. Mark didn't remember studying the verse that came naturally to his lips.

"Stand at the crossroads and look;
ask for the ancient paths,
ask where the good way is, and walk in it,
and you will find rest for your souls."[4]

"Stephen, do you want rest in your soul? The people of old did not follow God's advice and ask where the good way was. They chose to disobey God and he brought disaster on his people. Don't make the same mistake they did. Ask for his help now. Your Heavenly Father can rescue you from this turmoil and hatred, if only you ask."

"You need to forgive your earthly birth father, or this hatred and desire for revenge will destroy you. I'm not saying what he did is okay, it's not. And you don't even need to *feel* like forgiving him, or ever have a relationship with him. It's an act of obedience. However, every one of us deserves to be judged for our sins, and we will be held accountable. If you don't forgive him Stephen, *you* will be separated from God and live a miserable life." Another verse came to Mark, this one very familiar and comforting.

"And when you stand praying, if you hold anything against anyone, forgive them, so that your Father in heaven may forgive you your sins."[5]

"Stephen, you might be angry at God now, even question his very existence. Yet I believe that deep inside you know he is real. Would you risk leaving your own sins unforgiven for eternity? Your father doesn't deserve that kind of power over your life. I'll leave you with one more thing to consider from the Bible."

"Dear friend, do not imitate what is evil but what is good. Anyone who does what is good is from God. Anyone who does what is evil has not seen God."[6]

"I'm not saying it is easy Stephen, it's not. This is one of the most difficult things you'll ever have to do in your entire life. But you're not alone, Stephen. Again, you don't have to *feel* the forgiveness. It's a choice. Ask God and he will help you if you are sincere. The feelings may come in time. Everything is in God's time and in his plan. You have the power to choose Stephen. Choose God's goodness or Satan's evil. It's up to you."

The man who walked into Sara's kitchen several hours later was the Stephen she knew and loved, not the man she helplessly watched grow angrier and angrier over the past several months.

Cautiously Sara dropped the dishtowel and followed him into the living room. She could tell he was broken and had been crying.

"I went to the church."

She softly sat down next to him and lovingly squeezed his hand. She wanted to caress his hair and hold him tight as she did when he was younger and needed a hug, but he was a man now, and she didn't want him to feel awkward.

"Pastor Mark was there."

Sara remained quiet, patiently waiting. Nothing was more important than this moment. She was grateful dinner was in the slow cooker and would not need attending to for several hours. She didn't care if they ate at 10:00 tonight and knew Carl wouldn't either.

"I wanted to kill Rich Banks. A part of me still does."

Carl slipped in and sat on the other side of Stephen. He must have been in his office next door and heard him talking.

"God is going to help me forgive him, even if I don't feel it. I made a decision today to get on with my life with God's help. I'm choosing to find rest in my soul. I don't want to see him, talk with him or even pray for him, but I made the *choice* to forgive him so I can begin to heal."

Stephen's voice wavered as he spoke, but Carl and Sara could tell he was sincere. Stephen was ready for God to help him survive the tragedy of losing his mom and Marcie.

Carl finally spoke.

"We're so proud of you, Son, you know we love you, always will. Our prayer and hope is that you consider us your family forever. Your room in our home and our hearts is forever."

"Carl, I want to keep my own name for Mom's sake, but would you and Sara consider adopting me? I know I'm almost an adult now, yet I realized today that you truly are my dad, and without my mom here, I really want you to be my mom now Sara. Will you think about it, please? It's not money or an inheritance or the house. I just want to belong to your family."

Carl and Sara laughed and cried and said yes about a dozen times. They all hugged and rejoiced in a loving God who cared so much for their family.

Three months later, Stephen Washington Banks left for college on a full scholarship awarded for his artistic potential. He packed some clothes, but more importantly, added a few small mementos of his mother to display in his dorm room. He also carefully tucked in his favorite picture of Nate looking expectantly at his mother as she readied for another of their special Saturday outings. His worn Bible wasn't packed in a suitcase. He kept it close by in his backpack ready to reference when feelings of doubt and insecurity threatened to overcome his newfound faith.

CHAPTER 10
LOVELAND, CO

"TASHA, WE'VE been over this a million times, I don't think it's a good idea to try to find your birth parents. We haven't a clue who or where the father is and the mother didn't want anything to do with you. She wouldn't even look at you. She's never tried to contact you in all these years. We live in the same house today as the day you were born and all of our numbers are listed. We can't be that hard to find. I know it sounds cruel, honey. I just don't want you hurt, and if I'm honest with myself, I'm afraid if you do find her that our relationship will change."

"Oh Mom, please don't say that. You'll always be my real mother, and I love you even more knowing that you chose me in spite of where I came from. I could be the child of a drug dealer for all you know. Can't you see that I want to know the truth? We don't know the circumstances about why she gave me away. Maybe she's regretted the decision about giving me away, or wants to know what I look like, stuff like that. We know her name, my birth date and the hospital where I was born. Please let me at least try to find out where she lives."

"Have you prayed about this Tasha? Is this the best decision for everyone involved?" Joan tried to keep her carefully chosen words and voice calm and pleasant, but she could hear the self-doubt and anger coming through. "Please think about it and give it some time."

"Mom, how about you? Aren't you being selfish by not letting me find out the truth about my past? I will respect your decision, but this is consuming my every thought, and I know it's already affecting our relationship. Let's do this together, you, me and Dad. Then no matter what I find out, you'll be part of it and there to support me if necessary. Please?"

Joan could tell Tasha was expecting to find an ideal mother. She hoped to find a loving woman in a wonderful marriage who had been frantically searching years for her lost daughter. Joan knew better. Tasha's comment about her parents being drug dealers was more likely than not.

"Your dad thinks it should be your decision. He respects your judgment and knows you have thought this through. If you really want to know, Tasha, we'll help you. If we find anything at all, be prepared for the worst, okay?" Joan sighed for what must have been the thousandth time since Tasha learned about her adoption. They should have told her when she was very young. Some secrets are not meant to be kept. Joan also hated that she was so pessimistic. She normally saw the bright side of most situations. If she was honest with herself, fear drove her reaction to Tasha's desire to find her birth parents.

"Thank you Mom!" Tasha squealed and gave her mom a huge hug spinning them both around in circles until Joan was dizzy.

Joan tried to smile, but she was still very worried about what Tasha would find, and if it was as bad as she suspected, her daughter would be deeply wounded.

"I don't have much to give you, but let's go get the papers dear, and you can start searching on the internet. Newspaper articles and such will be easy to find, confidential information such as adoptions, much harder."

Tasha was glad it was Saturday and her homework already done. She had the whole weekend to do some background work. Maybe if she found something she could even go and photograph the locations. Tasha was so excited to get started immediately that she forgot the most important part ... to pray.

"She's been at that computer all day, Tom. Do you think she found anything? The pad of paper next to her is full of notes and she must have printed out at least 50 pages of articles."

"I'm sure there is more than one Westerly in Loveland, and Shelly is a fairly common first name. Give her time, and she'll come to us when she's ready. Let's just love her, okay Joan?"

"It's so hard Tom. So hard."

"It's hard for me too, Joan. Maybe this is a test for when we have to let her go completely in a few years. Give her to God."

"I'll try, but right now I'm going to do what I know best when I'm stressed. What do you want for dinner?"

He laughed, "How about if I ask for one of my favorite dishes so you won't have time to think about our daughter?"

"Perfect, what are you in the mood for?"

"Lasagna, a tossed salad, garlic bread and strawberry shortcake for dessert?"

"My, you do know how to keep a gal busy!" Joan gave a forced smile. "Give me an hour and a half and your wish will come true. No snacking though, and you'll need to go to the fruit stand to pick up fresh strawberries."

Tom ruffled her hair before they embraced for a nice long hug. "I love you. Always remember that."

"Me or my cooking?"

"Definitely you, but if you didn't know how to cook it would be harder," he teased.

Joan reluctantly left the embrace and headed toward the kitchen, while Tom ignored his own advice and headed toward Tasha and the computer.

Joan was right. Papers were scattered on the desk, floor and crumpled up in the garbage. Tasha rubbed her head in frustration.

"Any luck?"

"Oh Dad, yes and no. Do you think I'm doing the right thing? I mean, what if I find something I don't want to know? Already many of the articles are not too encouraging. But on the other hand, what if I have a chance at a good relationship with my birth parents? What if I have a brother or sister? Don't you see I have to try?"

"Yes, Tasha, I do see. We'll be here for you no matter what, okay?" He squeezed her shoulder and sat down next to her. "Mind if I look through what you've got so far?"

Tasha hesitated, but then nodded her head in affirmation. Most of the articles dealt with jail sentences and parole violations, but there was one article about a Shelly Westerly rescuing a child from a burning house. That had to account for something. The last article Tasha could find was dated five years ago when she was released from prison for abandoning a child in a motel, but it didn't say if the child was hers. A lot could happen in five years. Maybe she got married and now had a new name or moved out of town or the state.

"Have you checked the phone book to see if there's by chance a Shelly Westerly listed, honey?"

"That's the first thing I did. There are only five listed with the name Westerly, but I didn't want to call them without your permission."

Her admission touched Tom. She still respected their authority.

"Well, do you want to call them now? It's a good time, late afternoon on a Saturday, chances are they might be home."

"I'm scared, Dad. What if one of them is actually *her*?"

"Then you'll know. But there's no hurry Tasha."

"What if one of them is her and she moves while I'm trying to make up my mind? I have to know, Dad," Tasha reached for the phone book.

Four phone calls later no one had heard of a Shelly Westerly. "We just have one more phone number, Dad." She dialed the numbers slowly while Tom's heart felt like it was beating double-time. His forehead wrinkled in concentration, and Tasha knew her father was praying for her.

"Hello, this is Tasha McLeary, I'm trying to find Shelly Westerly. I got your phone number out of the local directory. Do you happen to know her?" Tasha timidly asked, waiting for another rejection.

"Yeah, I know her, wish I never did though," the gruff voice came across the line. Tasha sat there not knowing what to say, the silence was deafening.

"Hello, hello, anyone there?" the voice rasped.

Tasha hung up the phone and looked up at her dad. "He knows her."

"Why did you hang up, Tasha?"

"He sounded mean." Tasha reached out to her dad and started sobbing. "Dad, I don't want mean relatives."

Tom held her and prayed for the right words. "You don't have to go any farther than this Tasha. It's okay, honey, hush."

Tasha continued to cry into the familiar solid and warm shoulder. Her dad smelled like cedar and Dial soap. She loved the combination, it was so comforting. Finally, she got up, swept the whole pile of papers into the trash and said, "I'm going to help Mom. Dinner smells delicious."

Tom thought about that for a moment. It was obvious Tasha didn't want to talk about it right now. She could only handle so much at a time. It had taken months since she learned of her adoption until she got up the courage to actually do something. "Like mother like daughter," he muttered to himself.

Certainly there was the argument about nurture versus nature. How much of a child's personality and morals are really from their birth genes compared to their upbringing? Tasha loved being in the kitchen with Joan. From the time she was very small, whenever either of them had a meltdown, individually or with each other, they found solace in the kitchen. Sometimes they didn't even eat what they made, but the comfort of cooking, canning, baking, or whatever else they did in there brought healing. He patted his slightly rounded stomach, thinking of the many times he ate far more than he should have after one of their cooking sessions to make them happy.

He supposed it was the same as when he went out to tinker in the garage or work on the cars. They had their escape, and he had his. After a long time with these two women, he realized that every time he thought he understood them, there was another deeper level he hadn't even begun to touch. No matter, he loved them the way they were. Dinner did smell good, and the fragrant Italian spices took him out of his ponderings. According to his watch, dinner would be ready in about 25 minutes, and he hadn't gone to the fruit stand yet. Smiling as he rushed to the car, he looked forward to the meal that would make his small paunch soon grow a little bigger.

"Yum, Mom. That was delicious."

"Yes it was, Joan. Thanks for another wonderful meal."

"Well if you would give me your requests more often, we wouldn't have what I'm in the mood for all the time!"

"I'm happy with your choices, even *all* the vegetables. I'm kind of getting used to them, though if you never buy another eggplant, I would die a happy man."

"Hey, I want both of you around for a long time, and fruits and veggies are part of my plan. Eggplant is good for you."

"Okay, let's make a deal. The next time you serve eggplant, just make enough for you. Tasha and I will have double servings of the other choices on the table."

"Dad, what if she serves asparagus that night? It's almost as bad."

"Dip it in ketchup honey, and you'll never even taste it. At least asparagus doesn't feel mushy the way your mom cooks it."

"But Dad, it makes my pee smell!"

"No bathroom talk at the table or I'll serve both asparagus *and* eggplant tomorrow night! Ketchup, indeed. Now, how about dessert? Strawberry shortcake as requested, with fresh strawberries and real whipped cream? Thank you for picking up the fresh berries, Tom. They are beautiful and smell heavenly."

The bantering continued throughout the dessert, a game of Yahtzee and a movie with homemade popcorn. Tom decided to wait until after Tasha had gone to bed to discuss the phone calls she had made earlier with Joan. So, the enormous white elephant was tucked back into the corner for another night. No one wanted to talk about its presence, as if ignoring it would make it go away. They all knew better.

Chapter 11
Boulder, CO

"OH MAN, I didn't get all the classes I wanted," Josh complained to Stephen as he threw his well-planned schedule on the messy twin bed.

"This is only our first semester. We've got four years to take all of our required classes," Stephen replied.

"Which ones didn't you get? You don't even know what you're going to major in yet."

Looking forlorn, Josh replied, "Weight Lifting, Intro to Computers and Pottery."

Stephen rolled his eyes.

"Josh, you're built like a tank, you're a computer whiz and pottery isn't even listed as a general elective for non-art majors."

"Yeah, but the cute little blond who works in the cafeteria is an art major and I overheard her tell a friend she's in that class."

"Tell me again, why are you going to college?"

"Because my parents are footing the bill, and I'm not ready to begin a life-sentence of work in the family accounting firm. Years of writing tax returns is enough to ruin my social life. Bleh."

Stephen thought of how hard he worked for the scholarship, submitting dozens of photographs to numerous colleges.

Colorado University was his first choice, and he was grateful his mom was still alive when he received the acceptance letter giving him a full scholarship, including books, room and meals. She was so proud of him. While she made better money at the high school, college tuition was expensive, and it would have been a sacrifice for her to send him out of state.

Cathy only had her small retirement, an even smaller savings account and a $10,000 life insurance policy from work, so Stephen was grateful for the full scholarship. He felt the familiar sour-tasting bile rise in his throat as he thought of how his father had deserted them.

Stephen called up yet another prayer, his lips moving silently. "Jesus, help me not to hate him, it's so hard."

He had enough to get by during the next four years, and the Jeep was paid for. He wondered how much film the university would give him and how much he would have to buy himself. He knew it took as many as 100 shots to get the perfect one. At least he could use the lab on campus to develop his own pictures and eliminate that expense.

Josh was looking at him expectantly.

"What's that, did you say something? Sorry, I was miles away."

"Yeah, did you get all of your classes?"

"I register tomorrow, so I don't know yet. Hey, I'm hungry, want to go over to the cafeteria with me?"

"No thanks, I have a date in an hour and am heading for the shower. I want to look and smell my best for the lady in waiting."

Josh laughed and struck a mouth-watering pose that would have graced the cover of any GQ magazine.

"Besides, today is Friday and clam chowder is not my idea of anything edible."

Josh hesitated, then asked, "Stephen, do you have a girl back in Washington, you know, someone special?"

Stephen paused, and softly replied, "No, not anymore." After all these months, the pain was as fresh as the morning he learned Marcie had died. His face echoed his thoughts and his jaw clenched tightly.

"Care to talk about it?"

Stephen looked at the young, carefree man, and felt years older though they were the same age.

He shook his head and walked out the door, leaving Josh wondering what could be so bad that his roommate couldn't tell him. It had only been a week since he met Stephen, but it was obvious the man was hurting. He spent long periods of time staring out the window or reading his Bible, and the few times he called a woman named Sara, he reassured her that he was fine. Josh didn't agree, but he didn't know Stephen well enough to know one way or the other.

Shrugging his shoulders as the door slammed shut behind Stephen, he gathered his favorite, best-fitting jeans and headed down the hall to get ready for his date.

The young admissions clerk checked his student identification card and entered the number into the computer. She smiled at the handsome young man in front of her.

"Mr. Stephen Banks?"

"Stephen Washington Banks, will you please add Washington to my name?"

"Of course, we must have entered your name wrong in the computer when you applied."

Stephen didn't correct her. He just didn't feel like explaining his adoption just a few weeks before.

"Do you have your class schedule request sheet completed?"

Stephen nodded, hoping he would get his classes. He didn't really want to take all the required general education courses. However, he had to get through them with exceptional grades to get into the coveted upper division photography courses offered by the renowned Dr. William Guenther.

He handed her the sheet as she entered the course numbers and waited for the computer to generate a schedule. Stephen wondered at the power the inanimate object had over his life. It's ones and zeros decided what classes he could or could not have. It couldn't feel or think, yet his fate was in its impartial electronic circuits and wires.

The clerk smiled up at him.

"Good news Stephen Washington Banks, you got all of your classes."

He breathed a sigh of relief. As a brand new freshman, he had last priority in the registration cycle and had to wait until the last week before school started. Next semester he could register on the voice registration system like all the other seasoned students.

She handed him a printout of his class schedule. English, Math, Computer Science, Golf and beginning Photography.

"Thank you very much," Stephen smiled at her.

He didn't notice her lingering and hopeful glance as he gathered his papers together and stuffed them in his backpack. He turned to leave.

She gave a little cough, "Uh, Stephen?"

He looked up at her smiling face, and saw she was blushing.

"Yes, did I forget something?"

She looked down at her bare hands, and he noticed the clear polish on her pink rounded nails. It occurred to him that her cheeks matched her nails.

"No, but there's an outdoor jazz concert tonight in the Quad. I'll be sitting next to the fountain if you aren't busy and want to join me."

Risking a glance at him, she noticed the frown on his face and her own smile fell away.

Stephen hesitated, put on his backpack and walked away without answering her.

"Lord, will I ever be able to feel again? I can't forget Marcie, she's still so real to me. Other women don't interest me. I miss her so much, Jesus."

He felt bad about how he didn't answer the admission clerk's question. He stopped outside the office disrupting the flow of busy traffic as students went to their appointments getting ready for the new semester. He thought about her look of anticipation when she asked him to go to the concert and the feeling of regret increased. The nudge was overwhelming so he turned around and walked back into the office. She was helping someone else now, so he got back in line.

"This is ridiculous. Jesus is this from you or my mother's manner lessons?"

The clerk cleared her throat, and he realized she was done with the student in front of him.

He stepped forward and looked into her amused and embarrassed eyes.

"I'm sorry. That was rude."

"Yes it was," she grinned at him.

"It's just that I can't do this right now. It's not you. You seem very nice. I know it's just a concert and not a date, still … I can't."

She appeared to be enjoying his discomfort, then subdued her response at his solemn tone.

"I hope you have a nice time at the concert. Please accept my apology."

Stephen once again turned and walked out of the office, this time feeling better about treating the young woman with consideration. His heart was still heavy, but he knew he did the right thing.

"Thank you Jesus. It feels good to choose the right path, even though it's not always easy."

The young woman watched him leave and sighed as she signaled for the next student to step up to the desk.

"I would have liked to get to know you, Stephen Washington Banks," she thought as she put on a smile and asked for the next student's ID card.

Stephen walked around the campus, stopping to sit on a bench under an old pine tree. The shade felt good on the hot summer day. Before long, fall would come with her chilly nights and crisp clear mornings. The changing colors always brought joy into his mother's life. She loved each season for what it was, though fall was always her favorite. She collected the brightly colored leaves and put them in a small vase on the kitchen table.

As a boy, they made wax paper collages with crayon shavings and as many different types of leaves they could find. She hung them in the window and declared them as beautiful as any stained glass master could make.

His heart ached at the loss. She would have made a wonderful grandmother to the children he hoped to have some day. He promised himself he would be as good a dad as she was a mom to him. He would never run out and leave a young woman stranded with a young infant.

Coming out of the reverie, he noticed his stomach growling and decided to stop by the cafeteria before going to the bookstore to get his books. Josh might not like the food, but as part of his scholarship, the price was right and the people were friendly. The food was better than he expected, but definitely not as good as Sara's.

He got up, gathered his papers and continued to walk across campus. The breeze coming down from the Rocky Mountains felt good on his face. He knew that same breeze, rather wind, in a few months would be bitterly cold. Stephen was a good skier and looked forward to hitting some new slopes this winter at some of Colorado's famed resorts. He thought about the great shots he could take of pines adorned with snow, children laughing as they fell and helped each other up, and panoramic vistas from the top of the ski lifts.

Light, he thought as he felt the sun upon his face, warming him gently. Light was what it was all about. With the right light, he could create a beautiful picture out of anything. Even an old tennis shoe abandoned on a creek bed in the right light was art.

Itching to get his camera out, Stephen hurriedly made his way to the cafeteria. After a filling lunch of a burger and fries, with no one to remind him about remembering to eat his vegetables, he rushed over to the bookstore and picked out his books. The clerk entered his scholarship number into the computer and he was done. Classes started in two days, so it was time to explore.

On his way out of town, Stephen spotted a discount store and decided to stop and pick up some film. He bought 30 rolls and knew they wouldn't last long, but as soon as he got into his classes he would find out where he could get film cheaper. Sometimes he felt like an addict, working to get enough money for his next "fix."

The day was gorgeous. He still had several daylight hours left to get up into the foothills before the sun began to set. He briefly thought of the invitation to the jazz concert and brushed it aside. The young woman was nice enough but he knew he wasn't ready to start a relationship. God would provide the right woman when and if it was time.

Stephen noticed the houses became farther apart and fewer cars were on the highway as he started up the mountain pass. The hills turned into sheer cliffs where rocks were blasted out of the mountain to make a path for the highway. He downshifted his jeep as the grade became steeper and passed a bicyclist struggling to climb the hill. The man's face was taut and straining, sweat pouring down his jaw and neck, soaking his jersey. Stephen could relate to the extreme physical exertion from his football training in high school. Coach was relentless when pushing the players to run "just one more lap." At least the bicyclist had a reward of riding back down, the wind rushing past as gravity pushed him onward toward the plains.

Stephen had no idea where he was going, but he knew he wanted to get somewhere with decent elevation to see some vistas. After another 30 minutes of twists and turns, he finally saw a trailhead pointing to an overlook. Flipping the turn signal, he slowed and pulled into the small parking area. There were no other cars, which suited him just fine.

It was colder up here, about 45 degrees he thought as he collected a fleece jacket, his camera bag, a tripod and several rolls of film. He locked the Wrangler, though anyone who had a knife and wanted to get in could easily cut the canvas top. He looked in the windows making sure a potential thief could see that there was nothing to steal.

Taking a deep breath, Stephen followed the trail many hikers had taken before him. Yet it felt brand new, like he was the first to discover the tantalizing views he knew were just footsteps away. The sun was setting and dusk would soon be upon him, so Stephen quickened his stride to see where the trail would lead him.

He wasn't disappointed. As he turned the bend, breathing in the fresh pine mountain air, he gasped as the view unfolded before him. He quietly crept forward. A gift unwrapped before him, and he accepted it with gratitude.

The young doe and her two fawns looked up at him, but sensing no danger, dropped their heads and continued to graze on the tender green grass. He carefully set down his camera bag and tripod, wishing he had loaded the film before he left the Jeep. Sitting down on the grass to make himself less obvious, Stephen tore open the package and slipped the first small canister into his camera as quietly as he could. The click of the shutter sounded like an echoing gunshot in the peaceful setting. Stephen quickly looked up, but the deer continued to graze without notice.

He firmly screwed the camera into the tripod base and adjusted the legs to balance it on the uneven slope. Looking at the background, he decided to use a wide aperture to focus in on the deer and diffuse the background into a green and brown blur. After shooting several shots of the small family grazing, Stephen decided it was time to draw some attention to himself. He wanted the wild animals' alert and curious gaze caught in indecision. Should they run or was it still safe to remain in the lush and tender meadow? Looking down, he saw a twig next to his leg. Perfect. He picked it up and easily snapped the wood in two with his thumb and forefinger.

Oh yeah. Stephen's pulse quickened as the deer looked up in alarm. The shutter issued its hushed click, click, click as Stephen shot several shots before the deer lost interest and returned to their grazing. The sun was lowering in the sky, and Stephen wanted to get to the vista before his light was gone.

He gathered up his equipment, not bothering to take the camera off the tripod, but gathered the legs together for easier carrying over his shoulder. The deer trotted off, deciding this foreign object was perhaps not so safe after all. Stephen looked around and noticed a few lingering wildflowers. He made a mental note to come back next summer after the harsh winter's snowmelt to shoot the glorious display of delicate flowers. A miracle, that's what it was. Every year the hardy blooms showed their faces, though to look at their soft petals, you would never imagine they could survive the severe freezes and deep snow year after year, decade after decade until centuries passed in the blink of an eye.

"Lord, you care about the smallest details, don't you? You care about big mountains and small flowers, about the oceans and clouds, but more importantly, you care about me. Why,

God? I am so small and you are so big. Look at your wondrous creation. Why do you need me?"

The mountains were glorious in the high alpine terrain. Stephen hurried up the path, his breath shortening at the elevation. The trees were thinning, the sky becoming brighter and he knew he was near the top. It was a race before he lost his light as the earth continued its relentless revolution around the sun, giving the gift of a sunrise to another people far, far away.

Around one more bend, he could feel it. The tripod dug into his shoulder, but Stephen didn't care as he gazed out upon God's glory. He had heard about the Colorado Aspen trees, but they didn't become real until his own eyes drank their fill. The hills dripped golden honey among the deep green conifers and rugged brown rocks.

Stephen set the tripod down and tried to stop looking at the panorama long enough to get his camera ready. His soul sung with joy at the sight before him.

"Oh God."

That was all he could think of to say. Any words he came up with would not be enough. God knew his heart and his mind. It didn't happen often, but the tingle started at his toes and went all the way up his spine, through the top of his head and back up to the Heavens. He knew God was pleased at his reaction to the beauty of it all.

This was why he was made.

Click, click, click went the shutter again and again. A short pause to add a polarizing filter to bring out the dramatic effects of the orange and pink colors behind the puffy white clouds.

Stephen groaned as he ran out of film and had to stop and reload. The light was fading fast, and he still wasn't done shooting.

Once again, he looked through the lens and was rewarded with a flock of geese flying south for the winter. The leader was strong, his followers forming a perfect V formation behind him. The sun had set, but the sky was still bright with color, giving the geese a beautiful muted background. The tall pines almost touched their tired wings as they flapped up and down, working toward the goal of a warm winter.

Stephen shot a whole roll of film on the geese. He wanted a dark room ... right then and there on the mountain top to see his results. Regretfully, the light waned and he was forced to pack his equipment and start down the trail back to his Jeep.

As he tripped over yet another rock, he thought about how stupid it was not to bring a headlamp or flashlight along. The complete and utter darkness approached quickly in the mountains and Stephen had never been on this trail before. It couldn't be over a mile, but it felt like ten in the dark. Sounds of wild animals haunted him as his imagination ran wild.

Didn't he read about mountain lion attacks in the Rocky Mountain foothills? Or was that the Sierra Nevada in California? No matter, the shrill cry sounded like a mountain lion or something even bigger and stronger *and* hungrier. So much for my beautiful shots, he thought. They'll find me half eaten in the morning and someone else will develop my film.

The path took another turn that Stephen almost missed. The moon was coming up, and while not full, it helped aid his trek along the trail.

"How will I explain to Josh a big knot on my head from walking into a tree? He'll really think I'm crazy," Stephen thought.

Just then, he passed through what he thought was the meadow where the deer grazed earlier and hoped his Jeep was nearby. Sure enough, a few minutes later, the familiar site warmed his heart. Reaching deep into his pocket for the keys, he once again thanked God for a safe journey. A cheerful chirp signaled the unlocking of doors from the remote entry as Stephen pushed the button. Depositing his equipment in the back, he climbed into the driver's seat and started the engine. The heater soon warmed the small interior and despite the canvas cover, Stephen felt safe.

He wondered about the bicyclist. Where was he now? Already down the hill or in a cabin up the mountain, cozy and enjoying a huge glass of cool mountain fresh water? Maybe enjoying a bowl of hot chicken soup to replenish the calories he burned on the highway? Was he with someone special, or alone like Stephen?

Loneliness overcame him.

"Who will enjoy and exclaim or criticize the pictures I took this evening? Is there anyone who cares enough to share the beauty I saw?"

Oh, he knew Carl and Sara would exclaim over the shots, and that meant a lot to him. But he really wanted someone special, someone close with sweet smelling hair and a gentle smile to compliment him on a job well done. Someone to drape his arm over her shoulder in the darkroom as the images unfolded in their perfection.

"Lord, do you have someone for me out there? Have I met her yet? Are you taking care of my mom and Marcie? Did they see my work tonight?"

The ache in his chest deepened as he thought of Marcie that last night sleeping peacefully on their couch. She became more beautiful in his thoughts as his memory of her dimmed.

Silence, always silence.

"No, that's not true."

Stephen remembered God's approval he felt earlier tonight as he gazed upon his creation.

"Please keep me safe Lord as I go back to campus."

The prayer was as much a habit as a plea as Stephen pulled out of the small parking area and started down the pass back to his dorm room. If Josh was home from his date, Stephen could share his day. There were also several professors waiting for him to start classes in two days.

A new segment of his life was beginning.

CHAPTER 12
LOVELAND, CO

THE NEXT day after Tasha had called the Westerly phone number, she took the discarded papers out of the trash and put them in her bottom dresser drawer. She continued living her life, refusing to think about her birth parents.

The last two years were fairly normal, at least as far as teenagers go. Nothing was said about finding Tasha's birth mother, and both Tom and Joan went to bed each night relieved they made it through another day without having to face the situation. However, not knowing eventually got to her, and after many sleepless nights wondering what to do, she gathered enough courage to dig the papers out of her drawer. Her parents started worrying again, of course. But, in the itchy, hurt way it feels when a healing scab is torn off, they were hopeful that Tasha would get the answers she wanted. Then they could stop the "what-ifs" that plagued their nightly conversations.

Tasha called the number again and was relieved it wasn't the man who answered last time. The voice was a woman's and a little bit friendlier. It turned out to be Shelly's sister, Stella. Stella agreed to call Shelly and ask if she wanted to meet Tasha. A few weeks later, Stella called her back and said the following weekend would be okay, but she sounded reserved. Tasha tried not to worry and let Stella's tone upset her.

"Ready, honey? You don't have to do this you know." Tom felt like he had said those words more in the last month than in his entire life.

Tasha ran the rest of the way down the stairs, pulling on a jean jacket over her Old Navy flag t-shirt and a pair of worn blue jeans. "Do I look okay? I don't want to look over dressed."

Tom looked up at his daughter's freshly scrubbed face and hair brushed neatly into a ponytail. "You're perfect, Tasha. If they don't love you immediately, they're crazy. Your mom is in the car. I know she said she didn't want to come, but she changed her mind. She's in the back seat. Maybe you could sit next to her and hold her hand?"

"Sure Dad. I'm glad she changed her mind."

Tasha ran out the door while Tom locked up. She couldn't believe they were on their way to meet her birth mother, trying not to think about the fact they were driving to an address in a bad part of town. The home belonged to Stella and her husband. Stella refused to give any information about her sister or where she lived, stating that Shelly could fill Tasha in on the details of her life when they met ... if she wanted to. It was a relief to finally know the truth, but the whole situation seemed rather odd to Tasha.

Tasha tightly gripped her mother's hand, supposedly to give her mother support, but in reality, it was as much for Tasha's benefit too. The familiar hand felt comforting and secure. Before they knew it, her dad was pulling up in front of the address given to her on the phone. There was trash everywhere and a beat up old car in the driveway.

"Well, here we are," Tom forced the words out in a cheerful voice.

Neither Tasha nor her mom were fooled. They were as dismayed as he was, but didn't want to say anything unkind.

"Let's go." Tasha said, resolved to get this over with. She took a deep breath and pulled her mother out of the car with her. She wasn't about to let go of the lifeline that had always made her feel safe. Her dad stepped up beside them and she grabbed his hand too, feeling protected in the middle of her parents.

"Well, well if it ain't the happy little family," a bitter and slurred voice called out from the front window. The window was so dirty it was impossible to see the face that belonged to the voice.

"Let's go Tasha," her mom pulled back.

"No Mom, we're doing this."

The front door opened and a middle age woman walked out closing the door behind her. She was very thin and wore a threadbare and faded sundress, though the day was much too cool for her to be comfortable.

"I'm Stella. Today might not be such a good time. I tried to call you, but there was no answer. You must have left already. My sister just showed up, but she's um, not feeling very well."

"Let 'em in sis, I wanna see that girl I gave away for free." The voice with the unseen face yelled.

"It really is better if you leave. I'll call you." Stella urged, looking up and down the street and back at the door, obviously hoping no one was paying attention to the exchange and that her sister would stay inside.

The door flew open and the woman shoved Stella aside causing her to stumble and fall onto the dirty porch.

"Shelly, no!" Stella cried, laying in the cluttered mess where she fell. She had hit the porch rail and was rubbing her injured hip.

Before Tom, Joan and Tasha could move aside, Shelly tripped over a broken flowerpot and stumbled down the stairs into a heap at their feet. She pounded the ground with her fists, a string of profanity fouling the air with vulgar and hateful words. It was hard to see what the woman looked like, but Tasha could see her own blond tresses on the woman's head.

Her hair was matted and dirty while Tasha's was clean and shiny. Other than that, there was little in common.

Shelly was so thin she looked anorexic. It was probably because she starved herself to buy drugs and alcohol or the drugs affected her appetite and metabolism. There were dark purple streaks down the inside of her arm, most likely from a heroin fix. Shelly looked up at them, another string of foul profanity coursing from her mouth. Tasha saw her skin was tinged yellow and her eyes dull and bloodshot. Pock marks covered her drawn and sunken face, though it was difficult to tell if from a disease or scars from acne. Tasha held her stomach and struggled not to vomit, nodding her head back and forth in denial that this wretched person could possibly be her birth mother.

Her words were hard to make out because they slurred and ran together, but finally Tasha could tell the woman was asking for money. Shelly looked up at Tasha's mother and yelled even louder, the words full of hate and malice.

"You never paid me for her. How could you take her without payin' me? All these years you had a daughter and I got none. I'm suing you for every penny you got unless you give her back." The profanity returned as Shelly tried to get up off the ground. Tasha felt her mother's hand grip hers even more tightly until the purity ring she wore dug into her flesh. She fought to not cry out in pain.

"She'll make money for me, and then we'll be rich. Won't we girlie?" Shelly was struggling to sit up and Tasha got an even better look at her ravaged face. Tasha's stomach turned again in revulsion, but she couldn't turn away.

"You're a purty little thing. I bet you're still a virgin aren't you? That'll bring a pretty price. Take you on over to Denver. We'll buy ourselves a little home, just you and me with the profits. We'll learn all 'bout each other and it'll be jus' sweet." Shelly dropped back down to the ground and sobbed, her fists pounding the hard dirt.

Stella whispered, "I'm sorry. I didn't know it would be this bad, otherwise I would never have agreed to let you see her. It really is best if you leave now. I'll call you when I can."

Shelly turned her head to yell at them. "Yeah, leave, get on out a here! I never want to see you again. You hear? Never! Unless you got some money to pay me." The bitterness and anger on her face was frightening.

Tom, Joan and Tasha backed away slowly, still holding on to one another.

"Wait," Tasha cried, her voice ravished, and tears streaming down her face. "What about my father? Do I have a brother or sister?"

Shelly sneered. "Don't know who the dad was, probably some punk who raped me in an alley. Or one of them fancy guys used to take me to a cheap hotel from the strip joint. You had a brother so the doc said about six months after you was born, but I had one of them clinics take care of it when my pants got too tight and no one wanted me. Had to else I would of lost another job, just like you caused me to. Wasn't a real person anyhow."

"Go back to your happy family girlie. Leave me be." The sneer turned into sobs once more and Tasha turned and ran to the safety of their car.

Her mom and dad rushed to join her and they raced off from the miserable place, leaving each to their anguished thoughts.

"Pull over Dad, NOW!" Tasha cried.

Tom looked quickly and found a gas station with a field next to it. Screeching the tires as he jerked the wheel to make the driveway, he glanced back and saw Tasha retching. Her door was open before the car even stopped and he cried as he watched his daughter vomit in the dry grass until there was nothing left. Joan tried to help, but Tasha kept pushing her away. She finally gave up and got back in the car, sliding into the seat next to Tom.

"She used to let me help her when she was sick," Joan said in a broken voice. "Why won't she let me help her?"

Tom gently put his arm around his wife and pulled her next to him.

"It's okay Joan, she'll come around. She's not herself right now."

Tasha got back into the car after what seemed like an eternity. Her quiet voice was stone cold and void of emotion. "Dad, please take me to the church." The tears were gone and as her dad looked into the rear view mirror at Tasha's face, it reminded him of the wax statues he saw in a museum once. A fear gripped his stomach and he had a terrible sense of foreboding.

"Sure honey." He choked on the words. He was grasping for the right thing to say, to do, anything. It was one of those times when God knew the prayer without him having to say a word. Church was good. It was safe and loving and would fold them up in God's love. Jesus knew rejection, and he knew how Tasha was feeling right now. "Do you want to talk to the pastor?"

"No Dad, I just want to sit by the cross outside. Maybe God will tell me why. It doesn't make sense. I want to know why and he's the only one who knows." Once again, her voice was cold and empty.

Joan whimpered as tears silently fell down her cheeks. She looked back at her daughter and saw a blank gaze. It reminded her of an empty shell she found on the beach one day. Joan felt an unfamiliar terror rip through her body and knew this day had changed them forever.

"Where are you going Tasha?"

Tasha paused, and Joan looked at the angry retreating back walking through the kitchen door, wishing with all her heart that Tasha would turn around with the sweet smile she missed so much.

"Does it matter?"

"You know it does, honey. I love you. I want to know where you are going and what time you'll be back."

"To take some pictures, okay, Mom? See, I have my camera right here. I'm taking my car and I have my cell phone if I need to call you." Tasha answered with a resigned attitude. "I am 16 years old, remember? I have my driver's license. Why are you still treating me like I'm a kid?"

The closed look on her daughter's face scared her. "Tasha, letting your father and I know where you are going and when you will return is common courtesy. Your dad and I do the same. It is so we don't worry about each other. We are your parents and you will obey and respect us. Do you understand?"

"Yes, Mom." Tasha replied in the ever familiar toneless voice and rushed out the door before Joan could stop her.

"Dear Lord, please help me know what to do. I'm at a loss with this child of yours."

Joan uttered the same prayer she had every day since Tasha had learned of her birth mother. It wasn't getting any better, only worse. At least Shelly hadn't tried to contact them. Joan thought of that terrible day and the suggestions Shelly had made to Tasha. It made her furious all over again. Tasha still refused to talk about it. Would the pain never end?

Tasha escaped the questions by running out to the beige 1965 Volkswagen bug she bought with money saved from babysitting and other odd jobs. She named the car Gretchen. It had scratches and a large dent on the rear fender but ran well and was easy to maintain. She threw her camera bag in the back seat and decided to go to one of her favorite hideouts. Her lovely face turned into a frown as she wondered if she would be able to take any pictures today. Since the visit with that awful woman, she was in a rut. Nothing looked or felt right. Unused film filled her camera bag, a first since she developed an interest in photography. Her surroundings looked gray and lifeless to her, imitating how her heart felt. She couldn't remember the last time she called a friend just to chat or asked her mom to go shopping even though she didn't need any new clothes.

The miles passed and before she knew it she was at her exit. Just a few miles up the curvy road a small lake waited with a stand of ponderosa pines along the west shore. The sun would soon set and she knew the reflection in the water would be perfect ... if the wind wasn't blowing tonight. The bullfrogs would be competing with one another to make the loudest noise possible to attract a mate. It was time for the fish to hurl themselves above the surface, reaching with wide-open mouths in hopes to catch their dinner. Tasha thought the circles they made in the still water, expanding until they dissipated into the shoreline, were very interesting. Just like my life, Tasha thought. One small event, yet it was slowly consuming her entire being.

Tasha checked the glove box and was relieved she found a small bottle of mosquito repellent. She wasn't in the mood to get a host of bites that swelled up and itched like crazy. She threw the repellent in her camera bag and set out to walk along the lake.

Good, there was no one else here tonight. Sometimes she saw a few other cars alongside the road and felt violated. This was "her" place, a private sanctuary she didn't want to share. She knew she should not be alone here or actually anywhere, but this place was different, special and safe. There was one small cabin at the east side of the lake ... that someday she would own. She would watch the sunset every night from the front porch. It was a dream that would come true someday. It had to.

Tasha looked over the lake. It was perfect, just as she anticipated, but it still looked gray. Where were the green trees and blue water? Why was the sun so dull tonight as it sunk into the horizon? It barely looked orange, more like a brown color. The lake was too quiet. Tasha thought she might hear the bullfrogs, but there was only a slight buzz from the mosquitoes close by and even those were muted. She felt like she had earplugs in or a bad cold. What was wrong with her?

Tasha had a thought and checked her camera bag. Yep, there it was, a roll of black and white film. Just like she felt. She loaded the camera and looked through the lens. Sure enough, everything was black, white and varying shades of gray. Some people thought the contrast was riveting, though Tasha had never really cared for what she interpreted as dull photos, preferring vibrant colors instead.

It was an effort to pull herself out of what felt like a deep abyss to try to see beauty in her surroundings. "*Please God*," she whispered. "*I feel so heavy*." Shelly came to mind and Tasha actually felt a little bit sorry for her instead of the ever present anger. She looked down at her feet and saw some writing in the dried mud. Suddenly the scene from the Bible came to mind where Jesus was teaching and several prominent men dragged a prostitute into their midst, demanding she be punished for her sins. Jesus looked at them, and quietly began writing something in the dirt at his feet.[7] Tasha wondered what he wrote that had the spectators so captivated. Why did God have to leave that part out of the Bible? Finally, Jesus looked up and told them that whoever was without sin should throw the first stone. Slowly they all dropped the stones one by one and walked away, and Jesus told the woman to go and sin no more.

Tasha saw the correlation clearly, but refused to even think about Shelly being like the woman in the story. Tasha wanted a beautiful, successful and loving mother. Shelly could not possibly be the woman who birthed her. She was absolutely disgusting and offensive.

Shoving the thought from her mind, Tasha looked back into the camera and decided to take just one shot tonight. She pointed the camera down at the mud writings, angrily focused and shot the picture. It took everything in her to do just that one small motion. Still it was a small success. But where were the tears? Surely someone as wretched as she had the right to cry? Her eyes were as dry as her heart was cold. She felt like the walking dead. Getting back into her car, Tasha didn't even notice she had forgotten to put the repellent on and her arms and face were covered in mosquito bites. She also didn't notice the man crouching down in the back seat of her small car.

*

"Why isn't Tasha home yet? It's dark and her dinner is still on the table, probably ruined by now." Joan fretted, wringing her hands together.

"Did she say where she was going or what time she would come home?" Tom asked.

"No, she just said she was going to take some pictures and that she had her cell phone. I know I should have pressed further, but I didn't want to make her angrier than she already was. Sometimes I want to shake her until we both scream. I'm definitely messing up, but I don't know what to do. This is so hard. Sometimes I wonder if we will make it through in one piece."

"Joan, don't blame yourself. I haven't handled this situation in the best way either. I find myself working in the garage more or turning on the TV so I don't have to deal with Tasha's moods … sullenness, anger and disrespect to name a few. When is the last time you've seen her laugh or even smile?"

"Forever."

"I'll call her cell phone number, then we'll eat and she can eat hers cold. Your meal will be fine. Thank you for making it." He knew neither one of them felt like eating, but he didn't want to hurt her feelings.

"Lord, help me to not yell or isolate Tasha further. Please give me your words."

111

Tom dialed the familiar number. It rang, but there was no answer. He heard his daughter's cheerful voice message, recorded long before the terrible day Shelly entered their lives.

"Hi there, I can't answer right now, but I would sure like it if you left a message so I can call you back. Thanks!"

"Tasha, this is your dad. We're worried honey. Would you please call so we know you're all right? We love you very much, Tasha. Where ever you are, we want you to come home now."

"She didn't answer."

"I know, I heard."

"Joan, do you think we should ground her? Take away her car keys?"

"I don't know. I don't know anything anymore."

Tom tried to smile as he forced down Joan's delicious dinner. He hoped she didn't notice, but he saw the way his beautiful wife's clothes hung on her, knowing she was going along with the pretense he established for them that everything was normal.

CHAPTER 13
BOULDER, CO

"WHOOPEE!" Stephen yelled as he checked his email and read the note from Dr. Guenther.

Josh looked up from his magazine, raised his eyebrows in amusement, and said, "What's got you so excited, bro?"

"I've been accepted as an intern by Dr. Guenther for the next two years, that's what," punching his fist in the air and smiling ear to ear.

Josh went back to his magazine as he muttered, "No surprise, Stephen, you're the best student photographer CU has ever known."

It wasn't a remark stemming from jealousy, rather a known fact.

"Nothing is guaranteed, Josh, and besides, you're partial because you're my roommate and best friend."

Stephen basked in the good news, pleasure filling his soul as he considered two years of working directly with the famous photographer. Should he call Emma? Would she assume too much? He thought she was a great friend, but he also knew she wanted more. The inviting glances, awkward departures after a fun outing, and calls "just to see how he was doing" were all indications.

They met in the campus Christian club last year and quickly became friends. However, any time together was always spent in a large group of people.

"Safety in numbers," Stephen thought.

He really liked Emma, and was even willing to take a chance on a relationship. However, if he was truthful with himself, Stephen knew he was downright scared. What if something happened to her? Could his heart withstand another traumatizing loss?

"Is she the one, God?"

No answer.

Would Emma understand when he lost all track of time in the darkroom or poring over the countryside and local schools for the perfect shot? Stephen knew himself, and it was fact that he would not be as attentive to Emma as he should be if they were a couple. As friends, he felt no obligation to call her every day. Their relationship easily picked up where it last left off, even if it was several days or a few weeks before they saw each other.

Why then did he want to call her with the good news now? Wasn't Josh or Sara enough? He briefly thought of Rich Banks, wasting away in prison. He hadn't turned out to be a very accommodating prisoner so they transferred him from the minimum security prison to a penitentiary. He was guaranteed to serve at least 10 more years.

"Never," Stephen thought. "I will never call that despicable man."

A slight tug pulled at him, but Stephen ignored it just as he had hundreds of times before. Even though he forgave a few years ago, everything in him still screamed no at the thought of ever talking to the man who selfishly and stupidly took the lives of his mom and Marcie. But, the continuous thoughts wouldn't leave him alone. After all, his *birth* father needed salvation too.

Surely God didn't expect him to be the one to lead Rich Banks to Christ? There were plenty of visiting pastors who went to the jail or some other converted convict who could reach the man. Stephen wanted absolutely nothing to do with him. Ever.

Stephen returned the first several letters from the prison address unopened. He wrote a big "RETURN TO SENDER" in angry bold letters across the front of the envelopes. The letters finally stopped and he hadn't received another one in over a year. Just as well. His dad was never there when he was growing up, so why should he be there for him now?

"You're asking too much of me. God, I just can't do it."

Stephen once again buried the thought and forced his mind back to Emma.

She was lovely and everything he wanted in a woman. Soft spoken, pretty, but not glamorous, bright and interesting to converse with, and a devoted Christian. What was holding him back? It was two and a half years since he had lost Marcie and they hadn't even committed themselves to one another.

He called Sara.

"Hello?"

"Hi Sara, it's me."

"Stephen! What a surprise. Carl and I were just saying how quiet it is now that you're back in school after our nice summer."

"Sara, as long as I am able, I'll be up there when school is not in session, you know that."

"I'm still trying to adjust my cooking for just Carl and I. And, I miss your compliments at every meal. I know Carl appreciates me, but you express it more."

Stephen tried to find the words to tell her how much he loved her, but comparing her cooking to cafeteria food wasn't the best way. He would surely trip over anything he tried to say on that subject.

"I miss you, Sara. Carl too."

"Oh, Stephen, we miss you so much. Your college is half over, then you can come home if you want to, unless of course you find some nice woman to keep you there."

If only she knew where his mind was right before he called.

"Sara, I've got great news. I've been accepted as Dr. Guenther's intern for the next two years!"

"Oh Stephen, that's wonderful. Your mom would have been so proud. She knew this was your dream, and now it's really happening. You've worked hard Stephen, and God has given you real talent, this must be a gift from him. I know it's an answered prayer."

"Thank you for praying for me Sara. It means more to me than you'll ever know."

Sara could hear the catch in his voice over the phone and felt an overwhelming love for this special young man.

"How could I not? You are so dear to me, and you're my son."

"Stephen, I questioned God all those years when I wanted children so bad, but Carl and I never had any. Then you and your mom came along and we became so close. I don't know Stephen, maybe I was not supposed to have children because God knew I would get a son and you would need another mother. His ways are not ours, and we will probably never understand all that he does for us."

"I'll never understand why he allowed for my mother to die so young, Sara. It still makes me very angry. I do thank God for you and Carl though. Carl is the earthly father I never had and you are my special other mother. I remember the day you adopted me and how safe I felt. That feeling has grown into much more. I cherish our relationship. God chose the most wonderful people for me, and for that I am grateful."

"Ah," she muttered trying to get her emotions under control before she started bawling.

"When do you start working with Dr. Guenther? Are you finished with your other general education classes?"

"Finally. Those took forever. How is Group Communication or Intro to Computer Science going to make me a better photographer?"

"You never know … someday you might have your own business and actually have to talk with people or manage your bookkeeping on a computer."

"I suppose, but it just seems like a big waste of time to me."

"I'll see Dr. Guenther on Monday when the semester starts. That will give me this weekend to put together a portfolio of my best shots. Do you think it's presumptuous of me to ask him to critique them or should I wait awhile and see what he's like?"

"I would go ahead and get the portfolio ready and ask God for his timing. He'll let you know when and if you should share your work."

"Good idea, Sara. How is Nate? I miss him."

"He's good, a little white around the eyes, but other than that, you would never know he's getting older."

"I miss that dog. I wish they allowed them in the dorms. Will you please tell Carl hi for me? Big hugs to both of you, and Nate too. I'll call again next week and let you know how the internship is going."

Stephen gently put the phone back in its cradle. Josh had walked out sometime during the conversation, probably sensing his need for privacy. He felt at a loss as he looked around the dorm room. He and Josh had made it their own. They spent a day at the zoo while Stephen took all sorts of crazy pictures of the animals and of people making funny faces at the animals. Looking at the developed shots they laughed and wondered which side of the bars some of those people should really be on. Many memories of that day graced their walls along with some spectacular scenery shots Stephen took in the nearby mountains. One of his geese pictures had won an award in a local fair, so a blue ribbon hung from that one.

Josh was big into sports and adopted the Denver Broncos as *his* team while in college. Compliments of the devoted fan, their beds were covered with bright orange spreads and blue pillows. A huge football mobile hung from the ceiling reminding Stephen of his elementary school science project depicting the solar system. Josh had big footballs, medium footballs and small footballs all hung from miniature goal posts revolving around a plastic referee. The little man was dressed in black and white stripes and blowing mightily on his whistle. Josh had put a tiny Broncos cap on him which was obviously a conflict of interest for the other team.

Stephen decided to go for a walk around campus and grabbed his camera on the way out. Sometimes the campus newspaper asked him for "filler" shots if it was a slow week for news.

The day was unseasonably hot, close to 100 degrees, with little or no breeze. Most of the returning students were hibernating inside enjoying the comfort of air conditioning. A few sat under trees reading a book or napping. The real find was an impromptu volleyball game near the activity center. Someone had set up an old net and the two teams were playing hard. There were at least 50 spectators cheering them on. The score was obviously close by the screaming and yelling despite the hot day.

Stephen took a few distance shots then ambled up to the side who was screaming the loudest. Raising his voice, he asked an older man what the score was.

"Tied two games each, going for the best of five."

"What's the score now?"

"10-10"

"No wonder they're so excited," Stephen replied, but the man took no notice. He was on his feet, jumping up and down with the rest of the crowd.

Stephen began shooting. He took close ups of the audience, their excited faces cheering their team on or transforming into looks of despair when they lost the serve. Another shot of a player spiking the ball and the looks of determination of the receiving team showing they were not going to give up a point.

Someone had turned on a garden hose and was spraying cool water on the hot players. The sunlight caught the glistening water droplets as they cascaded down upon the flushed faces and sweating bodies of the players. Stephen hoped he captured the excitement of the game and got some good action photos for the newspaper.

He heard a final cheer and the crowd began to disperse. The old man picked up his newspaper and an empty bread bag and headed back home, shaking his head and mumbling about what a great game it was and what it would be like to be young again. Stephen took one more profile shot of the man living a day in a typical American life before continuing on his walk

A pretty young woman slowly walked ahead of him and he wondered if she was one of the spectators. Something about her was familiar and as he slowly caught up. He admired the tilt of her head and graceful step, and the knowledge filled him with fondness when he realized it was Emma. She sensed him behind her and turned to see who approached. Her face lit up at the sight of him. Stephen's heart gave a small lurch and he realized he was especially pleased to see her. They had talked a few times over the summer, but this was the first time he saw her since the summer break.

Her smile still lit up her face, but she seemed awkward.

"Hi, Stephen," she softly ventured.

He stared at her and finally questioned, "Emma?"

His heart was pounding.

"What's this God? This is Emma, my friend from the past two years. Why do I feel like a bumbling fool?"

"Stephen? Are you okay?"

"Uh, yeah. Hey uh, would you like to walk over to the, uh, the …"

What was wrong with him? He felt so confused.

"Stephen?" she asked and waited a long moment.

"I don't know," he finally replied miserably.

119

"Well, why don't we just sit down right over here in the shade and you can tell me about your summer, okay? How are Carl and Sara?"

He paused and finally got the words out he wanted to say, "I missed you Emma, I missed you a lot."

Stephen searched her eyes, looking up so intently into his. He hadn't realized how much he missed her until now.

"Ah Stephen, I miss you like that all the time, even when we're together. You're off in your own world that no one can reach, so even when you're with me, you're really not."

"I don't want to be alone anymore Emma. I want to be with you. I think God is telling me it's okay to be with you. Do you feel the same thing?"

Emma laughed, "Stephen, I think God told me you were the one the first day I saw you in church. I've just been waiting and praying for him to tell you, but you've either not been listening or now might be God's time for us."

He wondered at her confidence. How did she know for sure? Had she really been waiting for him for two years?

"Uh, Emma, do you mind if I take some pictures of you? You are so beautiful. I want to capture this moment, the way you look right now, forever."

"Stephen, don't run away from me, not now, not today. Please don't hide behind your camera," she pleaded.

"Just one roll Emma, then I'll put it away and we can talk, okay? Will you do this for me?"

She hesitated, not knowing if he was putting her off, then agreed.

With a slightly bemused smile, she said, "Where do you want me, and how should I look?"

"Just where you are, close your eyes and think about a few minutes ago when we first saw each other, okay?"

He looked through the viewfinder and felt his heart lurch again at the utter joy he saw on her beautiful face, now knowing her expression was from answered prayer, a prayer for him. Her cheeks glowed and a slight breeze came up and gently blew her hair across her pretty pink lips and chin. He wanted to reach out and touch the strands, so silky and soft. The shutter clicked over and over as he drew her in close then backed off. The willow they sat under offered its long branches to frame her naturally. A few fluffy clouds passed in front of the sun, reducing the harsh glare of the afternoon light. He ran out of film before he was ready to stop, but wanted to honor his promise.

Stephen watched her for another moment before she noticed he was done. He looked down at her small hand resting on the bench. Her nails were polished a simple clear varnish with their smooth white tips just reaching beyond the ends of her long fingers. Tentatively he reached out and gently laid his own much larger hand on top, curling his fingers around hers and gently squeezing.

He was relieved and grateful when she didn't pull away.

Her eyes remained closed as if she couldn't believe this was actually happening, but her fingers raised against his in acceptance of the simple gesture.

He wondered if the same butterflies filled her stomach that were playing havoc with his.

She slowly turned to him, not wanting to end the perfect moment.

"Stephen, what just happened?"

"I don't know, and I'm scared to death."

"Me too. Please don't hurt me Stephen. If you're not ready for this, walk away. Walk away right now. We can still be friends."

"Emma, I don't want to hurt you, not ever. But I'm afraid I will. I'm afraid I'll get too involved with taking pictures and my internship with Dr. Guenther, and you'll get less of me than you deserve."

"And what if you die, Emma? I couldn't stand it, not again."

"Stephen, you can lock your feelings inside for the rest of your life to prevent a tragic loss from ever happening again.

The real tragedy is that you'll never know the complete plans God has for your life if you don't take a risk. He will always be there for you no matter what happens. Do you want to be alone for the rest of your life? No Christmas mornings with little ones jumping in your bed to wake Daddy? No wife to prepare and share your favorite dinner after a long day? Who will you grow old with Stephen?"

"I don't know Emma, you don't know how it was, how it still is. I just don't know if the risk is worth it."

The words sounded hollow and empty to him. He wanted to love her, he knew with a little encouragement the feelings that were so real to him right now would grow into something beautiful.

"Oh God, what should I do?"

"He hears your prayer, Stephen, listen for his answer. Read the Bible."

Stephen eyebrows lifted in surprise. Did he say the prayer aloud? He didn't think so, yet how did Emma know that was exactly what he was thinking?

She gave his hand a final squeeze and with regret in her eyes let go and walked away.

Later in the darkroom, Stephen developed the roll of film. He felt an enormous loss as the beautiful images of Emma unfolded before him. She was breathtaking. His heart wanted to love her, but his mind told him differently.

"Why am I so afraid Lord? Did you give me a taste of what I cannot have or am I rejecting your will for my life? I am so confused."

He pushed the thoughts away and immersed himself in studying new techniques in photography. It was easier not to think, not to love. His list was growing, first his mom and Marcie, then his birth father and now Emma. It was getting harder to push the ever-increasing thoughts from his mind.

Dr. Guenther was eccentric and serious most of the time, but he had a great sense of humor. The difficulty was knowing when he was joking and when he was not. The man was a legend on campus, his art displayed in prominent places in every building. The University President decorated her entire suite with his photographs, most of them were published in one magazine or another. He had done several layouts for National Geographic that lay strewn about his office, mixed up with campus newspapers and hundreds of university flyers in bright colors announcing events that never got read.

Dr. Guenther took it all in stride, rather embarrassed about all the hoopla and changed the subject when students gushed about his fame. Rather, he measured success in how much he could teach his students in the too short time he had with them before they left to establish their own careers. Many great photographers had studied with him, and he took more pride in their work than his own.

He looked across the room at his newest young intern. Stephen Banks was intense, always serious, studying late into the night. There was not one part of a camera or darkroom that Stephen did not know. William had only one thing to teach Stephen and it wasn't the mechanics of photography. All of his undergrad courses had taken care of that.

No, William would attempt to teach him how to invite his audience to enter into the entire experience and setting of a photograph. Stephen's photos were good, but they lacked feeling. The boy needed to open up, to live and taste and smell. He sensed a deep hurt and pain, which could be used in itself to create great art. Yet to hide and close people out would only serve to limit his gift. The pictures of the young woman left in the dark room were excellent. He was sure there was more to the young man's explanation than finding a pretty woman seated on a bench. There was too much feeling in the photographs for a mere acquaintance or stranger. Maybe he didn't have that much to teach Stephen after all?

"No, Stephen, no. Your perspective is all wrong!"

They were tromping through the mud along a riverbank and it had been a long day. Stephen was discouraged and William frustrated.

"Sir, I just don't understand what you're asking me to see."

"Look at what's around you Stephen, look."

Stephen saw the river, pregnant and at the top of the banks from melting snow up the mountain. The trees were just beginning to bud and new grass emerged from the mud trying to suck his shoes off cold feet.

"I see a beautiful river, trees and new grass."

William groaned to himself, "Six months of trying to reach him, argh!"

"Booooooring. A thousand photographers have done it before. What will make your perfect photograph different from theirs? What do you want *your* audience to see?"

"God, please give me patience with this man. Help me be respectful and not give up. He's impossible! What do YOU want me to see Lord?"

Stephen looked again, trying to see God's creation through his eyes. The river was beautiful, but surely there was more? He stopped and listened. He smelled, felt and tasted. Something caught his eye and he looked down.

Several water bugs were swirling around in a pool frantically trying to escape the current. The mist from the rushing water reached up to caress and refresh his hot skin. The birds overhead sang a love song as they competed with one another to mate with the female working hard on her nest. She coyly pretended not to notice their attempts to win her over. He reached down and picked some miner's lettuce growing along the riverbank, and enjoyed its sweet and tangy flavor, savoring the taste of it as never before. The pungent odor from fresh cow manure nearby rose to fill his nose.

Every sense felt vibrant and alive. Stephen hadn't felt this way since before his mother died. The tingle started at his toes and quickly filled his whole body. God was in this place. Surely, God heard his prayer?

Stephen pulled his gear out and set up the tripod. Dr. Guenther must have thought him crazy when he started to shoot the water bugs and then the robin high up in the tree. And, what about the miner's lettuce? What beauty was there in that as he zoomed in on the curious plant? That is what God showed him, so those were the pictures he would take. Forget Dr. Guenther!

Stephen didn't care about the mud as he lay down to capture the mist over the river. He even took a few shots of the cow manure dotting the trail meandering up the mountainside, smelling its earthly scent once again. His knowledge of filters and apertures and light was ingrained now, and the subtle changes came naturally as he tried different combinations to create the perfect mood.

William sat on a rock and watched his protégé, delight filling his soul that Stephen had finally understood and entered into the experience. His work was done with the exception of some fine-tuning of the mechanics and more complex dark room techniques. He would sit on the cold rock until there was no light left for Stephen to use before he would dare interrupt this breakthrough. He saw it a few times in his best students, those who had gone on to become great photographers. He had the same hope for Stephen, but still felt an uncanny need to know more about the young man's past. What made him tick? What were the secrets that held him captive?

Stephen sat down and began to clean and carefully put his equipment away. He felt like his very life was drained from him, yet he felt full and complete at the same time.

"Is this what you want from me, Lord? Everything?"

Everything, that's what God wanted and craved. Stephen knew it, understood it and accepted it. He accepted it because of the reward he received this afternoon. He saw what God wanted him to see, not what his own eyes saw. The difference was immeasurable.

"Humans are so limited in what we expect from our short life on earth."

"Yes, we are, aren't we?"

Stephen startled, not realizing the thoughts were spoken aloud.

"Let's get back to the darkroom, Son. We're not waiting until tomorrow to see what you've got here."

Dr. Guenther flipped on the lights in the darkroom. The film was developed and the photos hung to dry.

"You did it Stephen. You drew me inside of you. I see what you saw this afternoon. Thank you for a precious gift, a gift of yourself."

William was overwhelmed. Stephen had captured the essence of the river this afternoon, even more than William had "seen" with his experienced eyes.

"Sir, it wasn't me that took these pictures."

William lifted his brows in question.

"It was God."

"God? Like in the almighty creator of the universe, God?"

"Yes sir. I asked him to show me since I couldn't see it. We were both tired and frustrated and I didn't know what you wanted me to see, so I asked God. These pictures are his through my limited hands and eyes."

William felt the time had come.

"Stephen, what happened to you? Why are you so bitter and full of pain?"

"Not anymore sir. I'm done living with the pain."

"What do you mean?"

"I can live now. I'm not afraid to risk having a relationship, even love if that's what God wants for me. You know the pictures of the girl I took last fall? On the bench? I wanted so bad to let my feelings grow for her, but I was too afraid. Tomorrow morning I'm going to call her and ask her out, that's what I'm going to do. I hope she'll still want me. I don't deserve her though. I haven't talked to her in over nine months."

"Stephen, I don't understand. Why couldn't you live before?"

Stephen paused; something was different. Then he realized that the old ache was gone.

"My mother and a very special girl in high school were killed by a drunk driver six months before I graduated from high school. My birth father who deserted us when I was an infant turned out to be the man driving the car."

William walked over to Stephen and laid a hand on his shoulder.

"I am so sorry son."

He had never told anyone before, but William knew the time was right now. He was tired of the struggle, of the hopes and disappointments. Small accomplishments faded into nothingness as he failed once again.

Eyes down, William softly said, "Stephen, I drink, too much sometimes. I've never killed anyone by driving drunk, but I'm frightened that I will someday if I don't get this under control. I've tried many times but failed. Do you think your God could help me too?"

Stephen turned around, an unexplainable love filling his eyes.

"Dr. Guenther, all you need to do is ask. God doesn't want you to be a prisoner to alcohol or any other addiction. After my mom died, I was so angry. I turned away from God, blamed him for what happened. It's a lonely place, and I never want to experience it again."

"Would you like me to pray with you?"

William looked up, uncertainty in his eyes, "I don't know how. Besides, we're in a darkroom. Shouldn't we be in church or something?"

"God already knows your heart, sir. Just say the words you just told me and ask for help, they don't even have to be aloud. You can say them anywhere, anytime."

"What makes you think he wants to help me?"

"He created the universe, the ultimate 3D photograph. But, he was lonely, Dr. Guenther. So, he created man and woman to worship him and have a relationship with him. He gave them free choice to choose to worship or not. It wouldn't mean much if he ordered them to love him, even though he had the power to do so. He's been waiting your whole life for you to make that choice."

"I don't think I really understand it all, but I do know living each day waiting for my day here to end so I can start drinking is very concerning. Then I stumble into bed each night, waking more than I care to admit with a terrible taste in my mouth and a throbbing headache. The pull is so strong. If I don't have any booze in the house, I'll stop at the store to buy some. Will the temptation cease after I pray?"

"God doesn't give us more than we can bear. I'm not saying you won't want a drink, especially at the beginning. But, God will give you a way out of your temptation if you ask him and choose the alternative. Plus, if you read his words for you in the Bible, as you get to know him better, you want to live his way for it brings the most joy and fulfillment in your life. I bet your art will get even better once you see God's world the way he intended it to be seen."

"I want to stop drinking. This is very awkward, but I'm going to pray aloud Stephen ... so you can hear my prayer."

William began, his voice shaking and uncertain.

"Dear God, I've tried and failed, many times. But, you know that. I can't do this on my own anymore. The temptation is too great. It's not just the drinking God. I want to see anew what you showed Stephen today. Please show me your world as you want me to see it. Help me to become a better photographer by taking pictures of what you want me to share with others, not only what I think is important. I want to live for you, God."

William looked up with a big smile and Stephen walked over to hug him. Tears were in both their eyes.

"Do you feel any different?" Stephen asked. "Some people do and some don't, but it's your decision that matters, not how you feel."

"I feel a sense of hope and peace, and also a little fear that I'll fail."

"If you fail, it will be because you are human. If you try to do it on your own, then most likely you will fail, just as you have in the past. But we have a God who loves us so much that even after we mess up, he is still there, filled with grace and mercy."

Stephen felt so privileged to be part of this moment, but he knew it wasn't enough. He had never brought anyone to Christ before.

"There's one more thing, Dr. Guenther. Do you know who Jesus Christ is? Salvation and healing are more than just believing in God."

"No Stephen, the only time I've heard the words Jesus Christ is when some poor chap drops a bowling ball on his toe or gets a flat tire." Dr. Guenther grimaced.

"Jesus Christ is the son of God, sir. God sent him to earth to show us the character of God and to save us from ourselves. He placed the baby Jesus in Mary's womb. She was a virgin and had never known a man. Mary birthed the child and named him Jesus. He spent his short life teaching and doing miracles to show God's power, unlimited grace, mercy and love.

Jesus said, "If you have seen me, you have seen the Father."

"Then he was rejected by his own people and crucified on a cross for our sins. After three days he rose again. Many saw him before he rejoined the Father God in Heaven and left the Holy Spirit for us. His death means life for us. You just asked the Holy Spirit to rule over you, sir. But you have to understand that it was Jesus who died for your drinking and every other sin you might have. God, Jesus and the Holy Spirit are one."

"I know it's a lot to grasp. I'll bring you a Bible tomorrow if you don't already have one. Please come to church with me, and I can introduce you to our pastor. He can answer any questions you may have since I'm obviously not that good at explaining the whole thing."

"Stephen, you did fine. The peace and hope I feel is real. I'm willing to believe in Jesus Christ because I see what he's done in your life. I would treasure a Bible from you to learn more about Jesus, and yes, I will go to church. I would rather go with my mother though. She's been hounding me for years, though I haven't listened. It would make her so happy if I finally agreed. She says it is a Bible believing church, and if I hear anything contrary to what you've just told me, I'll ask you about it. Okay?"

"Only if you read the Bible too. It's our responsibility to read God's word and use only that as his authority for our lives."

"Deal?"

"Deal."

The two men started to shake hands and knew it wasn't enough after such a profound and life-changing experience. They grabbed each other in another huge hug and both lifted a prayer of thankfulness to God.

The next morning, Stephen called Emma with his good news. She was happy for him, but the conversation was awkward. He asked about her classes and family. She asked him about how the internship was going. After several long silences in the conversation, she finally admitted she was seeing their youth pastor and that they were tentatively planning a fall wedding.

"Stephen, I waited for months but you never called. I thought ...."

"No, Emma. You're right. I wasn't ready and it's obvious you're very happy. God chose the perfect man for you, and it's my loss."

How could he have not noticed? Occasionally he saw her at church but chose to sit on the other side and quickly slip out after the service before risking a chance encounter with her. Still, the youth pastor? He should have been more aware.

For some reason, Stephen was both relieved and happy for them. He knew she was special and would make someone a great wife. It was obvious God's plan for him was with someone else though. He finished the conversation with Emma telling her how happy he was for her. He promised to keep them in his prayers for at least a year to help their marriage start strong and stay strong. She returned the promise for his career and that perhaps God would put someone special in his life as well.

Stephen knew his next phone call would be much more difficult but necessary. He pulled the old faded number out of his wallet and dialed the Washington State Penitentiary to see what visiting hours would be next week while he was on spring break. It was time.

CHAPTER 14
NEAR DENVER, CO

"WHY ARE you keeping me here? Who are you?" Tasha asked for the tenth time in as many days.

The man refused to answer. He was as dirty and smelly as she was by now. Tasha longed for a bath and clean clothes. At least the mosquito bites had healed and no longer itched. She hadn't been hurt, only forced to drive to this old run-down motel where she was kept tied to the bed for the last ten days. The days were okay, but the nights were very cold and she didn't have a blanket.

At first she screamed and kicked the wall, but after three days she still hadn't heard a sound besides the scratching of small rodents. It was obvious this place was abandoned and that they were the only two people here. The man hadn't uttered another word after he held the gun to her head and told her where to turn. He didn't look mean, though it would be a stretch to say he was attractive. He was big, over six feet tall and at least 220 pounds. Short brown hair, brown eyes, brown clothes … everything about him was brown.

"My parents don't have much money if you're kidnapping me for a ransom. I'm not famous or beautiful or that smart. I'm too old if you want to steal a child of your own. My car is old and beat up, but you can have it if you let me go. What do you want with me?"

No answer, not even a look.

"Can you hear, are you deaf?" Tasha screamed.

Maybe he is deaf. How could anyone ignore another person for this long? Well at least Tasha found she had a will to live. She didn't want to die in this place. The brown man brought her one meal a day, usually a peanut butter sandwich and a glass of water. She was getting sick of peanut butter sandwiches and vowed to never eat another one if she got out of here alive. It wasn't enough food and she found her pants didn't stay up very well when she was allowed her three bathroom visits per day. The bathroom window had a thick board across it and was bolted shut so even if she broke the window, she wouldn't fit through the small space. The brown man only gave her a minute before the door was yanked open and he tied her to the bed again.

Her wrists were so sore. They were deeply scabbed from the pulling she did in the first few days trying to get free. It was no use, she was stuck here until someone came to get her. He walked out the door, locking it from the other side. She knew he would be back in about six hours with a sandwich and to let her use the bathroom. At least the plumbing worked so she could get some water from the sink to drink, though it too was brown. Escaping her plight, she willed herself to sleep and began dreaming about voices.

She screamed, "HELP! HELP! GET ME OUT OF HERE!" Tasha kicked the wall and cringed as the ropes dug into her flesh again.

"Shut up girlie." The door opened and Tasha woke with a start and sat up, realizing the voices were real. She shrunk back into the bed when she saw Shelly was with the brown man.

"You done good, Harley. She looks skinny and younger, about 13, you think? The guy I got lined up said no older than 14 and he's willing to pay big bucks."

"She's real pretty Shell. It was easy following her to the lake. She left the car unlocked so I just hid behind the back seat like you said. It was cramped, though. I took the plates off the car I stole before I followed her. It's been hard keeping my paws off her Shell. I done my fair share of looking and trying to catch her on the john, but she's too darn quick."

Shelly scrunched up her face and turned on him, "You didn't ruin her did you?"

"No, you said I could have half the take, and I need cash more than I want her skinny little bod. Too young for me. I like 'em more like you, experienced," he snorted and reached over to fondle a sagging breast.

Shelly softened at the attention and pressed her body against him promising more of the same later.

Tasha closed her eyes tight not wanting to see the foul exchange. She felt the ropes on her wrists being untied, but didn't move. *Oh God, I'm so scared, please help me.*

"Couldn't you have tied her more loosely? Look at this mess on her wrists. How am I going to sell her like this?" Shelly screeched.

"I had no choice," Harley yelled back. "She tried to escape."

"We'll think of something, maybe some of those pretty bracelets. Or some guys like their catch tied up, we could use them red silk cords."

"How are you going get her to do him? She kicks and screams real loud."

"Not if she wants to see her parents alive, and drugs will help loosen her up and enjoy it."

"We got no cash for drugs, Shell."

"Yeah, you're right. Maybe we can get a loan or promise the dealer he can have her next for free. Just not the first time." Shelly scowled at Tasha curled into a ball on the bed, eyes closed tight. "Get up girlie and take a shower. Tonight you become a *real* woman. If you don't clean yourself up, Harley will do it, and he likes it rough. Got the bag, Harley?"

"In the head."

"Good, there's soap and shampoo, a brush, a towel, clean purty lacy underpants and a dress. No makeup or hair dryer. Put the barrettes in your hair up front like to keep your hair outta your face. You better come out looking like a little girl." Shelly yanked Tasha off the bed and forced her towards the bathroom. "You got five minutes. Don't be late or Harley will come in after you."

Tasha moved her feet one in front of the other and stumbled into the bathroom. She closed the door and turned on the water in the dirty shower. It was cold and brown but she quickly stripped off her clothes, grabbed the shampoo and soap and forced herself to shower quickly. In spite of herself, it felt good to be somewhat clean. *"God what do I do? Please help me get out of this horrible situation. This cannot be your will."*

Tasha rinsed the soap off as best she could in the cold water and dried off with the towel, if you could call it that. It was more like a large worn dishrag. The dress was clean, but the style was obviously for someone much younger. It was pink gingham with puffed short sleeves and bows around the high neckline. The skirt was ruffled and came to just above her knees. The panties were soft white cotton with ruffles on the bottom and new. She also found some white socks with lace that folded down at her ankles and black Mary Jane patent leather shoes.

Who still dressed like that at 13? No one she knew. She saw the doorknob turn and froze. Was Harley coming in? She called out the best she could, though her voice shook, "I'm almost done. I just have to brush my hair." The knob stopped turning, and Tasha breathed a sigh of relief. She brushed her wet hair and put the pink barrettes in to hold her bangs back. She looked up again at the window, but it was still bolted shut.

Trembling, Tasha opened the door and found Shelly and the brown man kissing again. Her stomach turned in revulsion and she worried that she would throw up and they would be mad at her. She coughed instead and they both turned to look at her.

"My, oh my, aren't you the purty little girl? Not my choice for the dress, but the client gets what he pays for." Shelly slurred and reached over to run her fingers through Tasha's wet hair and over her soft cheeks. "Never would of thought something so purty could of come out of me."

Tasha cringed away from the touch and Shelly hardened again.

"Time to go, can't keep the customer waiting."

Harley opened the door and Tasha noticed it was dusk. Her Volkswagen was still out front, and when she saw they were going to use her car, a small flicker of hope filled her. Surely her parents had reported her missing and gave a description of the car?

"Tom, call the police. Something is very wrong. Tasha is in danger, I can feel it."

"Honey, the police have been over here every day for the past nine days searching for leads. There are posters up all over the city, and probably all over the state and country by now. Tasha's picture has been on the news. There's nothing more that can be done now that hasn't already been done. We've searched and searched. Maybe she doesn't want to be found."

"Fine, I'll call them Tom. I can't shake this feeling. It's different, urgent. Pray Tom, pray hard."

Joan dialed the familiar number and got the dispatcher. "Please, you have got to listen. I know my daughter is in terrible danger."

Tom overheard one side of the conversation, Joan first tried reasoning, and when that didn't work, yelling, desperate for the police to help their daughter.

"I don't know how I know. I just know. She's in trouble. Do something!" Joan hung up the phone, doubled over, wracked with very real pain squeezing her heart.

Tom sat down beside her and held his wife tightly. He prayed as only he could right now, the comforting and familiar Psalm he memorized as a child.

"The LORD is my shepherd, I lack nothing. He makes me lie down in green pastures, he leads me beside quiet waters, he refreshes my soul. He guides me along the right paths for his name's sake. Even though I walk through the darkest valley, I will fear no evil, for you are with me; your rod and your staff, they comfort me. You prepare a table before me in the presence of my enemies. You anoint my head with oil; my cup overflows. Surely your goodness and love will follow me all the days of my life, and I will dwell in the house of the LORD forever."[8]

"The Lord is with her Joan. Trust him."

Shelly drove and insisted that Harley sit in the back seat with Tasha. His knees were forced into the seat in front of him since the car was so small. Tasha took small satisfaction that he was so uncomfortable. The dress scratched her neck, and she was glad her mom didn't make her wear frilly clothes when she was small. If she wasn't rescued or could not escape, she knew what would happen tonight. Her mom explained the facts of life, and that is why she wore the purity ring now. She wanted to save herself for the right man, the man God chose to be her husband someday. Tears ran down her face at the thought she wouldn't be pure for him, if she lived at all. Who was he, where was he now? Did his parents raise him as a Christian?

"God, I want to be pure for my husband. Please save me!"

Yet the car continued to move forward down the deserted road toward Denver. It was such a big city. How would they find her?

"Harley, we need to stop and find something to hide her wrists. Any ideas?"

"There's that truck stop up ahead. They might have a gift counter with some cheap jewelry. Or if you could find some of them cute baby sock things, we could cut off the feet and just use the tops. Maybe they would match the socks she got on now."

"Harley! I didn't know ya had it in you. Good thinkin'." Shelly reached down and pulled out a huge bottle of Vodka. She looked in the rear view mirror and took a long swig.

Tasha noticed the bottle was almost gone and desperately racked her brain for ideas on how to get out of the car. She could also try to get help when they stopped, unless they crashed first. She started squirming and tried to make her face look worried. It took a few minutes before Harley brown man grunted.

"Would you sit still! Do you have ants running up your legs or what?"

"I have to go to the bathroom. I must have drank too much water in the bathroom when I was taking a shower." Tasha's voice quivered and she forced her face to look even more worried and squirmed more.

"Well we're not pulling off the side of the road. It would be just like you to start running and mess up your clothes. Then what good would you be? You got to wait."

"She has to go before we get to the motel Harley. The client is not going take too kindly that she has to go to the head first thing. Her *daddy* can take her at the truck stop, but don't you dare let her out of yer sight. Then we stop at the dealer's house for a little fix for her. If he won't give us one, she can have some of this." Shelly lifted the bottle of Vodka and laughed. "We can mix it with a coke from the truck stop so she don't choke."

Tasha turned her head toward the window so they wouldn't see her cry. She had never done drugs, drank or had sex. "Would she lose her innocence of all three in the same day?" Fear and despair gripped her and Tasha's shoulders trembled. She tried not to sniffle but to her horror she started hiccupping.

"Ah now look at her Shell, she's crying. Her eyes are going to get all swollen and red."

"Listen girlie, if you mess this up for us, you'll be real sorry, and so will those Ozzie and Harriet parents you got. Cut it out now if you ever want to see your mommy and daddy alive again."

Tasha quickly glanced up at the rear view mirror and saw Shelly's angry pitted face. Her stomach lurched. Would they do something to her parents? She had no doubt Shelly had it in her. The woman was the definition of sin itself.

Tasha forced herself to think of something else, anything. She racked her brain and settled on the day they went to church after meeting Shelly for the first time. It worked, the tears were replaced by anger. She had thought to find hope and encouragement, but her heart was so bitter with disappointment and anger that all of her other feelings were drowned out. Oh how she had prayed for God to give her a relationship with her birth mother, a sweet, kind and loving woman.

Tasha glanced up at the rear view mirror again and turned away in disgust. What kind of God would give her a mother like that? It wasn't fair, in fact it was downright cruel. She couldn't think of a worse example of a mother than Shelly. Her brain knew it wasn't God's fault, but her heart hurt and God was the easiest to blame. Now she was in this terrible predicament ... frightened, scared and alone. She was afraid for both herself and her mom and dad. She knew Harley and Shelly would hurt them if she didn't cooperate. They were both disgusting and cruel.

The car slowed down and Tasha saw they were pulling into the truck stop. There was only one truck and a few cars in the parking lot. Not a good chance for someone to be in the bathroom.

"You are going to go to the bathroom, relieve yourself, wash your face and come directly back to the car with me. Don't talk to no one, don't smile at no one, no tears or you never see Ozzie and Harriet alive again. Understand?" Harley threatened. "You got three minutes, tops."

"But I have to go second," Tasha whispered her head down.

"What do you mean, second?" Harley growled.

Tasha's face flamed, "You know, number two."

"Oh for crying out loud, fine, five minutes."

Tasha breathed a sigh of relief. Maybe someone one would come in to the bathroom.

"Shelly, go on in there and make sure no one's using the john and there ain't a window for her to escape. I'll keep anyone else from going in while Little Miss Priss takes a dump."

Tasha's hopes deflated, "How would she get help now?"

Harley and Shelly escorted Tasha to the bathroom, trying their best to look like the all-American family out on a little road trip. Tasha glanced around, and her stomach sunk. The place was deserted. There were just a few men at the counter eating a late lunch and a waitress checking if anyone needed more coffee. No one even looked their way. The bathroom was in the back of the restaurant, and Shelly quickly checked to make sure it was empty and there were no windows before going off on her errand to search for something to cover Tasha's wrists. Harley gave her a little shove and warned, "Five minutes, no more or I'm coming in, and I'll do a lot worse to you than your sugar daddy will tonight."

Tasha ran inside and desperately looked around. Nothing. She did have to go to the bathroom, but she decided to wait and use the ploy again later. Perhaps even wet her pants if necessary. She saw a garbage bin and ripped the bag out dumping the contents on the floor. Just a bunch of wadded up paper towels, wait, what was that? A discarded lipstick tube, almost gone, but enough. Tasha quickly started to write on the mirror, but changed her mind, thinking Harley might check before they left so she ran into the first stall, hoping there would be enough lipstick. She wrote,

HELP! 2 Denver – VWBUG - NSA349 - Tasha

Harley opened the door, "Two minutes, hurry up."

Tasha waited for the door to close and ran to the other stall. Thankful, there were only two. She wrote the same thing. Harley opened the door just as she exited, noticing all the paper towels on the floor. "What did you do that for?"

"I didn't, this place is a mess and the bathroom is gross. I went second. Please let me go now Harley! I'll never tell Shelly you helped, and I won't tell the police. Please?" Tasha pleaded in a whisper.

"What about all the dough she's paying me tonight afterwards? You going to pay that?"

"My parents will, double, please Harley?"

At that moment Shelly rounded the corner with a small bag. She had a smile of victory and held up a pair of ruffled baby socks and a pair of scissors. "Ready?"

Tasha gave a pleading look to Harley who just shrugged. He followed Shelly out the door dragging Tasha along like a rag doll. Tasha considered screaming for help and looked back. The waitress glanced up, and Tasha pointed to the bathroom and silently cried "HELP!" Harley yanked her arm hard and pulled her into the parking lot.

"Don't try nothing stupid girlie, come on. This'll be over before you know it. Close your eyes and pretend nothing's happening. That's what most of you do anyhow. Then get on with your perfect life. Shelly said she's leaving you in the motel room and getting out of here as soon as the goods are delivered. You're too much trouble to keep. But, if she hears you don't act nice like, your parents are history. Got it?"

CHAPTER 15
BOULDER, CO

"OH TASHA, how terrible!" Winnie exclaimed. "Did anyone find your note?"

Tasha stared off in the distance, not answering, the memories coming back anew as she remembered her story. Her hands were clammy and cold, and her neck felt stiff. It still seemed like she was talking about someone else. Did this really happen to her? You read about things like this in the paper, but they didn't happen to people you knew or worse yet, yourself.

Where was God when it happened? How could he have let her go through something that terrible? She thought about her future husband. What would he say when she told him? If she ever got married ... it didn't seem like she was going to ever be a bride at this rate.

"Tasha? It's okay, dear."

Tasha looked over at the woman speaking. Who was she? Why was she sitting in the dark with an old woman? It all came back, the terrible morning, the photographs on Stephen Banks' walls and the woman in the park.

"Yes, I'm okay. This is the first time I've told anyone what happened, other than my parents and a few close friends when I was in high school. Thank you for listening Winnie. I think I should go now. It's dark and you probably have to eat dinner or something." Tasha stood up and looked around. She didn't know where she was or how to get home to her apartment, and Winnie didn't drive. What about her cat? Penelope must be starving by now. It dawned on Tasha that the only one missing her was her cat. No one else. It was disheartening.

Winnie stood up and said, "Let's go inside. You're right, it is dark and the mosquitoes are out. We wouldn't want that pretty face of yours full of welts."

Tasha followed Winnie inside her lovely apartment as Winnie turned on the lights and shut the blinds.

"Do you have someone waiting for you dear, someone you would like to call so they don't worry about you?" Winnie gently questioned.

Tasha shook her head no, "I have a cat who would probably like to be fed, but other than that, no."

"That settles it then, you'll sleep here tonight on my hide-a-bed, and we'll take the bus to your home tomorrow morning. I know *all* the bus routes. I'm sure your cat is special, but one night without food won't kill her." Winnie called her daughter and asked if there were any leftovers from dinner. There were, as usual, and delivery service via the oldest child was on its way.

Tasha was at a loss. Not wanting to impose, but she didn't want to be alone tonight either. The thought of staying with this kind woman was reassuring and comforting. Winnie proceeded to pull out the hide-a-bed and Tasha hurried over to help. Clean sheets were already on the mattress and Winnie produced a soft blanket and down pillow from within the wicker corner table at the end of the couch. It had a hinged top that hid the contents, and Tasha thought it quite clever. The bed looked wonderful and inviting, but she didn't want to go to sleep until she finished her story. The rest had to get out and maybe she would be purged of the nightmares, depression and anxiety if she could just say it out loud. Maybe God did put Winnie in the park today just for her. It was a comforting thought that God would arrange that especially for her.

There was a knock on the door and a handsome young man in pajamas held out three Tupperware dishes with a smile. "Here Gram, Mom sent these over. If you could eat it all I would be most grateful. Beef stroganoff and beets are not my favorite, ugh. If you don't want the vanilla pudding, I could take that back with me though," he said hopefully.

"Thank you, dear. All three dishes can stay. We'll save some pudding for you if you promise to come visit me tomorrow."

"Sure Gram, I'll see you after school. Don't eat it all!" The door slammed shut and it was just the two of them. Winnie busied herself getting plates and two glasses of milk, "For the bones you know," and dished up the meal.

"This is better than living next to a restaurant. My daughter is an excellent cook, and she always has enough for me if I don't join them for dinner."

The food did indeed look good, and Tasha realized she was hungry. She had no idea how long she had been talking and was grateful for Winnie's patience. They ate in silence, each absorbed in their own thoughts until Tasha continued.

CHAPTER 16
DENVER, CO

THERE WAS no one home at the drug dealer's house, so Shelly mixed Tasha a vodka and coke and ordered her to drink it out of an old cup she found under the car seat. Tasha noticed it was from Hardees, her favorite fast food place. She must have left it there who knows how long ago. Tasha took a small sip and gagged. It was awful. She longed for the normalcy of driving Gretchen to the restaurant right now, by herself, free from these two evil people.

Shelly took off for downtown Denver and Tasha lost all hope as they got closer and she still didn't hear police sirens.

"Can I roll down my window, please? I think I'm going to vomit." Tasha whined.

"As long as you don't jump out and don't throw up. Puke makes your breath stink, I know that from doin' it myself," Shelly warned.

Tasha rolled down the window and put her head out. Shelly and Harley were arguing about where the place was. While they weren't looking, she poured the drink out the window. The lace around her neck still itched terribly and now the new socks on her sore wrists hurt as well. "Mom, Dad, where are you?" Tears came to Tasha's eyes again. She was so frightened. She hoped the man wouldn't beat her or worse yet, kill her. Would it hurt? How could she ever expect to find a good Christian husband who would want her after tonight? Her mind filled with despair and hopelessness. Maybe she should have drunk the vodka so she wouldn't feel it as much.

"There it is, told you I was right. You are so stupid, Harley." Shelly gloated. "Give me the cup, girlie." Tasha handed it over. "Good, you finished it all. It'll take the edge off. You do what the man says, and you see your parents tomorrow. Got it? You don't and all three of you are history. If you like it, tell him, and we'll set you up in a nice apartment and all of us will get rich. We could be like a real mom and daughter if you want." Shelly sounded hopeful and shrugged her head to the side.

"You go to room 20 right next to that blue car over there, three doors down. I'll go check it out, then you come on over when I give you a cute little wave, like you was in some beauty pageant. Don't you dare run or Ozzie and Harriet are goners."

Tasha turned away from her and glanced quickly about for last minute help. Nothing. Despair filled her and Tasha groaned. She might as well get this over with. She wanted to see her mom and dad so much and didn't see any other way out. The waitress at the truck stop obviously didn't understand what she tried to tell her and the bathroom messages didn't work. The motel looked sleazy and dirty. They already had a key so check-in wasn't necessary much to Tasha's dismay. Shelly parked outside room 16. Figures, she would always remember the room number by the age she was when she lost her purity.

She saw Shelly use the key to unlock the door and open it slightly. She said something that Tasha couldn't hear, then gave her little wave and called for Harley to bring the girl over.

Harley opened the car door for her like a perfect gentleman. He leaned down and grunted, "Get out, and look like you want him bad. Swing that sexy bottom of yours a bit. Guys like that."

"Please Harley, it's not too late. Get in the driver's seat now and get us out of here. I promise my dad will pay you a ton of money and Shelly will never know where you are, please Harley, please?"

"Too late, girlie, too late. Get outa the car, now."

Tasha unbuckled her seat belt and timidly got out. She kept her hand on the familiar metal of her car and had the desperate urge to run, but her feet wouldn't move. Not forward or backward. They were stuck to the ground. Her knees trembled and she could feel her hands shaking. Who was behind the door?

She saw Shelly nod, and terror filled her stomach.

"Oh God, now please, help me NOW."

"He likes the look of you girlie. Come on. If you go along with him, it'll be over in a few minutes, otherwise he'll rape you. That's the way it works." Harley grabbed her arm and pulled her towards the door.

"Wait, will you be here to take me home when it's over?" she questioned the rough man who obviously had at least a small soft spot for her.

"No, there's a phone in the room. When he leaves, call your parents and tell them where you are. See you kid, thanks for the dough. It's been real good looking at you and dreaming of us together, once you grow up into a real woman, that is." His back to Shelly, he grabbed his crotch in a suggestive way and leered at her.

Tasha gagged and looked down. She forced her feet to take one step at a time towards the awful door. She tasted bile in her mouth and swallowed it back down. She had to or they would kill her parents. She must have looked younger than her 16 years in the dress because she heard the man gush, "Oh yeah, Shelly you did real good. This one is even better than the last one."

Suddenly she saw bright spots light up behind her and heard "FREEZE! This is the police. DOWN, NOW, on the ground, all of you."

Tasha screamed and dropped to the ground. An irrational thought that she would soil the dress crossed her mind and

Shelly would be mad. The asphalt scraped her knees and she felt sticky car oil against her cheek. Someone stepped on her leg and ground her knee further into the pavement. She heard gunfire above her head and heard herself screaming. She kept screaming, drowning out all other sounds, her mind and senses consumed with the terrible sound. Fear crippled her to do anything except to scream. Her eyes closed tight and even when the gunfire stopped, she refused to open them. Her screams turned into whimpers. Then she felt a soft touch on her cheek and she flinched away. Was it the man?

"Tasha, it's okay, it's me, Mom. You're safe. No one's going to hurt you. They're gone, forever." Her mom reached down and gently touched her cheek again.

"Mommy?" Tasha dared to open her eyes, and her mom's sweet face was there right next to hers, wet with tears. "Oh Mommy, Mommy," Tasha cried. Joan pulled her daughter into her lap and held on to her so tight it hurt, rocking back and forth.

"Thank you God, thank you. Oh Father, thank you."

Joan wept. Tom rushed towards them from behind the police officer and dropped to the ground, pulling his wife and daughter into his embrace and hugging them fiercely. He didn't know how he could ever let Tasha out of his sight again. She trembled uncontrollably. He looked over at Shelly and the strange man on the ground, both of them dead after foolishly pulling guns on the police. The bitter taste of hate filled his mouth. The man from the hotel room was sitting in the back of a patrol car, and Tom fought against the impulse to beat him to shreds. He knew Tasha needed him more than ever now. Certainly, he wouldn't be much help if he was in jail. His baby, what had they done to her? Tom's sobs and tears joined his wife's and daughter's until they became one small pristine puddle on the filthy ground.

The next morning Tasha found herself snuggled in her parent's bed, right between them. She smelled clean from the thorough scrubbing she gave herself in the shower last night, but she doubted she would ever feel clean again. Her parents reassured her they wouldn't ask any questions and she could wait until she was ready to talk to them. The police, however, needed a statement this morning so they could file charges against the man in the hotel. It was too late for Shelly and Harley. They would receive their judgment by the ultimate authority.

Gathering up courage to open her eyes, she found both her parents watching her, concern and love in their eyes. She attempted a small smile, but she felt awkward and knew her heart was in danger of closing them out again. She opened her mouth, but no words came out so she closed it again. Tears ran down the sides of her face into the pillow, and her mother gently wiped one side of her temple with a soft finger, while her father did the same to his side with a much rougher finger. That undid her and the sobs started all over again. Would she ever stop crying?

"I'm okay, they didn't hurt me." she hiccupped.

"Thank you God," her mother breathed.

"How did you find me?"

"A waitress from a truck stop called the police and said some girl named Tasha had written a desperate note on the bathroom door. She said there were two awful looking people forcing a young girl out of the store. I had just called the police earlier, knowing something was terribly wrong so your name was fresh in their minds. They called me back right after her call. The police put out a full APB on your car. Some undercover officers saw your car and picked it up immediately. They followed you discreetly to the motel. The dispatcher radioed that we needed to come to the motel immediately, so the police called us and told us where you were. Thankfully, it was only about 10 minutes away or we would have been too late. You were so smart, Tasha, writing that note, otherwise we might never have found you."

Her father picked up one of her hands and kissed the sores on her wrist. "Oh honey, they did hurt you. I'm grateful they didn't rape you or hurt you physically any worse than they did, but your heart, your trust and your innocence need to heal. Tasha, don't turn away from us. Don't let this terrible thing take you from us, please? We're here for you, always."

"Oh Daddy," Tasha cried at the pleading in his voice and turned to him, her arms lifting for a hug. "Help me, Daddy, help me."

Tom hugged his daughter so hard he worried he might crack her ribs. He never wanted to let go.

"I feel so dirty, Daddy. I scrubbed and scrubbed myself in the shower last night, but I still feel dirty. What did I do wrong?"

"Nothing baby, nothing. You did nothing wrong, and you're still as pure as a fresh-fallen snow. You're clean, Tasha, clean and pure. Look at your sweet mother, baby. She is wholesome, pure, committed first to God, then to me and you. Look at how beautiful she is. You have that same beauty to offer your God-given husband someday Tasha. Please know and believe that."

"Mama?" Tasha looked hopefully at her mother for much needed reassurance.

"Daddy's right, honey. You did nothing wrong. Absolutely nothing. God gives each one of us a choice. What kind of love would it be if God ordered us to love him? Where is the beauty in that? You've chosen to love God, Tasha, and he rejoices and accepts you for who you are and your decision to choose him. Not everyone makes that choice, Tasha. In fact most don't. Christ died for every one of your sins, not that I believe in any way you caused this terrible thing to happen. But ... if you believe you did even one thing wrong, if you ask for his forgiveness, it is forgotten, as far as the east is from the west. If you feel dirty, Tasha, he can make you feel clean. You only need to ask."

"I don't deserve it." Tasha answered in a small voice.

"None of us do, Tasha," her mother answered. "None of us do. It's a gift that you either reject or receive with thankfulness."

"Baby, why don't you think you deserve Christ's gift?" her father asked.

Tasha looked at her dad, then her mom and back to her dad again. She was afraid to admit the words even though she knew she had to say them.

"Because I wanted to know my birth mother and father. I wasn't happy enough just having the gift God already gave me with you. And I went off by myself that day, knowing I wasn't supposed to."

"Oh honey, it's perfectly natural that you would want to know your birth mother and father. It's human nature and not your fault it turned out so awful. More importantly though is that your actions and behavior have *nothing* to do with Christ's love for you. He loves you just the way you are! He made *you* Tasha. He formed you and knew every one of your days before even time began. No matter what you do, he will still love you, even more than we love you, which seems impossible to me."

"As far as going off by yourself, that wasn't a wise choice and it was disobedient to us. We only want to keep you safe, not make up rules to frustrate you or make you mad. For that you can ask forgiveness from both of us, and Christ when you're ready. But it's not your fault you were abducted."

"For now, though, how about experiencing another of God's greatest gifts to us … a big bowl of … chocolate ice cream, with a chocolate brownie and of course warm fudge sauce and topped with whipped cream. What do you say, a sundae for breakfast?"

Tasha giggled and Tom's heart lifted.

"Only if you let me beat you in checkers."

"Two out of three and your mom gets to help if I make a stupid move."

"Deal."

CHAPTER 17
LOVELAND, COLORADO

"**I** DON'T WANT to go to school. Everyone will whisper and stare at me. They all know. It's been in the newspapers for days. Can't you just home school me for the next two years until I graduate? In fact, I'll do the work in one year and leave for college early. Or better yet, let's move to another town. A fresh start, you know? Oregon. I've heard Oregon is nice. Dad could get a job there easily. Please Mom?"

"We've talked about this over and over again Tasha. We gave you two weeks, but it's time. You can't run away. If you don't face this, you'll regret it forever. You're already way behind in your classes." In her heart, Joan wondered if this was the best decision, but everything told to them by their pastor and school counselor indicated Tasha needed to get back into a normal and safe routine.

Tasha's stomach turned and she felt worse than the time she went to the fair and agreed to go on the rock-o-plane ride with a friend. She screamed the entire time to be let off the sickening ride, and indeed did throw up in a nearby trash can soon after the horrifying experience ended. Tasha thought about the verse in Ephesians drilled into her by more than one Sunday school teacher.

"Children, obey your parents in the Lord for this is right. Honor your father and mother – which is the first commandment with a promise – that it may go well with you and that you may enjoy long life on the earth."[9]

She sighed, sometimes it was so hard to do what God wanted her to do. "Okay Mom, let me go brush my teeth and I'll be back down in a minute. To be honest, she looked forward to going to school just a tiny bit. She had only been there a few weeks when *the incident* happened, and some of the classes she really did enjoy. Photography was her favorite. Her teacher said she had great promise, and the other students were probably already learning how to use the darkroom by now. Wandering around the house all day with nothing to do but think and remember was no fun. Every time she turned around, her mom was following her and asking if she needed anything or wanted to go anywhere. Tasha knew she was just trying to be helpful and loving, but it was driving her nuts.

Tasha decided it was a good morning to floss and use both the electric toothbrush and Waterpick. That way she would get there just minutes before the first bell rang. She didn't want to be late, but early would have been even worse. The old building looked the same. Kids everywhere, backpacks slung over t-shirt clad shoulders, some hurrying to class and others catching up on the latest gossip in small groups.

"Bye Mom, I'll see you after school. Pick me up right here and on time, please?"

"Of course, honey. Right here at 3:00 sharp. Did you remember your lunch money?"

"Mom," groaned Tasha. "I'm not six anymore."

"Sorry, I keep forgetting. You were six just yesterday, you know?" Joan looked longingly at the daughter of her heart. "I'll be praying for you all day, honey. Be strong. Soar like the wings of eagles and know God is protecting you. I love you."

"Thanks Mom. It means more than I can say. I love you too."

Tasha stepped out of the car and grabbed her backpack from the back seat. Slamming the door, she turned away with determination in her step, her pretty head held high as she walked toward the building. The bruises and scrapes on the outside healed, but the wounds were still deep inside where only God could see them.

Joan saw the kids stop talking and turn toward her daughter. Some pointed toward her and turned to whisper to one another. Tasha kept walking, her back ramrod straight. Oh how Joan wanted to run after her and pull her back into the car. Oregon wouldn't be so bad.

"God, please help her get through this day and the next and the next. Be there for her since I can't."

Joan saw a handsome young man standing alone near a tree. He saw Tasha and ran over to catch up with her. Coming up behind her, he reached out and gently touched her shoulder. Tasha stopped and turned. Joan watched in amazement as he reached for her hand and led her towards a lovely bench under a tree. He dropped his backpack and put one arm around her as they sat down, not talking, just looking at one another. Then he looked up toward the sky, and Joan was sure she saw tears on his face, even though it was so far away.

Who was this young man? How did Tasha know him? Obviously, he meant something to her. Did she have a boyfriend they didn't know about? Did Tom know? Joan caught herself staring and didn't want to draw any more attention to her daughter. She slowly drove off, talking to God, questioning, arguing, pleading, bargaining, until finally she turned her daughter over to her Savior.

"She's yours Lord, just as she always has been. Thank you for knowing what's best and taking care of her."

Joan drove off and found herself in their driveway, though she didn't know how she got there. She sat in the car and wondered how to fill her day. Old Mr. Gregory next door was out pruning his prize rose bushes before it got too warm. She could go and talk with him, but thought perhaps she would first bake him some cookies. With a purpose in mind, she went into her kitchen and started baking. All day until it was time to pick her daughter up from school, Joan baked until her cupboards were bare. She made her best casseroles, cakes, cookies, pies, and muffins, every one of Tasha's favorite recipes that she could remember from the time their daughter was a little girl. When Tasha came home, she could have her choice for snack and dinner and Joan would put the rest in the freezer. What she would do tomorrow while Tasha was in school, Joan didn't know. But for today, she had kept her mind and hands occupied … one day at a time.

Joan noticed Mr. Gregory's roses looked very nice when she left to pick Tasha up from school, and only then did she realize she never did take him a plate of cookies. There would be plenty to share after Tasha chose what she wanted first.

The eyes, the whispers, Tasha could feel and see them everywhere. Her stomach was in knots, but she kept her face devoid of emotion. Not one crack could show or she would lose it.

"Oh, God, help me. I need you."

The sidewalk to the front door of the school seemed so long. Would she ever get there? Suddenly she felt a gentle touch on her shoulder and an overwhelming sense of peace flooded over her. She was afraid to turn to see who it was, but something compelled her, there was no choice, and her body stopped and turned on its own, drawn to the presence.

Kind brown eyes, filled with tears and compassion looked right into her own, uncertain and frightened, despite her resolve to be strong. Warmth, and though she couldn't explain it, a gentle light and beautiful smell like right after a spring rain surrounded him. He reached for her hand and gently drew her towards a nearby bench. Tasha willingly followed, her hand in his as she looked up into his kind face. Who was this guy? Tasha didn't recognize him, but it felt like she knew him, or at least she trusted him. After her experience, she didn't trust anyone other than her parents enough to touch, much less hug them, and this action was totally out of character for her. Tasha didn't think about that now, only that she was hanging on to a lifeline, to let go would mean to drown.

He looked up into the sky, then back down at her, tears in his eyes reflecting her own. He whispered, "It's okay, I am with you. As long as you need and want me, I will be your friend." His voice was low and soft, comforting and soothing, kinder that anyone's voice she had ever heard.

Tasha held on to his hand tighter and nodded her head. The fear was falling away and she noticed his thumb softly move over her fingertips. She started to feel like her old self again. Would things ever be the same? Would she ever be innocent again? Suddenly it didn't matter who he was, he wanted to be her friend, and he *knew*. Not just about what happened to her, but how she felt. He understood and just wanted to be her friend. She didn't want this moment to ever end.

"Hey Tasha, we missed you!"

"Yeah girl, what took you so long to get back? I can help you with your math if you want after school, not that you probably need it."

"Mr. Stellar asked about you too. It's okay that you're better than us in photography and he obviously likes you more. We're going to start in the darkroom tomorrow afternoon, so you have to take some pictures like today so you'll have something to develop. I'll help you with the chemicals and stuff. It's been so boring learning about lights and fluids and paper. I'm ready to actually see what I've taken."

"It's okay, go. I'll be here when you need me."

Tasha didn't want to let go but he gently nudged her away.

"Wait, what's your name?"

"It doesn't matter, I'll be here when you need me. I'll know." The kind eyes reached all the way into her soul and she felt her heart swell.

"C'mon girl, the first bell already rang and you don't want to be tardy to the old warden's class. You'll get a detention for sure and spend your afternoon picking up trash instead of taking pictures."

Tasha found herself being pulled along and when she looked back her new friend was gone. She was not late to her first class and her normal seat was vacant and ready for her. By lunch she knew everything would be okay. There were still the whispers and stares, but Tasha felt the presence of her new friend and was reassured that everything would be okay.

Her true friends didn't say a word and acted as if nothing had ever happened except for the more than normal touches on her shoulder or light squeeze on her arm. They were truly happy to see her and didn't act like she was dirty. She knew it would have to come out, or there would always be that big white elephant in the corner that everyone knew was there, but no one wanted to acknowledge. How many times had she heard her mom say they needed to get rid of the big white elephant?

When she was little, she would actually look around the house for it, but could never find one. She smiled at the memory. As usual, her mom was right, it would eventually come between her and her friends unless they talked about it. Right then and there she decided a slumber party was in order. Plus, it would give her mom something to plan and do. She might ask her to cook a few of her favorite desserts and order pizza in. Tasha was feeling very good about her day when she ran out just in time to see her mom pulling up the street.

When they walked in the kitchen, Tasha's mouth dropped at all the food.

"Mom, how are we ever going to eat all this? Are we having a huge party I didn't know about?"

"It's too much?" Joan asked, hurt in her voice.

"Oh, no, it's fine, I just don't know where to start with my snack, and dinner and breakfast, oh, for the next three weeks! It all looks great now but we'll have to put some in the freezer or it will turn fuzzy and green by the time I get around to eating it all."

They looked at each other and burst out laughing at the same time.

"You're right, honey. It is a bit much. I needed to keep busy today. Why don't you make a plate or ten up for Mr. Gregory and tell him I noticed how lovely his roses are?"

"Okay, Mom, but first do you think I could have a slumber party this weekend, with about five of my best friends? I see we have plenty of food to eat and you won't have to go to any trouble. We'll sleep downstairs so you and Dad won't be disturbed."

"It's not too soon?"

"No, Mom, you were right, it's time to get on with my life."

"Okay, honey, I'll rent a feel-good movie for you and your friends and a John Wayne western that I'll suffer through with your dad."

"Sounds good, thanks Mom. I'll tell them to come over about 5:00."

Tasha picked out a little from as many of the dishes she could fit on the plate for Mr. Gregory and grabbed her camera to take some shots of his rose bushes for class tomorrow. He would be pleased, especially if she framed them or entered one in the photography competition at the fair next summer.

After the door slammed, Joan whispered her thanks to God and realized she forgot to ask Tasha about the young man at school this morning.

"That was so good," Lisa gushed, still sniffling and laughing and crying at the same time. I just love Meg Ryan. She's my favorite actress. Do you think her love life is that romantic for real? *Sleepless in Seattle* was my favorite movie until now, but I think this one might replace it. I hope she never stops making movies."

Empty popcorn bowls, pizza boxes and a plate of cookie crumbs shared the coffee table along with an untouched tray of carrot and cucumber slices. Tasha's friends were all snuggled in their sleeping bags, laid out across the living room floor. Their fingers and toes were freshly manicured, but their normally beautiful locks of hair were currently being held prisoner under clear plastic shower caps to soak in a deep seaweed conditioner. They all had green clay masks on their faces which had dried and cracked except for the slimy spots where their tears had fallen during the romantic movie. Tasha thought that would be a great picture for the yearbook. They would die of embarrassment though and never trust her again. Her dad had looked in on them on his way to the kitchen an hour ago, stood there for a minute, then turned and backed out the way he had come in, shaking his head and not saying a word. Tasha smiled, thinking of the look on his face. No doubt, he was glad to be a man.

Tasha thought about why she invited her closest friends over and her stomach clenched. Then she remembered the guy at school on Monday and felt a calm reassurance consume her. The big white elephant loomed above her and she wanted it gone, right now. Her friends were still going on about how good the movie was, so Tasha sat up and cleared her throat. Lisa noticed her first and nudged the girl next to her. Soon they were all quiet, looking at Tasha with questions in their eyes.

"God, help me, I need to do this, but I can't do it without you."

"Um, I need to talk about what happened to me."

No one got up and walked away, no one said a word, just small nods of their heads and acceptance in their faces. Tasha was encouraged and went on. The words rushed out.

"I am adopted. I found out two years ago. I wanted to meet my birth mother and father so I searched until I found my mother. I wish I never would have. It was awful. My birth mother didn't even know who the father was. She didn't want me so she gave me away, then she aborted my baby brother. She was a prostitute and a drug addict who had me kidnapped and then tried to sell me into prostitution."

Tasha gulped and continued, "They tied me up and kept me in a dirty abandoned motel for ten days. I only got one peanut butter sandwich a day to make me lose weight to look younger. This woman, my *birth mother*, made me dress up to look like a little girl. Then they took me to a sleazy motel so this business man could have my virginity for a lot of money. The police shot them in front of me and arrested the man. The kidnapper and my birth mother are both dead now, and I feel so dirty. I never knew people could be so awful. I wasn't raped or anything like that, but I still feel like I was violated."

"I was mad at God for who he gave me for a mother and father, and I'm sad that she turned out so bad because I longed for her to be loving and kind and for us to have a great relationship. I feel guilty for not appreciating my real mom and dad more, and I'm afraid no man is ever going to want me because I still feel dirty like I did something wrong. I'm afraid of all the evil in this world. And I don't know who I am anymore." Tasha broke down and sobbed, her shoulders shaking."

First two hands, then two more until ten hands rested all over her, some rubbing her back, some wiping tears from her face and others just resting on her shoulders. She heard Lisa's sweet voice first, then the murmuring of all her friends in prayer. They were all praying for her. Tasha felt an overwhelming sense of love and wished with all of her being that she was worthy of accepting it. She knew she would never be the same again. Still she was glad for her friends. She opened her eyes and looked down, then burst out laughing. They all stopped and looked at what she was looking at. The tissues were green, all of them. Soon they were all laughing and crying and hugging.

"Come on, let's get this stuff out of our hair and faces." Soon the kitchen, both bathroom sinks and tubs were green with seaweed conditioner and clay. The girls quickly rinsed the mess and met back together in the living room, hair softly drying around their glowing faces. They were shy at first, then each girl told Tasha how glad they were that she was their friend and felt honored to be invited over for the "cleansing."

The girls reassured her that she was in no way at fault and they would have done the same thing. Tasha appreciated their words and knew in her head they were right, but still her heart couldn't accept them. However, she knew her relationship with them was closer by sharing what happened, probably better than it was before, and was very glad she did it. She imagined the white elephant getting smaller and smaller until it disappeared.

Tasha thought about the guy at school and wished she could find him again. She asked her friends if anyone knew him, but they couldn't remember seeing him on Monday in front of the school, which was very odd, since they pulled her away from him to get to class on time. Tasha wanted to thank him and very much wanted to get to know him and ask him to be her friend. She vowed to watch closely at school next week and chase him down if necessary.

The girls finally drifted off to sleep and woke to the smell of hot chocolate and Belgian waffles with warm blackberry compote for breakfast, even though it was well past noon. Her real mom was at it again, and Tasha felt an overwhelming sense of gratitude and love for this beautiful woman.

She was going to miss her when she went off to college, her dad too. They had offered for her to stay home and go to a trade school, or even work for a few years before college. But she wanted to study photography at the University of Colorado in Boulder. She heard great things about the program and was anxious to finish high school and start college.

Lisa was also going to Colorado University and they decided to room together on campus for two years, and then get their own apartment. It would be great. She could get a new start to put all this behind her. Tasha vowed she would email her mom and dad every week and come home to visit between semesters and spring break. They promised to let her keep her cell phone so she could call whenever and they could talk as long as they wanted. She was looking forward to the time when she would be on her own.

CHAPTER 18
BOULDER, CO

RICH BANKS was proud as he sat in the reserved section for relatives of the graduates with the highest honors. Stephen was graduating Summa Cum Laude, with a 4.0 grade point average, even in what he thought were the *useless* general education classes. Two years ago after Stephen's phone call and prayer, Rich turned his life around. He had a reason to live. His son wanted a relationship with him, and albeit slowly, wanted to get to know him.

Every day since the accident, Rich had tried to convince himself that it was anyone's fault but his own. He justified that Cathy shouldn't have been out on the road that early in the morning. The snowplow drivers weren't fast enough to keep up with plowing the roads. His tires wore out too quickly, and he should have sued Firestone. The excuses went on and on, but deep inside, Rich knew it was his fault those two women were dead. Forever dead. And he, Rich Banks, took away his son's mother and girlfriend in one quick stupid, incredibly stupid, moment. All for a night of celebration for a son he never knew and probably never would. The guilt ate away at him every day and he took it out on anyone who crossed his unfortunate path.

The inmates knew to steer clear of Rich Banks, lest they end up with a black eye or cracked rib.

Rich basked in the aftermath of the phone call, replaying his son's words over and over before asking the warden to call the visitation pastor to schedule an appointment the next time he was on the grounds. He had hope, in a hopeless environment. The pastor had been trying for months to talk to Rich, but he scoffed at him and told him to take his religion elsewhere. Look at where it got his dead ex. That afternoon, sick from the lies and guilt, he asked Jesus into his heart and started living his life for the Lord.

His fellow prisoners wondered at the change, but most everyone kept to themselves. Rich had already earned his respect soon after he entered the prison with his tough attitude and unapproachable persona. The wardens noticed the change as well and soon began giving Rich extra responsibilities and privileges. When his parole board hearing came up last month, the third since his conversion two years ago, amazingly every single warden and guard recommended that he earned an early release, in time to attend his son's graduation. It was approved, and Rich broke down and cried, thanking them and his Lord.

He was granted a one week pass to go to Colorado, and Rich once again, was overwhelmed at the goodness of God. After the graduation, he was required to return to Washington and remain on parole for a minimum of six years.

The day was beautiful. Spring flowers were still in bloom, but the sun shone brightly overhead promising warmer days soon. Rich's only regret was that Stephen decided to stay in Colorado rather than return to Washington. Stephen wanted to continue his freelance work and keep the small apartment he and Josh shared. The two men moved out of the dorm last year when Stephen began making more money. They wanted to experience life in a residential area of the college town.

The seats were filling up and Rich anticipated seeing his son walk across the stage to accept his diploma. He wished he could have helped Stephen more with the expenses not covered by his scholarship, but what was in the past couldn't be changed. He had the future now, and was determined to make the most of it.

The pomp and circumstance music began and the campus president and faculty dressed in full regalia took their seats on stage. Excitement mounted as the students began the procession down the aisles and took their seats.

Rich stood and strained to see Stephen among the hundreds of graduates. There he was! His gold honor cord shone brightly against the dark gown. Unashamed, Rich stood up on his chair, put two fingers in his mouth and gave a loud whistle. Stephen and almost everyone else looked his way. His son finally saw him and enthusiastically waved back. Giving him a thumbs up sign, Stephen turned to the student next to him and whispered, "That's my birth dad," not caring about the tears that welled up in his eyes.

He worked so hard for this day. Carl and Sara stood next to Rich and they were both in tears too. He wondered how that was going, but everything looked okay from where he was standing.

"Mom, Marcie, do you see me? Look, I accomplished one of my dreams!"

The day would have been even more perfect if they could have sat in the seats next to Carl, Sara and Rich. But he felt a warmth flow through him that was from more than just the sun's rays beaming down on his shoulders. It was the son filling Stephen with his presence, confirming his love and that he would be with him always.

"To Stephen, may your career be fulfilling and glorify God!" Carl boomed out in his large voice with a toast to the graduate.

"Hear, hear," everyone else joined in.

The kitchen and coffee tables were laden with appetizers and finger foods that Sara had prepared early that morning. Carl hung streamers and bought a big bouquet of balloons to make the place more festive.

Stephen looked around at his family and closest friends. It was a small group, but each one was precious to him. His birth dad, Dr. Guenther, his parents Carl and Sara, Josh and a few other photography majors were present in the small apartment. The mood was gay and full of laughter as they each recounted fun or embarrassing moments in Stephen's life.

The phone rang and Stephen contemplated letting the answering machine take the message, but felt an urge to pick it up. Grabbing the cordless, and out of breath from laughing so hard, he said hello as best he could with the background noise.

"Just a minute," he said trying to stop laughing while he walked down the short hall to a quieter room.

"Hello? Mr. Banks?" The voice on the other end of the line yelled.

"Yes, that's me. I'm sorry for the commotion. We're celebrating my graduation today."

"I know. I've been waiting for weeks to call you. I was going to call on Monday but was afraid someone else would grab you up."

"Who is this?"

"Ed Hauser, editor of *Colorado Insight*. We're a fairly new magazine that targets the 30 to 50 age group. Our focus is on outdoor activities in the state. We've noticed your work in some smaller publications and would like to offer you a job working for us starting immediately. What do you say?"

Stephen gulped and tried to place the magazine. He knew there was a new magazine some of his friends were raving about and wondered if this was the one.

"You haven't been offered another position have you? I told myself I should have called weeks ago, but I didn't want to rush you during your last few weeks of school."

"No, no, I haven't accepted a job from anyone else. I just thought I would continue to freelance for a while until I decided for sure what I wanted to do."

"Well, why don't you come down on Monday and check us out? We're located right here in Boulder. You can peruse our past editions and decide if we fit. This is our second year and we have quite a following. I think you'll be pleased at what you see. We've been using freelance photographers until now, but our owner and staff agree that hiring you full-time would be in our best interest. Your work is exactly what we're looking for and we think you'll be perfect for our magazine. What do you say, Mr. Banks?"

"I'll think about it Mr. Hauser and call you on Monday. I'll talk to my family and Dr. William Guenther with whom I've been studying. I'll also need to pray about it. This is a big decision for me, you know, my first job and all. I would want to do my best for you, and I need to feel right about it in order to do that."

Ed really wanted this man. He knew Stephen Banks would be a perfect fit with *Colorado Insight*. He wasn't a believing man himself, but he liked what he saw in Stephen's work. Trying to tone down his enthusiasm that Stephen was even considering calling him back, he replied, "Sure enough Mr. Banks, sounds quite fair to me. I look forward to hearing from you. Our number is in the book. Have a good time celebrating your graduation. You deserve it!"

Stephen turned the phone off and sat on the bed for a moment. Looking out the window and up into the clear blue sky, he asked God, "Is this what you want for me? You know it's been my dream, but I want it to be yours too. Please show me."

Walking back into the living area, he cleared his throat to quiet the group.

"I was just offered a job with a magazine called *Colorado Insight*. What do you think?"

One of Stephen's friends pulled a magazine out from the backpack lying at his feet. It was this month's issue of the magazine.

"Oh, man, you have to take this job. Check this issue out. It's quality stuff if you're into the outdoors."

Stephen grabbed the magazine and started thumbing through the pages. It was a good magazine. However, looking at the glossy pages, Stephen knew he could make it better.

"Can I keep this? Just for the weekend until I pick up my own copy?"

"Sure man, it's yours. I've already read it cover to cover and plan on visiting some of those trails out of Estes Park tomorrow."

"Is this what you want, Stephen?" William's voice softly interjected.

"Do you want someone else telling you what to shoot?"

"As long as they don't tell me how to do my work, it would be fine. I kind of like the idea of some job security and benefits for a while."

"Then I recommend you ask them just that if you go see them on Monday. Make sure when they give you an assignment they let you go with it."

"Thanks for the advice sir. If I feel God wants me to take this job, I'll make sure that's one of the stipulations."

"Carl, Sara? What do you think?"

The couple sat side-by-side holding hands on the couch. Their demonstration of love for each other after so many years touched him.

Carl began, "Stephen it would make us so happy to have you back in Washington, but this is your life, not ours. This magazine sounds like it's off to a good start, and if for some reason it fails, you still can fall back on your freelance work. I think it sounds like a great opportunity."

Sara nodded her head in agreement and smiled at Stephen. "Read your Bible Son, and see if God gives you further guidance."

Later that night, when everyone was gone and the apartment cleaned up from the festivities, Stephen prayed and opened his Bible. It felt a bit strange with Josh gone. He was staying with his family at a resort for a few days before moving back home to join his family as an accountant. Somewhere in the past four years, Josh decided he really did like numbers and was looking forward to working with his dad and sister in the family firm.

"What do you have for me tonight, God? Please show me what to do about this job offer."

He knew the answer might not be obvious, nor might it come today. God's timing was not his, much to Stephen's consternation. Patience was a virtue he needed to work on.

Opening his Bible, Stephen was tempted to close his eyes and let the page open where it fell, but he decided to continue his reading from the night before in his study of Psalms. He was not much into poetry, and the verses were hard to read. Yet, God saw fit to put these passages in the Bible, so Stephen felt obliged to read them. His eyes fell to Psalm 67.

May God be gracious to us and bless us and make his face shine on us so that your ways may be known on earth, your salvation among all nations.[10]

Stephen thought, "I wonder if I can use this magazine to show people God's ways on earth? It's not a religious publication, but surely if I can capture God's ways and his creation to share with thousands of people, I might be doing some good? Maybe this is my life assignment?"

"God, am I stretching this a bit to get what I want?"

The answer wasn't obvious or clear to Stephen, and he still wasn't sure after reading his Bible, but he didn't think he got a "no" either.

Sighing, he turned out the lights and let sleep overcome him. It had been a long day, and Stephen didn't even realize it was his first night to sleep alone in his entire life.

Josh did stop by the next morning with a gift. A friend at the public library let him check out every back issue of *Colorado Insight* since its inception.

"They are due in two weeks mind you, so don't turn them in late or I'll get fined," Josh warned. Then he was off to enjoy a few days at the lake before beginning his new job.

Stephen made a fresh pot of coffee, enjoying the rich fragrant aroma. He flung open the windows on this gorgeous day and settled down in his favorite chair to peruse the magazines.

He liked what he saw. Snowboarding, skiing, hiking, rock climbing, windsurfing, sky diving, river rafting, outdoor concerts, this magazine had it all. He dreamed about inspiring adventures by having the opportunity to go to these places to take the pictures for the layouts. It would be like a paid vacation every week! Could he communicate God's creation and love for his people? That was the ultimate goal.

"God, will you help me show your world through this job? Is it the right thing to do?"

Stephen waited a moment and rose to stretch his legs. Looking out the window, life proceeded as normal. Teenage boys mowed lawns, a little boy triumphantly rode his tricycle down the sidewalk, and an elderly woman watered her well-tended rose garden. Still not sure, Stephen did know he had a freelance job to finish before Monday, and he also wanted to set up Josh's old room as a darkroom. As a graduate, he lost the use of the campus darkroom. He wondered if the magazine would let him use their darkroom for his freelance if he bought his own supplies?

He headed off to the local skateboard park to finish the assignment about activities to help keep kids occupied and off the streets. It was for a community newsletter, and Stephen enjoyed getting to know the kids in town doing different things.

Boulder started several new programs and wanted to get word out to the parents. At the park, Stephen knew without a doubt that this was God's career choice for him. Photography was in his soul, ingrained deep from the time he was a small child, along with his mother's contagious enthusiasm for life and delight in God's creation. How could anyone even consider this a job? He once again thanked God for his gift as he captured kids defying gravity as they sped up and down the ramps, wind blowing through their hair and clothes. Their faces were so transparent, showing smiles of glee upon landing after an exceptional jump or embarrassed blushes after a fall.

"Mr. Hauser, how do you feel about God?" Stephen asked the direct question as he sat down in the comfortable leather wingback chair in the editor's office at *Colorado Insight*.

"Well, I guess I haven't thought about him all that much," Ed answered truthfully, wondering where this conversation was leading.

"I spent quite a bit of time praying this weekend, and I'm still not sure this is the job God would have me take. I've had a lot of freedom with my freelance work, and every picture I take has his signature on it."

"What do you mean, Stephen, God's signature?"

"Well, I ask God what he wants me to see and then I follow his lead. I'm afraid if you direct the pictures I take, I wouldn't be able to have the freedom to ask God what he wants me to do."

"I guess that is a problem isn't it? Do you plan to continue to take the kinds of pictures I've already seen in the publications where you've been hired as a freelance photographer? How do they direct your work?"

"They give me an assignment with full freedom to take the pictures as I see fit. I turn in the developed product and then they choose what they like. Since the work is freelance if they don't like what they see, I don't get paid. But so far, that hasn't happened."

"Sounds risky to me, on your part that is. If you decide to take this job, and I'm still offering the job, the only difference is that you'll get paid regardless of whether we like the shots or not. If you continue to do the type of quality work I've already seen, I doubt there will be a problem, with or without your God. You're welcome to invite him along for the ride."

"I guess it's settled then Mr. Hauser. When we talked on the phone you indicated you wanted me to start immediately. What is my first assignment? I have my own equipment, but if you prefer I use yours, that's okay as well. Do you have a dark-room and the necessary supplies on the premises or do I need to build one of my own?"

Ed breathed a quiet sigh of relief. If God was the only stum-bling block in hiring Stephen, it was settled. He had no doubt in Stephen's skill and vision as a photographer, and had a gut feeling their magazine would soon double its subscriptions.

"We don't have a darkroom on the premises, Stephen, but you are welcome to scout out facilities to rent, and of course bill the charges to the magazine. Your first assignment will start tomorrow morning in . . . are your ready for this? Leadville."

"Where is Leadville, sir? I've never heard of the place."

"Well, it's not exactly Leadville, but nearby. There is this group called the Highpointers, founded by a man named Jack Longacre. Their goal is to climb to the highest point of every state. Each year they have a convention, and this year their goal is to climb to Mt. Elbert, the highest point of Colorado. While the climb is not technical, at over 14,000 feet and about a 10-mile hike, not just anyone can do it. There will be at least 300 of the members, kids included, all trying to ascend to the highest point of our beautiful state. After the climb, you'll be treated to a fine dinner, the group's award ceremony and recognition of those who have completed all 50 states. They will also select the location for the next convention. Are you up to it?"

"Sure, sounds interesting and I bet the people are a lot of fun and from all over the United States. I'll check out a map and head over there tonight to settle in and check out the surroundings. As far as the darkroom, I have an extra room in my apartment that I would like to setup if that is okay with you. I'll just send you the bill for the materials as I would like to use the darkroom for my own work outside of the magazine, so there won't be any rent charges."

"That works for me. Be sure to keep track of all your expenses and keep receipts so we can reimburse you for your lodging, mileage and meals. I'll see you next Monday. Here's my business card if you have any questions or would like approval for extra expenses. And this is your reservation confirmation for the hotel."

"You sure were confident about me taking the job, weren't you, Mr. Hauser?"

"Actually, I was worried you wouldn't but had a backup photographer lined up in case you said no, but I'm really glad you didn't. Welcome to *Colorado Insight*, Stephen. We're glad to have you on board. If you stop by Ellen's desk on the way out, she can have you fill out the necessary paperwork for your taxes, benefits and details about your salary, which I'm sure you'll find generous for a new college graduate. It's quite a package for such a new organization."

Stephen filled out the necessary paperwork and walked out the door, a man with a great job the first workday after graduation. He spotted a church down the street and found his feet walking toward the inviting building. It was a pleasant little place, brightly lit with a pretty stained glass window behind the pulpit. The pews were light oak with padded moss green upholstery and matching plush carpet. He thought perhaps only 100 people would fit inside the small building. No one was in sight, so Stephen dropped into the front pew. The sun shining through the stained glass window made pretty patterns of light across the floor in front of him. He watched their dance, and then looked up at a simple cross.

"Jesus, you are so good to me. Use me. I will follow your lead in all that I do. Thank you."

It was difficult, but Stephen remained quiet, letting his Lord fill his soul. At first, he felt nothing, but then a gentle warmth and a feeling of complete peace surrounded him.

"You are mine, it is written in my Book of Life. You will show the nations who I am through my creations Stephen. You will bring many sheep to me through your work, my good and faithful servant."

"Oh, Lord. You honor me. I don't deserve you."

"It is I who chooses who will do my work. Everyone has a special purpose and yours is to show those who do not know who I am. It is your gift. Use it wisely."

"Thank you Lord, I will do as you say. Help me to know how to reach your people."

"Continue praying, Stephen, and I will show you."

The words were so clear, as if God spoke aloud. Stephen opened his eyes and looked around. He was still the only one in the sanctuary. He knew then God gave him an even greater gift than his love and skill with photography. He had an assignment from God, the Almighty Creator of the Universe! With a light step, he stood up, left the little church and started a mental list of all the items he would need for his trip to Leadville.

CHAPTER 19
BOULDER, CO

WINNIE SIGHED. Oh, to be young again, to experience joy and love, pain and loss. No, she liked being old, not that she knew everything, but life's experiences gave her wisdom and she truly hoped and prayed she could be a friend to this special young woman. Again, she thought about the uncommon urge to go to the park and knew God had set up the divine appointment. She didn't even know how to respond to the terribly frightening ordeal Tasha went through. *"Lord, give me the words."*

She looked over at the young woman, deep in thought, with a wistful smile on her face. Tasha had stopped talking, but it was apparent she was remembering something very nice, thank goodness, after the horrible part of her story she just told. Winnie took the opportunity to get up, stretch her old muscles and give her bones a change of position. She cleared the dishes and washed them by hand in the sink, the warm water and suds comforting and soothing to her wrinkled hands. She had a small dishwasher but she preferred to wash the dishes by hand. There were so few. Besides, she loved the smell of Dove. Her mother and her mother before her used the same detergent and the pleasant scent brought comfort. You were never too old to miss your mother.

She rinsed the dishes and left them to dry in the rack. Winnie went to the restroom and returned to find Tasha walking around the room.

"Oh, there you are," she exclaimed. "I thought I bored you to tears and you went to bed."

"Never, dear. Your story is fascinating and I feel honored that I am the first one you shared it with besides Lisa. Such tragedy, tsk, tsk. Do you mind if I ask you one question?"

Tasha hesitated, "Sure, I just won't answer if I'm not comfortable with it."

"I like an honest woman," Winnie replied. "Throughout your childhood and what you've told me so far, you seem to have a deep and trusting relationship with God. Yet I don't sense that now. What happened?"

Tasha frowned, thinking about the question. "You're right Winnie. I know I need God, and in fact, just this morning, I was praying to him and it felt good to come back. It has been a long time."

CHAPTER 20
BOULDER, CO

"**I**SN'T SHE just the cutest thing you ever saw"? Lisa gushed to Tasha.

"Lisa, you know we aren't supposed to have cats in our apartment complex. It's against the rules and if we get caught we can get kicked out."

"I named her Penelope. Doesn't she look just like a little grey fluff-ball? She's just 10 weeks old the lady outside the grocery store said. She had 10 kittens in a basket, and I picked this little sweetie pie. I got her some kitten food and a litter box that I will hide in the laundry room closet and change every day. No one has to know. Tasha we can't take her back, she needs a home or she'll go to the shelter." Lisa looked up at Tasha, eyes pleading to let her keep the kitten. She held the tiny kitten out to her best friend.

Tasha sighed and took the kitten. She was soft, softer than anything she had ever touched and her bright eyes were so green against her fluffy gray fur. Penelope snuggled up into her neck and started purring, her tiny sharp claws kneading Tasha's chest.

"Oh, she is sweet isn't she?" Penelope nestled in closer and gave Tasha a rough lick on her neck. Tasha smiled and admitted defeat. "Okay, we'll keep her, but if you don't change the litter and this place smells like a cat, you'll have to find her another home. Deal?"

"You got it. Tasha, she's so adorable. Imagine all the pictures you can take of her as she grows up. Maybe you can publish a book on how a kitten grows, for kids, you know, about how to take care of them. You do the shots and I'll find a cat expert to write the text."

"Now that's a thought, but you know how busy I am. I only have one year left in college and Guenther expects a perfect portfolio before I graduate. I doubt a bunch of cat photos will be pleasing to him, though one or two might be okay."

"How many more do you need?"

"Well, I almost have enough now, but some of them are not as good as I would like. I still need at least five outdoor shots. I want a good job when I graduate, so I need a great portfolio. I'm scared though, what if someone really does want to hire me? You know what I went through Lisa. You're the only one I trust besides my parents. What if my employer wants me to go somewhere remote, you know, by myself? I don't think I could do it."

"Tasha, I know it was bad, but it was over five years ago and your birth mother is dead. You haven't been on a single date, you never go anywhere unless there's a ton of people around, and you sleep with your light on every night. You're letting fear rule your life, and what kind of life is that?"

"You don't know anything about what it was like, and don't pretend you do. What about my birth father? What if he knows about me and has been watching and waiting all these years? He might live right down the street for all I know. You're not me, Lisa, and I have every right to be frightened," Tasha replied grimly, anger in her voice. She hugged the little kitten tighter and it mewed in response.

"You're wrong, Tasha. Your parents raised you to know Christ, and he wouldn't want you to live this kind of life. You say you're a Christian, but you're sure not living like one. Guenther wants those outdoor photos for your portfolio. All you have now are buildings, fruit, parks and people. They're great, but it's not complete and you know it. I'll go with you and sit quietly so you're not afraid, but even I'm not enough, am I? You've got to hear it, Tasha. Get counseling, talk to our pastor, do something. Get over it!"

"How could you, Lisa? I thought you were my friend, that you understood," Tasha sat down, tears welling up in her eyes.

"I am your friend Tasha, that's why I can't stay quiet any longer. Real friends tell the truth, and I hope you would do the same for me. You've only got one more year Tasha, let me know how I can help, and I'll be there. Stop hiding. You know your parents would say the same."

"These are very good, Tasha. I hope you're as pleased as I am," Dr. Guenther stated. He opened the darkroom door and indicated she was to follow him out. "You've got the indoor lighting shots down, no shadows unless they're intentional. The baby portrait is perfect. I know how hard it is to get babies to cooperate. I didn't ask for animals, but the regal pose of the German shepherd in the park and the little grey kitten in the laundry basket are both very good. Your portfolio is almost complete. I am going to ask you to do an internship with me for your last year, but I don't want to divert your attention away from the last requirement of at least five outdoor shots. Is there a reason why you haven't done them yet? Do you need transportation or ideas of where to go? I can arrange that if necessary."

They arrived at his office and Tasha felt the familiar churning in her stomach. Her palms were damp and her hands shook as she nervously tucked her hair behind her ears. She hated it when she did that. It made her look so stupid.

"Yes, that would be helpful," she blurted out. Wait, what in the world made her say that? She had a car and enough money for gas, why did she say she needed help with transportation? Who knows who he would stick her with? They might not have any patience, and of course, would notice how frightened she was when they arrived and she had to get out of the car. "Uh, no, I don't need transportation, I can get myself places. Thanks anyway."

Dr. Guenther looked at her, obviously wondering why one of his favorite students was so ill at ease and nervous, even frightened. "Tasha, is there something wrong?"

"No, of course not. I'm fine. Are we finished now?" she asked, backing out of his office into the hall.

"Okay, but Tasha, let me know if there is anything I can do to help. I would still like you to intern with me, but not until you've got a start on those last five photos," he said to her retreating back, puzzled. "What was that all about?"

Tasha all but ran down the hall and outdoors, breathing heavily. Her heart was beating so fast. She didn't stop, she ran and ran not knowing or caring where she was going. As long as there were people around, she was fine. Maybe she would never graduate. There were always people on campus, on the grounds, in the dining and lecture halls. Even in the darkroom she rarely had the place to herself. Finally gasping for breath, she spotted a bench under a budding dogwood tree. Spring was her favorite time of year. Her stomach still churned as she wondered how she was going to get out of this mess. Dropping her backpack on the ground, she knelt over and rested her head between her knees. Her mom always said that helped when you were light headed.

After a few moments she opened her eyes, and saw the most incredible flowers, blooming right under the bench. She knew they were a variety of freesia but didn't think they bloomed this early. She took in their delicate scent and still upside down reached for her backpack, and took her camera out. She thought with amusement, I don't think I've ever taken pictures upside down before. Her stomach settled as she began taking the shots, slipping off the bench and lying on her stomach to get closer and different angles. She backed up and got a great shot of the freesias, bench and blooming dogwood in the background. Totally lost in what she was doing, she didn't notice the stranger sit down on the bench until she put her camera away. She felt drawn to him and had a sense that she knew him from somewhere, but couldn't place it. Then she smelt it, like it had just rained, and she felt the peace slip over her and she knew. It was the young man at her high school the first day she went back to school … afterwards. Carefully she sat down next to him on the bench.

"You," she breathed in awe. "Where have you been? Where did you go? I tried to find you the rest of the year."

He smiled a gentle smile and reached out to touch her gently on the shoulder. "A friend in need, that's who I am."

Tasha's shoulder felt so warm, she didn't want him to remove his hand. "What's your name? Do you go to college here too? Why haven't I seen you here before?" The questions rushed out all in a tumble of words, but Tasha didn't want him to go away, ever.

"You haven't needed me until now. I am here, and that's what matters."

"I never got to thank you, you know for that day you were there for me. I was so scared, and you made it okay. How did you know?"

He smiled, "You're welcome," and left it at that. "I noticed some of your photos in the campus newspaper. You're very good. Those little flowers under the bench will probably be in the next issue if you submit them."

Tasha felt shy all of the sudden. "Thanks a lot. I'm glad when I can bring joy to others through my work. The freesia shots I just took will go into my portfolio if they're as good as I think they will be. Hey, what's your major?"

He laughed, "Oh, I'm not a student."

She looked confused, "A professor then?" He looked much too young though.

"No, not a professor either, just a friend in need. I saw you running across campus and thought you might need some company and a little help."

"You can't be real, yet I feel I already know you, and yes, I do need help. I'm not sure why I'm telling you, except I just know that I can trust you. I feel safe with you. What do I call you besides 'friend in need'?"

"I think Joseph will do nicely. Hi Tasha, I'm Joseph, and I'm very pleased to meet your acquaintance." He gave her a mischievous smile and she laughed.

"Hello my old and new friend, I'm pleased to meet you too. Do you want to go for a cup of coffee? I know a great little place just around the corner from my apartment. Then I want you to meet Lisa, my roommate and Penelope, our illegal kitten. Lisa's been hearing about you for years and it would be nice to introduce you two, plus get to know you better."

"The coffee sounds great, but I'll pass on meeting your friend for now." They walked the few short blocks to the coffee shop, enjoying the smell of spring. Tasha had never felt more comfortable and warm with anyone in her life. She wondered if it was love at first sight. It didn't feel romantic, just so good and right. Before she knew it, they had their coffee and scones, and he had already paid and was walking her to her door.

"Tomorrow is Saturday, and I know you don't have any classes. I would love to take you to a beautiful spot for a picnic. Will you meet me here at 5:00 a.m. sharp?" Tasha quickly nodded her head in agreement, again not knowing why she completely trusted him. "Oh, and Tasha? Bring your camera and lots of film." He flicked her gently under her chin and was gone in a heartbeat.

"Joseph?" He was already gone. Tasha realized she hadn't told him she needed help, yet deep down she knew that he understood. The picnic was a guise to help her get those scenic shots she needed.

"Lord, did you send him? I haven't been talking to you much lately. If it is you, then thanks. And thanks for Lisa and Penelope too. You know how much I need them. And my parents."

"Lisa?" Tasha called. "Lisa? Where are you?" Penelope rushed over and started batting Tasha's shoelaces. Not wanting to step on her, Tasha picked up the little grey fur ball and the luscious sound of purring filled her ears.

"Oh Penelope, you're precious, but where is Lisa?" Tasha exclaimed. She had to share the news of Joseph with her. Lisa would understand. Her friend knew everything about that day and reassured Tasha that she would meet the stranger again someday.

It was Friday and Fridays were off limits for studying, a roommate pact that they formed when they moved in together. So where was she? Walking over to the kitchen counter to dump her backpack, Tasha saw the blinking light on the answering machine and felt a lump in her throat. Not tonight, she couldn't have plans tonight, of all nights when she finally met Joseph.

Tasha made herself press the button and waited for bad news.

"Hey Tash, it's me. Running a bit late, but I'll be home by six with pizza and Breyers Rocky Road so don't make anything, okay? Bye!"

Relief flooded over Tasha and Penelope gave her a look that said, "See, why did you worry?" "I know, I know, I can be insecure sometimes. I don't know what I'm going to do if Lisa ever marries some great guy and leaves me. Let's go take a bath, Penelope. You can play with my toes through the bubbles as long as you play nice."

CHAPTER 21
BOULDER, CO

"HEY STEPHEN, what are you doing for Christmas this year?"

Ed Hauser would never have believed how successful *Colorado Insight* had become if he hadn't seen it for himself. And Stephen Banks was a huge part of the reason. The guy was phenomenal when it came to capturing a perfect moment, and he had the guts to go anywhere.

"I thought I might go up to Washington. It's been awhile since I've seen Carl and Sara. When I talked with them last week, they said the bald eagle sightings along Beauty Bay on Lake Coeur d'Alene, Idaho are exceptional this year. Sighting reports are coming in of over a hundred different eagles, and the season still has almost a month to go. They feed on the salmon after they spawn. The fish are easy pickings when they die and float to the top of the lake."

"Okay, but if you change your mind, we would love to have you over for the day, or you can join us the week after at our cabin in Estes Park. There is no reason for you to be alone during the holidays."

Ed knew one of the reasons Stephen was so driven was because he was lonely. Not that Stephen would admit it, but he saw the longing in his eyes when his own wife and children came by the office for a quick visit. The children excitedly called "Daddy, Daddy" and ran to him ready for a hug and tickle before he let them go to greet his lovely wife. Stephen took it all in, then usually quietly left the room.

Ed once found him looking at past archives of pictures of families after one such visit. The magazine layouts that Stephen took of women and children called for the viewer to share his desire. The tender feelings invoked by a mother laughing with her baby at a comical raccoon's antics would make any man want to jump right into the picture with them. Stephen rarely took pictures of couples unless Ed asked him for a specific reason. Soon after joining the magazine, Stephen took an assignment on romantic bed and breakfast locations. When he returned from the shoot, he was moody and irritable for a few days, quite unlike his normal pleasant disposition. Ed had a freelance photographer do a similar assignment the next year rather than put Stephen through such torture again.

Ed wondered why Stephen couldn't find and marry a lovely young woman. The man was ruggedly handsome. His own wife said Stephen should be on the other side of the lens in their magazine. Oh, they had tried several times to subtly introduce him to friends and acquaintances. Stephen was polite and friendly, but never asked for their numbers or to see them again. Ed thought it might have to do with his religion. Stephen had once said something about being unequally yoked whatever that meant. "Surely, there was someone in that church he attended faithfully that would make a good wife?"

"Ed, are you there?" Stephen was talking to him and Ed hadn't heard a word he said.

"Yeah, sorry, just daydreaming, what were you saying?"

"If you email me your cabin phone number and address I might stop by after my Washington trip if I decide to cut it short. Otherwise I'll see you in January."

"Sure enough Stephen, I'll do that this afternoon. Tell Carl and Sara hi from me and don't fall into that lake and drown, or worse, get carried off by an eagle. Have a nice Christmas."

Stephen decided to drive up and surprise his adopted parents for the holiday. He had a week before Christmas, and if he left tomorrow morning that would give him time to stop along the way and hopefully get some good shots for his freelance work. He had so many requests in the last six months, it was difficult to keep up along with his work for *Colorado Insight*. Lately he was feeling uninspired for the magazine. Ed gave him a variety of assignments, but they were starting to all feel the same. Stephen felt the stirrings of anticipation and excitement for the trip and that perhaps he would even make it a loop along the Pacific Coast on the way home. Those feelings had been absent for the past several months, and he hurried to finish his last assignment before going home to pack.

The snow crunched under the old jeep's tires. It was still dark outside on Christmas morning as Stephen pulled into the familiar driveway. He grabbed a small suitcase and two huge stockings stuffed with small treasures for Carl and Sara. Quietly he walked up the stairs to the front porch, careful to miss the squeaky board that always alerted Nate that a visitor was approaching. That's all he needed, for the dog to start barking in the still morning and spoil his surprise.

Sure enough, the key was still hidden under the milk can. Both the can and key felt like ice to Stephen's warm fingers. He thought it must be close to 10 degrees this morning. Slowly, and carefully, Stephen opened the old door, whispering to Nate in the darkness.

"Hey boy, it's me." Sure enough, he heard the soft click of nails on the wood floor and felt a warm lick on his hand.

Stephen dropped his packages and sat down on the floor, hugging the dog tight and burying his face in his soft fur. Nate gave small whimpers of welcome, and Stephen felt an overwhelming sense of home.

"Thank you Lord."

"Shhh, come on Nate." They walked over to the couch, and Stephen unfolded his long body, squishing up against the back of the couch as close as possible so Nate could join him. Sara found them like that as the sun rose in the eastern sky, boy and dog, both grown now, but still as close as when they were growing up together. Stephen's hair was tousled and he had an arm flung over Nate, holding him close. The dog watched her movements through the kitchen, but didn't get up and ask to be let out as was their usual routine. Sara's heart was full and she too uttered up a silent prayer of thanks to God as the day to celebrate Jesus' birth began.

The smells, wonderful smells greeted Stephen when he slowly began to wake. Coffee, fresh squeezed orange juice and bacon, could it get any better? He caught his breath at the view out the front window of freshly fallen snow draping the ponderosa pines in the sparkling sunlight. Stephen felt the urge to unpack his camera, but he was too comfortable. Nate contentedly remained beside him, and while the dog might have a bladder made of steel, Stephen did not. Besides, he was dying for a cup of Sara's coffee.

"Move over boy, it's time to get up."

Nate slowly wagged his tail, thumping it against Stephen's leg, but he made no other move to get off the couch. Sara smiled and shrugged her shoulders, suggesting it was Stephen's problem on how to get the big dog to move.

"Come on, Sara, help me out here, please?"

She laughed, "Nate, time to get up, your breakfast is waiting." Walking over with the bowl of dried food, she waved it under his nose. "Christmas morning, boy, bacon drippings for you!" At that, Nate's ears perked up and he rolled off the couch. Stephen noticed the dog was finally beginning to show his age. A grip of angst took hold of his stomach as he realized that Nate had already passed his normal life expectancy. His rational mind knew that dogs did not live as long as humans, and it was to be expected that Nate could die at any time. He looked at Sara with new eyes. She was showing signs of age too, graying hair and more wrinkles, though she was still slim and walked with a bounce in her step this morning.

"God, please don't take them yet. I'm not ready."

The kitchen door opened and Carl stomped in.

"Whew, it's a cold one out there all right." He stepped toward Sara.

"Oh no you don't, you warm up by the stove first before wrapping those big arms around me!" She ran to the other side of the kitchen laughing.

Stephen's eyes welled up with tears of both joy and sorrow. This couple was so special to him, he felt safe and at home here. Yet he also wanted the same kind of life for himself.

"When, God? How long must I wait?"

"Oh Stephen, you shouldn't have!"

Stephen grinned as he watched Sara unwrap the last gift from her stocking. The small gifts on top were some of her favorites, but nothing special. A candle, dark chocolate, bubble bath and some gourmet coffee. His heart swelled as he watched her pleasure in the last gift. It was very small and delicate, and he found it in an old antique store close to the university. The treasure was a gold filigree locket, polished until it shone. When opened, the left side showed a miniature picture of Carl and Sara on their wedding day, and on the left a picture of him and his mom on the day they got Nate.

"Where, when, oh how did you find these pictures? It's perfect Stephen!" She ran over and gave him a huge hug. Stephen gladly accepted, never did he refuse her hugs no matter how old he became.

"I'm glad you like it Sara. The secrets are my own however," he smirked mischievously.

She turned to Carl as he opened his gifts. Similar to Sara's he received his favorites as well. A bag of smoked almonds, a new pair of leather work gloves, the latest John Grisham novel and a 1000 piece puzzle. Carl paused as he reached down deep inside the stocking for the last gift. His eyes lifted to Stephen, questioning if he should open it now.

Stephen smiled and nodded for Carl to continue.

Sighing with pleasure, Carl pulled the last gift out and slowly began to unwrap it. He heard the tinkling of small metal objects, and knew Stephen must have searched long and far for the treasures. A simple farmer, it was an unusual hobby, but Carl had always enjoyed collecting valuable and interesting coins from faraway places. Never having been to the places of his collection, he still had an insatiable interest in ancient history. He had several coins hundreds of years old. Sure enough, Stephen found some he had been trying to find for years. These were from Greece and very old. Carl could almost hear the women bartering in the common square market as he looked at the coins.

"Where did you find these Son? How did you know?" Once again, Stephen smirked and accepted Carl's hug of gratitude before he rushed off to put the coins in his treasure box.

"One for you too, boy. A brand new collar, leash and smoked marrow bone for you." As he took the old worn collar off and replaced it with the new one, the dog's soft brown eyes looked up with love and gratitude.

"It's just a collar, Nate." Stephen knew it was more than that. It was the unconditional love the dog had for him, no matter how long between visits. All Nate expected was a simple caress and the privilege of lying next to his feet. Stephen felt humbled and wished he could be as gracious and appreciative of the ones he loved.

"I don't know Sara, it's a great job, but I'm feeling like I'm ready to move on. The assignments are starting to all seem the same, and there's so much more I can do."

"Have you considered going back to freelancing?" Sara replied. She hoped and wondered if he would move back to Washington, but knew it had to be his decision with no pressure from her.

"Yes, that's always been my dream," he sighed.

"Well, then do it. God will provide for you if this is something he wants you to do."

"But how do I know for sure?"

"Pray about it, and if you feel a peace and the doors of opportunity easily open for you, I would say that's a yes. You've established a reputation and if I'm not wrong, you have plenty of opportunity for assignments. Once the word is out that you are freelancing full-time, you'll probably get even more requests. Last resort, you can advertise or ... take school pictures for a living!" She held her hands up in front of her face and ducked, knowing he wouldn't throw a pillow at her, but she couldn't resist teasing him.

Stephen shuddered, "Oh no, not the dreaded school picture photographer."

Sara laughed, "Those guys have a difficult enough job getting kids to smile, not to mention their mothers to be satisfied without a dozen retakes. What did you have in mind that you would like to do?"

Stephen stared out the window a moment before replying. "I want to show who God is through my work. It might be relationships, forces of nature, his majestic creation or just everyday life. My question is … who will buy and publish such works?"

"You would be surprised. When's the last time you went to the library and looked through the many publications? Not every magazine has to be National Geographic, you know."

"Okay, Sara. I'm going to pray about it, and I would appreciate it if you would pray for me too. Assuming God doesn't say no, I'll give my notice to *Colorado Insight* when I return. I'll offer to do one shoot a month for them until they hire someone else. Sound fair?"

"More than fair. Do you think you'll continue to work in Colorado or relocate?" Sara held her breath waiting his reply. She tried to keep her voice even and hoped the longing didn't show through in her question.

Stephen didn't even notice. "Oh, I'll stay in Colorado. It's where I'm established and have my studio. I like it there, and well, it's where I got my start after, you know, when Mom and Marcie …" his voice trailed off and they both thought back to that awful day.

Sara walked over and gave him a hug. "I know Stephen, I know. If Carl ever decides to retire, maybe we can come visit you more often. Especially once you choose to settle down and grandkids come along," she winked, then paused, knowing she hit a sore spot and regretted her light-hearted comment.

He pulled back and looked in her eyes. "Sara, do you think God will ever give me someone of my own? I pray for the right person every day, but so far it just hasn't happened. I'm so lonely sometimes it hurts. I see you and Carl, and how fulfilled your lives are together. I want to be married and have a family, more than anything."

"I know, I'm sorry Stephen. We have been and will continue to pray for you. I'm sure God has someone special in mind for you, and if not, well his love is sufficient."

Nate whined and brushed against Stephen's leg. "You want to try out that new leash, old boy?" Nate's tail thumped against the floor, and his ears perked up. As Stephen walked toward the door, the dog jumped up and ran back and forth. "You would think you're a puppy again!" He clipped the leash on Nate's new collar, pulled on his warm fleece coat and grinned at Sara before taking the dog out into the cold, clear day. He laughed as Nate growled and bit at the newly fallen snow, throwing it into the air in play. He gave up on the leash and started throwing snowballs for Nate, laughing at the old dog's perplexed look when the ball dissipated after hitting the ground. Stephen changed his mind about the walk and decided to build a huge snowman in the driveway instead. The snow was a bit dry due to the cold, but with a little perseverance, he soon had his first ball growing as he pushed it around the yard. All the while Nate ran to and fro.

When Stephen finally hoisted the last of the three big balls on top of one another and filled in the flat spots, Sara came outside with the "snowman" basket as she called it. Sure enough, he remembered she always kept one on hand for days such as this. In it he found a fresh long carrot for a nose, two lumps of charcoal for eyes, strings of red licorice for the mouth, an old beat up hat and scarf, and of course a broom for the snowman to hold in his improvised tree branch hand should he decide to sweep the walk. There was also a bag of birdseed to spread for the birds who chose to stay for the winter and a snickers bar for himself.

"When you're done, I have hot cocoa waiting for you," she called as she let herself back into the warm house and watched him finish the final touches on his masterpiece through the front room window. Unlocking his jeep, Stephen pulled out the small disposable camera he kept in the glove box for emergencies and snapped a shot of Nate growling fiercely in play at the newcomer. His heart filled with gladness and again he was happy he made the long trip up here for Christmas. The talk with Sara confirmed that he was ready to become a full-time freelance photographer if God answered his prayers. Carl and Sara's delight in his coming and their small presents filled him with love only a family can bring.

"Thank you, God, thank you."

He went inside to enjoy his hot cocoa and a rousing game of Monopoly. He had a week before going back to Colorado, and he fully intended to enjoy every moment, even if it meant Carl had him fixing fences and tractors!

Stephen walked back into his rental, and decided right then and there to move. He had enough in savings to put a good down payment on a house. If he was going to be a freelance photographer, he wanted a house of his own, with a room to make into a studio, another room for portrait shots and a bigger darkroom.

Ed groaned at his resignation, but said he had known for some time that Stephen was ready to move on. He was grateful for the agreement that Stephen would continue to do one layout a month for the next six months, then he might be willing to freelance for him later on given time in his busy schedule. Word was already out, and Stephen had more assignments than he could possibly finish in the next six months. The clients were patient and willing to wait, "… if he would only accept their proposal." So, Stephen accepted and told them he would do the best he could.

Stephen called the church and asked if there was a good real estate agent in the congregation. The secretary gave him two names, one of which she had used herself and was very pleased with the results. Stephen called the one she recommended, and told him what he was looking for. He had an appointment the following morning to look at a house on Mapleton Street, an established neighborhood near downtown. The downstairs could work for his photography business, while the upstairs had several bedrooms and a bath for his residence. It sounded … too good to be true.

Stephen looked through his assignments and prioritized them by the date they needed to be finished, and if he was honest with himself, his preference in the subject matter. Then he went to the grocery store around the corner and asked for empty boxes. They hadn't crushed them yet in the recycler, so Stephen helped himself, and took several home to start packing. He had no idea when he would be moving, but who knew when he would have a free afternoon again? There wasn't much to pack so it didn't take long, and Stephen daydreamed about the house on Mapleton. He hoped it was empty and ready to move in.

The house was perfect. Stephen noticed the huge trees in the front yard right away, welcoming him up the walk to the beautiful brick home. It had a front porch for morning coffee or cocoa and several windows to let in the afternoon sun and offer natural light.

"I'll take it."

The realtor guffawed and said he hadn't even been inside yet, or what the price was.

"I know, but I know God wants me to have this house and it will work out just fine."

The inside was even prettier than the outside, and indeed the house was vacant and within Stephen's price range. He completed the paperwork, and Stephen slept in his new home just eight days after he decided he would move, having the option to rent until the closing date. It was definitely an answer to prayer.

He transformed the hall and front parlor into a reception area to welcome guests and display his favorite photos. He turned the two downstairs bedrooms into a darkroom and a portrait studio. Both were lovely rooms, and he hated to cover the darkroom's windows, but it was necessary. The studio had two large windows for either natural light, or he had several different pull-down shades for backdrops. His new home also had four bedrooms upstairs, one for himself and hopefully a wife someday, one for an office and the third for guests.

Stephen secretly longed for a baby to fill the fourth room with gurgles and laughter. He daydreamed about a faceless woman with a gentle smile hushing the baby as she rocked back and forth. His mom had a rocking chair that Sara kept, but he knew she would give it to him for her first grandchild. The house was perfect, now if God would just answer the second part of his prayer.

CHAPTER 22
BOULDER, CO

"**Y**OU WAITED," Tasha exclaimed, out of breath. "I'm sorry I'm late. My roommate Lisa and I stayed up late talking, and I'm afraid I overslept."

Joseph looked at her tousled hair swept back into a haphazard ponytail, pillowcase wrinkles still marking her soft cheeks, and gave her a gentle and sweet smile. "I knew you were coming. I don't mind. Besides, it's still dark. We've got time."

Tasha's heart skipped a beat and melted.

"Do you want some breakfast before we get started?" Joseph nodded toward the bakery.

"Oh, a cup of coffee and a bagel would be great. Have you eaten yet?"

"No, I waited for you. Let's get something to go so we can be off before the light gets too bright for your pictures. I know you'll get some good ones today."

Soon Tasha was driving Gretchen, her beloved Volkswagen bug into the foothills following Joseph's directions, sipping hot coffee and enjoying her blueberry and cream cheese bagel. She cringed at the thought of her mom lifting her brows and asking if this was a balanced meal. Actually, Tasha didn't mind. She was quite used to her mom bugging her about eating healthy. Secretly it made her feel loved. In her classes where she learned about the food pyramid, she usually scored very well when writing down what she ate every day. She would make up for it later with a big salad.

The scenery was getting more familiar as she turned where Joseph told her to and Tasha started to feel uncomfortable. No, she was very nervous and felt her heart beating wildly, her palms were so wet she worried they would slip on the steering wheel, and she was having a difficult time breathing. The last turn Joseph told her to make brought her to the same parking lot of her abduction almost five years earlier.

"I … I'm sorry, I can't stay here," Tasha turned to the nice young man next to her, fear and panic radiating through every pore in her body.

Joseph gently reached over and touched Tasha on the shoulder, then her cheek.

An immediate peace and calm overcame her. The shaking stopped and she found she could breathe again, though she refused to look out the window. She knew she would see what once used to be her favorite lake and a small cabin on the distant shore … the cabin she dreamed about owning one day.

"Who are you? Where did you come from?" she breathed.

Joseph smiled and his whole face lit up, though the sun was just rising into the sky. "I'm your friend in need, Tasha, I told you that already. Now, God is displaying his light over his creation so beautifully, don't you think you better get your camera ready for those portfolio shots before it's too bright?"

Tasha nodded in understanding, all her fear gone and replaced by awe. She turned and grabbed her bag, loaded the film and stepped out of the car. Joseph knew she wasn't ready to be alone, so he followed her as she went about snapping pictures of everything God created in sight. He handed her another roll of film when she ran out and safely stored the ones already taken in the side pocket of her bag. An eagle soared over for an early morning breakfast while beavers busily built a dam. A mother doe and her twin fawns cautiously went to the shore for a drink before quietly moving off for the new spring shoots of grass and buds. God displayed his glory over the lake and trees, giving the most spectacular sunrise Tasha had ever witnessed.

Joseph even led her around the small lake to the cabin Tasha had admired and she took several shots, wondering if indeed she would ever have the courage to come back here alone, much less own it someday. Before they knew it, the sun was high in the sky and the light too harsh and bright. Tasha took nine rolls of film, and she was sure there would be more than five good shots for her portfolio.

As they walked back to the car, Tasha realized they hadn't said one word to each other, yet she felt like she had known Joseph forever. She was so grateful that he brought her here and helped conquer the fear that had gripped her life the last five years. She watched him look around at the beauty and thought he was extremely handsome. That wasn't as important as he was kind and generous. She thought he looked enormously pleased at the success of the morning. He looked down and smiled that special smile before reaching for her hand to give it a gentle squeeze before letting go.

Tasha's stomach fluttered again and he gave a slight frown. He hadn't meant for her to feel that way. It wasn't supposed to be like that, only friendship and to help her lose the fear. That was his purpose. If it became romantic, that wouldn't do at all, no not at all. It was time to go again, he realized with a slight disappointment. He knew he had filled his assignment, yet he wanted to stay longer.

Before Tasha knew it, they were back at her car and her stomach was growling. "Joseph, that was incredible. I'm not afraid anymore. At least not as long as you're with me. You know, don't you? What happened, and that it was here?"

He nodded and squeezed her shoulder again.

Wow, every time he touched her, Tasha felt so warm and loved. She didn't want him to let go, ever.

"I'm glad Tasha. You don't ever need to be afraid again. God is with you always. He was with you the day you were abducted, he is with you today, and he will be with you every day here on earth and into eternity. You don't need me to be with you because God is with you."

He touched right above her heart.

"In here, Tasha, that's where God is because you asked him to be. He will never leave you."

Tasha choked up and felt a burning sensation on her chest, the warmth filling her.

"I know he's there, thank you for reminding me and helping to take away the fear." Tasha struggled for words. Her stomach growled again, and she realized they forgot to bring a picnic.

"Do you want to stop for lunch on the way back, Joseph? I am so hungry!" Tasha asked, her tone and expression hopeful.

"No, thank you. You know the way back and it's time I move on. I have a ride coming soon. I'll just meet him up the road. Take care, Tasha. Remember, I know whenever you need me. I'll be here for you, okay? Always." Joseph gave her a small hug, let go, gave a little wave and started walking away.

"No, don't go!" Tasha cried. "Stay!"

Joseph looked back, longing in his eyes. "I want to, but my father has many who need help and it's time for me to go."

She watched him turn and continue to walk away until he faded into nothing. Tears coursed down her cheeks as she felt both an extreme sense of loss and joy at the same time. Tasha turned to open her car door and looked over once again at the small cabin. She gasped. A perfect double rainbow arched over it from one side to another like a door beckoning her to come in. It only lasted for a moment, but she knew it was for her. No clouds, no rain, it didn't make sense. But she saw it and believed. As she looked around the lake one more time, she knew her fear was gone and trust filled its place. *Thank you,*

God," she whispered, knowing she belonged to him forever. His plans were her plans.

"Tasha, these are exquisite," Dr. Guenther exclaimed. "The light, the colors, the mood. How did you find this place?"

Tasha shrugged her shoulders and blushed, "I've known about it for a long time, but it's taken me awhile to go back. I'm glad you like them."

"Like them? I love them! Most of these are good enough to be published, in fact I recommend we do submit a few to the amateur competition coming up in *Photography Today*."

Tasha felt warm all over with pleasure. He liked them, her fear was gone and God was the sole reason. A sudden thought crossed her mind and before she lost her courage, Tasha asked, "Dr. Guenther, can I share something with you?"

"If you tell me the secret to your success, sure," he joked.

"Those pictures really aren't me, you see, uh, I'm a Christian and God, you know, the God of the universe, all creation? Him? He helped me with those photographs. He showed me what he made, gave me the light, the beauty, the backgrounds, the urge to take particular shots in various ways." Tasha trembled, even though her words were self-assured and strong. She hoped he wouldn't scoff or laugh at her.

Instead, Dr. Guenther looked at her intently for a moment, and just when she thought he was going to tell her there was no such thing, he agreed. "I know exactly what you're talking about, Tasha. When I first started teaching, I didn't know God, and while my work was good, there was something missing. A few years ago, I had a promising student very similar to you who introduced me to your God, and my life and work have never been the same since. I want you to meet him someday. I think you two would make a great team."

"Oh, Dr. Guenther, I am so glad you understand, but I'm even more glad I can be my true self with you and that we'll be together in Heaven some day!" She beamed as she gathered her supplies and the developed photographs and headed toward the door. "Have a glorious day, Dr. Guenther!" She felt like she was practically floating through the air.

"Wait, Tasha! I expect that internship application by next Tuesday before you register for the fall semester. You'll need my signature in order to add the class."

"Yes, sir!" She was definitely floating.

CHAPTER 23
BOULDER, CO

"OH, JOSEPH, where are you? I need you, your touch, your kind words and peace. I am so afraid. The fear was supposed to be gone, and it was ... but then some creepy guy followed me out of the grocery store to my car to ask for money, and my doubts and fears started to return. The more I thought about that guy, the more I saw the horrors of this world in the newspapers, television news and from friends telling me about bad accidents and murders."

"Joseph, I know I should be talking directly to God, and I've asked him to send you, but you haven't come. Why not? You said you would be here, and you're not. You're not here, and I am all alone." Tasha finished writing in the journal she started shortly after Joseph entered and exited her life the second time. "Where was he?"

She looked at the front door and tried to gain enough courage to walk through it. She knew there was a name for this kind of fear, but she didn't want a name for it, only for it to go away. Over the past year, she thrived under Dr. Guenther's internship and mentoring. She told him about her fear, and he prayed for her and encouraged her to face the fear and not let it rule her life. She forced the tremors and anxiety down as she drove to higher and farther distances searching for the perfect shots.

Getting out of the car was the hardest part, but once she immersed herself in the photography, she lost all sense of herself and time. She found rushing waterfalls and broad, colorful plateaus, roaring rivers and peaceful lakes, rugged mountain passes and serene meadows. Lisa worried about her as she forgot to call and often walked in after midnight. A few magazines and the campus newspaper published her work on a regular basis. People started to recognize her around campus and congratulated her. That scared her too. Being anonymous was better because no one would follow her or try to kidnap her.

Why should she continue to pray? "God obviously doesn't care about me or he would send Joseph to help." She sat back down on the couch, refusing to look at the front door. Lisa was leaving soon. They both graduated and her friend had a great job offer back east. How would she survive without Lisa? She didn't want to move back home, though her parents had offered. Her mom had been acting strange lately and it worried her. She was 22 years old with a promising career except for this crazy phobia. Yeah, call it what it is, a phobia.

Tasha sighed and read the want ads for a job. What could there be for a photographer who was afraid to go outside? She didn't want to be a waitress or work in a convenience store, for both of those jobs encountered creepy people all the time. There were ads for teachers, and while she liked children, she needed more education to earn a credential. "Wait, what was this one?"

Wanted: cheerful and friendly photographer to take children's school and sports pictures. Must be experienced. Reasonable pay plus benefits. Send resume to PO Box 4325, Boulder, CO.

"I can do that," Tasha thought. "I am cheerful and friendly … when I'm not afraid. And children can be fun." Obviously, the job didn't offer her the freedom and flexibility of traveling to different places with different subjects and it could get boring or frustrating, but it did look safe. And, safe was very important. Tasha decided to apply. Dr. Guenther was not very happy giving her a recommendation, but he understood.

"Tasha, don't get stuck there. Trust in God. You are good, Tasha, even gifted. Your gift will be wasted taking hundreds of pictures of the same thing every day, month after month, year after year. There's nothing wrong with taking good pictures of school kids, but you've been given a greater gift. Keep trying and continue to take photos of what you love. Don't stop submitting your photographs to magazines and studios, promise me?"

"I'll try. This job is just temporary until I conquer my fear. I know I will. Thank you for the recommendation. I appreciate it, sir."

"Don't try to do it on your own, Tasha. Pray, and seek help first from God and then talk with your pastor and get some counseling from a Christian professional. Call me when you are ready. I know just the place that would be perfect for you, okay?"

"I know this is what I need right now, sir." Just the thought of working in a studio where they gave her assignments, especially those that required travel, made Tasha feel nauseous. "I'll call you when I'm ready for more of a challenge, I promise."

Tasha gave the kind professor a warm hug. She would miss him, but she also knew she would always be able to find him. The thought was reassuring. She turned and waved goodbye with a lump in her throat. If she wasn't mistaken, his eyes were very bright, and she was sure he was holding back tears. Tasha forced herself to leave before she broke down and agreed to have him place the call. She knew she wasn't ready, and with regret and a sense of loss, didn't know if she would ever be.

"Okay, Tasha, Mrs. Barton's sixth grade class is next, then we'll be done with this school," Barb, the administrative assistant from the photography studio informed her. Tasha sighed. After three months of taking school pictures, the children were very predictable in their behavior. The schools all seemed the same. At least the sixth graders could listen to instructions, even if sometimes they were more than she could handle, full of hormones and trying to impress the opposite sex. Why did it have to start so young?

The younger grades were usually first so their nice clothes and combed hair wouldn't be ruined at recess. They had their own challenges too, shy kids, wiggly kids, giggly kids, messy kids and every other kind of kid she could think of. While she liked children, this job certainly wasn't what she expected, but it paid the bills and she felt safe. There was a little more traveling than she expected, but only to schools within a 30-mile radius, and once there, she was okay in the busy and crowded environment. Principals, teachers and children, what other population could she find that would be safer?

After Lisa moved back east after graduation, she left Penelope with Tasha. They were able to find a nice little guest house to rent that was perfect for the two of them. The owners lived in the main house and were so friendly, she felt secure and at home there too. She still didn't want to move back home with her parents. Her mother seemed even more different lately, absent-minded, and her dad had enough on his mind without having to worry about her too.

"Here they come, at least you got them before lunch, though they are itching to get out there on the playground," Barb gave her a tolerant smile and it brought Tasha's thoughts back to the job at hand. Tasha could tell she was ready to be done for the day too. It was Barb's job to make sure the children's clothes were tidy and hair somewhat presentable, otherwise there were too many requests for re-takes from parents who expected their child to look exactly the same as when they went out the door that morning. This group of faces looked sweet, even if they were pre-teens. She could tell the teacher had the class under control and the students respected him. Oh, the innocence she saw in each one. How she longed to preserve it forever, to protect them, but it wasn't possible. Her stomach clenched in fear thinking that one could be hurt, and she would read about it in the newspaper or hear on the news. Every time she saw a child on television, she wondered if she had taken that child's picture. Probably.

Every once in a while, she could tell when children were sad. There was a haunted look about them, and Tasha wondered about their home life. Were they abused? Did they have a gravely sick family member, or were they helpless victims of an angry divorce? Those were the kids she especially wanted to take home with her. She would lavish them with love and kindness until the vacant look in their eyes disappeared and a sweet smile returned. She wanted to make it all better, but was at a loss how. For those special kids, she kept a stash of happy face stickers in her bag, and as they passed by after she took their picture, she winked, put her finger over her lips to let them know to keep the secret, and passed them the small gift. She gently brushed their small fingers with kindness as the sticker passed between them. She smiled thinking about the pleasure she received from doing one small act to help make up for all the cruelty in the world.

Sometimes she shot a whole school and never gave a single sticker away, but today was disheartening as she recalled the face of each child who had received a sticker. Her stash significantly depleted, she gave out far too many. She knew she was right on, because happy kids usually turned around and gave her a big smile, a thumbs-up or high-five. Today from each of them, all she got was a couple of silent tears, a shrug of the shoulder, a slight smile or no acknowledgement at all. Her heart was heavy. Briefly she thought of changing her career to adolescent counseling, but discarded the idea because she couldn't even take care of herself, much less counsel others.

After she finished the shots and packed her equipment away, Tasha decided to go ahead and start developing the pictures that afternoon. She stopped at home for a quick lunch and went to the studio. It wasn't necessary. The school expected the pictures back in about a month, but Tasha liked to keep ahead of schedule and the parents were pleasantly surprised to get their portraits back in a week or two instead of waiting until their fast growing child didn't even look like the picture they received. The prompt service usually yielded a few secondary orders, making more profit for the company. Tasha's supervisor constantly praised her about the quality and promptness of her work.

She often received invitations to after-work parties, but Tasha wasn't interested, preferring to read a good novel or pore over photography magazines to learn more about her trade. Sometimes she called her dad to chat for a bit. Her mom didn't want to talk on the phone and when she did sometimes the words didn't make sense. She knew she should go visit, but the thought overwhelmed her. She liked to use the internet to shop for clothes or to dream about places to travel. With the internet, she hardly ever had to leave her little house except to shop for groceries once a week or so. While her life was far from exciting, Tasha resigned herself to the day-to-day routine that was so familiar and comforting.

CHAPTER 24
BOULDER, CO

"STEPHEN, YOU have got to see these photos. Listen to me!" William pleaded.

"You know I respect you sir, but you don't know my schedule. I've got more work than I can handle, and if you must know, I don't want to work with an intern right now."

"She is not an intern. She graduated four years ago and has been wasting her talent in a less than challenging job. I think she's finally ready to start her 'real' career. I've waited long enough, it's time someone knows of her gift and helps to realize her potential. You know me Stephen, I wouldn't recommend just anyone, and she needs you as much as you need her. I know you like working alone, but look at you man. You've got more work than you can handle, and frankly, you need a life. Why can't you hire someone to help you?"

"My work is my own, I don't want anyone interfering, that's why. Besides, what's so special about this one? What makes you think we can work together?"

William replied, "Stephen, I know you, I know Tasha. You both studied under me, though to be honest, I learned just as much from you two as you did from me. This is the right person. She will challenge you in ways that will make you a better photographer, and you can continue to teach her in ways that I couldn't. At least look at the photos I snuck from her and let me know what you think. Have I ever asked this of you before?"

"Snuck from her? What do you mean, *snuck* from her? Did you steal her work?"

"Well, maybe borrowed is a better word. She refused to let me have any of her work to share with potential employers. I lifted just a few without her knowledge so I could present them to her upon graduation as a gift of her portfolio. After graduation, she started a job taking school pictures, so I kept the photos, waiting for her to get bored and ask for another recommendation. You're the only one I'm going to share them with because I trust you. If I give them to her now, she'll just put them in a closet and continue in her dull, comfortable and wasted life. I can't let her do that. She's too good."

"William, that is immoral and illegal. I can't believe even you would stoop so low!" Stephen cringed, wondering what else his favorite professor might have done.

"I was desperate, and it's the first time I've ever done anything like this. I knew you had to see these." William used his most persuasive voice to convince Stephen. He felt so sure about Tasha and Stephen working together. What else could he do to convince his protégé?

Stephen wondered at the bizarre behavior William described and thought perhaps it was time for the professor to retire.

"Send them over, but don't hold your breath waiting for me, okay? I've got three shoots already scheduled this week, so don't expect to hear from me before next Monday. I'll have to spend my weekend thinking and praying about this."

William breathed a sigh of relief, "You won't regret this Stephen. I promise you won't." He thanked him as he hung up the phone.

Stephen groaned and went back to setting up the portrait studio for his appointment in 30 minutes. It was for a dog food advertisement, and while he normally didn't take commercial clients, this one included a golden retriever puppy. The client promised him that he could keep the puppy if he did the shoot. Stephen wondered at the wisdom of agreeing to take the puppy, but after Nate passed on last year, he knew it was time for another dog. He thought the loss would be overwhelming, but besides a bit of sadness, he remembered the good times most of all. The shot of Nate attacking the snowman from Christmas graced his bedroom wall, and he still missed his childhood companion immensely. A new puppy might be just what he needed, especially now that he had a nice yard.

The doorbell chimed, and Stephen went to answer it. William stood with a large package under his arm.

"You, you, oh, you're a scoundrel, that's what you are! Did you call from your cell phone right outside my house?"

"Well, right around the corner," William grinned. He pushed Stephen aside and made his way into the front parlor. "I'll just set these here and be on my way." He was gone before Stephen knew what hit him.

Just then a puppy ran into the house when William opened the door to leave. Stephen's heart melted as the little guy plopped right down in front of him and started chewing on his shoe laces, just like Nate. A man in a business suit ran in next, apologizing profusely for the puppy getting away as he held an empty collar and leash in his hand.

"No problem," Stephen replied. "As you can see, we're already getting acquainted."

They both looked down at the puppy making a mess of Stephen's shoes, and again the man apologized.

"Hey, after the shoot, he's no longer your responsibility. What do you say little guy? What shall we call you?" Stephen picked up the golden ball of fur and whispered nonsense in his ear.

"Actually, it's a little she, the dog is female."

"Oh?" Stephen asked the little dog. I've praying for a woman in my life, but this isn't what I expected." He picked her up, and his heart swelled at her adorable little face. "You'll do just fine. The studio is ready. Are you ready for some breakfast? I think I'll call you Annabelle, Annie for short. What do you think of that?" Stephen gushed over his new roommate.

She kissed his cheeks and nose and chewed a bit on an errant lock of hair. Stephen had forgotten the pungent smell of puppy breath, but didn't mind as he sat her down on the table and prepared for the shoot. He had several new toys for her to play with including a ball and rubber duck. Annie found a dirty pair of rolled up socks and much preferred those to keep herself occupied while Stephen setup his camera and lighting.

"Is there anything I can do?" Acutely aware puppies were foreign objects to him, he certainly hoped the photographer didn't need assistance.

"Yeah, get behind me and bark, please."

"Bark?" The man asked incredulously.

"Well, whatever you can do to get her to look this way with an expression that means she wants your puppy kibble."

"Okay, I guess I can try." He looked around to make sure no one was watching as he stepped behind Stephen.

"Errr, ruf ruf," he choked. The puppy continued her industrious chewing on the sock.

"You've got to do better than that."

"RUF RUF, RUF RUF" he tried again. Annie looked up for a brief moment, but finding nothing interesting, turned back to the sock.

Stephen sighed, and decided to let the man off the hook. "Press the play button on the tape recorder behind me."

He found the tape recorder and pressed the button. All of the sudden, at least a dozen barking dogs, real dogs, filled the room with their combined voices, each vying to outdo one another.

Annie dropped the sock, sat up on her fat little butt and barked back. Click, click went the shutter as Stephen caught her ferocious reply. The tape recorder's voices changed to a quiet but distinct meow, and Annie cocked her head, eyebrows and ears lifted as she tried to determine what the new and foreign noise was and if she should be concerned about it. Click, click went the shutter. Stephen was very pleased at her reaction and knew he had some great shots of the puppy.

The man however was not happy, "Were the barks you requested of me really necessary?"

Stephen smiled, and said, "Not really, I didn't mean to offend you, but I did want you to know what I was up against, trying to get a good layout for your advertisement." He lifted a huge bag of the dog food behind Annie, tore open a corner and poured some on the table. He then drizzled some of the spilled food with a tiny amount of warm bacon drippings from his breakfast and placed her in the middle of it, making it look like she had chewed the bag open. Stepping behind the camera, he took several more shots of her happily munching on the delicious treat. Annie showed her pleasure by rapidly gobbling up her gourmet breakfast. Stephen took several more shots, grabbed her leash and picked the little pup up before she got sick. He had a veterinary appointment just around the corner in fifteen minutes, and he didn't want to be late.

"How did you know you would be done that quickly?" the man asked, confusion obvious on his face.

"I know dogs, and especially golden retrievers. They're so predictable. Ready Annie? Let's go meet my friend Max. He's going to love you." The three of them walked out together and Stephen locked up. "The photos will be ready tomorrow afternoon if you would like to come pick them up. Thanks for being such a great sport about the barking."

He hummed a bright tune as Annie tried to figure out the leash and sniff all the wonderful new smells at the same time. Stephen already knew he was going to love her, and was glad for the opportunity of doing the commercial shoot and getting a new friend at the same time.

For just a moment, he forgot about the photos in his front parlor and his crazy friend William.

Hours later, Annie was fast asleep on a rug in front of the crackling fireplace. Her appointment with Max had gone well. Her hips and heart were strong, eyes and ears clear and her fat little tummy soft and pliant. The big adventure wore her out, and for a few minutes anyway, Stephen had some time to himself. He sat on the floor next to her in the midst of the photos William had dropped off earlier. He hated to admit it, but he was impressed. The artist showed depth and feeling in her work, and he was drawn back again and again to ponder over them. Who was she? The photos were all scenic shots except for a few of a gorgeous cat, but he felt that each was a sanctuary in its own way. He felt drawn in and wanted to know where she took the shots. To be honest, he wanted to know more about the photographer.

"What do you think God? Should I tell William yes?"

It wasn't an audible and resounding answer, but Stephen felt a tremendous urge to call Tasha. He wanted to find out more about her past, what the places meant in her life and her plans for the future. He had never felt this way before, and it was unfamiliar. He was disappointed when he realized he didn't have her phone number or even her last name. It was late and it would be rude to call William, besides he didn't know if he wanted to give the old coot the satisfaction of knowing he was right.

Absentmindedly he stroked Annie's soft silky fur. Her little tail thumped back and forth even in sleep showing her enjoyment of his affection. Stephen couldn't resist and picked her up to cuddle the soft, warm body in his lap. She gave a little grunt, but continued sleeping, draping her small head and two paws over his arm. The fire was warm on his back and Annie's sweet smell drifted up to him. Stephen realized for the first time in years he felt a glimmer of hope, even anticipation. Was it because of Annie or Tasha's pictures? Not sure, he just knew if felt good, peaceful and ... right.

Waking Annie much to her protestations, he took her outside to the spot they both determined would be her place to "hurry up." Stephen didn't want to take her to public place and tell her to "go potty" so he decided the words "hurry up" made more sense. Annie seemed to understand for she quickly relieved herself and romped back into the house, straight into her warm basket by the fire. It was a long day for the puppy and despite her nap she was ready for bed. Stephen however, knew his night had just begun.

The sun rose as Stephen hung the last matted and framed photo in his front parlor. He chose different earth-toned hues, pulling out the dominant colors in each scene. He used an assortment of rich deep tones made from walnut or lighter oak and pine for the wooden frames depending upon the mood he felt the artist wanted to convey. The photos transformed the room into an inviting haven to sit and enjoy the lovely surroundings, especially with the windows opened to his tranquil front yard.

Several months ago when spring tempted the senses with fragrant scents and tender new buds, Stephen joined in the celebration and spent a few Saturdays planting flowers and putting together some hanging baskets. His neighbor asked him if he wanted some mismatched wicker furniture she was going to throw out, and he jumped at the chance to make his front porch a comfortable place to spend summer evenings.

Stephen stretched his arms forward and back then rolled his head back and forth to relieve the stress in his neck from the long hours spent leaning over his work. His eyes felt heavy, and he was ready for bed. Annie on the other hand needed to go out and she would soon be getting into mischief. Stephen was glad he had a big fenced back yard, though he knew the puppy would soon learn how to dig and chew if he didn't find enough for her to do. Stephen took Annie out to "hurry up" then filled her bowl, sans the bacon drippings this morning, and retrieved William's phone number.

His stomach fluttered as he dialed the number. When was the last time he was nervous like this? It had been a long time. Meeting Tasha must mean even more to him than he originally thought. Sometime during the long night, Stephen realized, though he had never met the artist, he knew part of her from the photos. What was her story? It was curious how interested he was in meeting her. He never felt this way about other artists who wanted to share their work with him before. Odd.

William gruffly answered the phone, "Do you know what time it is? The sun's barely come up!"

"Hello to you too, good friend."

"Oh, now I'm your good friend, eh? What do you want that couldn't wait until a decent hour?" William's voice was irritated, yet Stephen knew he wasn't really mad at him for the early wake-up call.

"You know what I want, William. There's no way you could have dropped off those photos knowing I wouldn't be interested. They're amazing. I want to see Tasha as soon as possible. But *you* have to explain to her how I got her photographs. Will you call her for me? I'm in the studio for the next two weeks before I go out in the field again."

William sounded wide awake now, his voice bright and enthusiastic. "You'll see her Stephen, really?"

"Yes, I said yes." Stephen laughed. "I'm going to hang up now so you can call her. If I don't answer the phone, it's because I'm off to bed. I was up all night with your little project and now I'm extremely tired."

"Uh, Stephen, I'll call her, but I won't tell her," William hesitated. "I can't bear to look in her eyes when she finds I betrayed her trust, even though it was for her own good. You can tell her the truth, even if she hates me for doing it. Maybe if she hears it from you, explaining why I stole her photos, knowing you're the only one who has ever seen them, she'll get over my deception. Please, Stephen? She means so much to me."

Stephen was silent and after a minute, William thought he might have hung up on him.

"William. I don't like it, but I can see your point. If you had done the same to me, I don't think I would have understood. This will give her time to sort out her feelings. If she lets me, I'll tell her your reasons and that you care deeply for her. It's obvious, or otherwise you would never have done it. You can lose your job over this William!"

"I know, but if I do, it's time I retire anyway. Maybe they'll hire you and make you department chair."

"No thanks, teaching is your department. I'm happy with my freelance work, and hopefully my new assistant."

"Thank you Stephen. You're a good man. You won't be sorry. I'll see if she can come tomorrow at 11:00, okay?"

"Thank you William, that would be fine," Stephen yawned, hung up and pondered what he had just done. It still felt right, and if possible, the urge to meet Tasha was even stronger than last night.

Annie gave a little yelp then started barking furiously at something behind the sofa. Stephen peeked over and found she must have pulled the electric cord from the lamp out of the socket. It was unplugged and she still had her fur ruffled up on her back.

"Oh, NO Annie! Don't play with electricity!" She looked downright angry at the offensive object. He laughed and reached down to pick her up. "Let's put you outside for now until we find a safe place." She was soon chasing birds and investigating the chew toys he had bought for her. Stephen sighed and wondered if he would make it through the first year of her puppy stage, knowing it would be hard but worth it. He headed up the stairs to catch a couple hours of sleep in his cozy bed before getting back to work on Annie's layout. Remembering the puppy's adorable face and expressions, he knew the shots were good. But it would take all of his concentration to finish it with his thoughts on Tasha and their meeting tomorrow.

What would she be like? He felt nervous thinking about her and hoped he would make a good impression. "I wonder if she likes tea or prefers coffee? Many women like tea," Stephen pondered to himself and made a mental note to pick some up at the grocery store later. He remembered that his own mother had loved coffee and made sharing a cup their Saturday morning tradition. Oh how he still missed her. She would have adored Annie. "Mom? Please pray for my appointment with Tasha. I love you."

Looking out the window at Tasha's retreating back, Stephen offered up a fervent prayer to God.

"*Please oh Lord, be with her. Help her to understand William's deception. Take away her pain and help her to trust again. Most of all Lord, help her to know you. Please give her your peace, yes Lord, your perfect peace. You know her past, present and future, God. If it's your will, please let me know it too.*"

Stephen wanted to run out the door and follow her, to beg her to come back. He felt awful about the way she left, tears pouring down her face and looking so vulnerable. What if she didn't come back? He desperately wanted her to. Still not quite understanding the pull he had toward this young woman, he just couldn't let it go. Yet he also knew she wasn't ready to talk with anyone right now, particularly the person who just turned her world upside down.

He heard a little yelp at the back door and went out to join Annie. Her whole body wagged back and forth in her delight to see him. Stephen smiled and sat down on the porch step and gently caressed her soft fur. Soon she ran off and came back with a stick, a green one with a few newly budded leaves that hadn't been chewed off yet. "Oh Annie" he groaned, wondering which of his prized bushes kept her busy this morning. She growled at the stick and ferociously shook it back and forth then dropped it at his feet, ready for a game of fetch. Surprised that she knew the game already, Stephen picked up the stick and threw it. Sure enough, her plump little body ran across the yard and picked it up. She raced back towards him, tumbling over her too big feet twice, but tail still wagging enthusiastically as she dropped it, slobber and all. They played the game until she dropped down next to him, sides heaving from exertion.

Stephen's mood was also lighter from the little dog's enjoyment and beautiful day. He picked her up and drank in the fresh outdoor smell of her. Her fur was so soft, it was all he could do not to squeeze her too tightly. It didn't take long before Annie was fast asleep in his arms, making little puppy noises and twitching her legs in a dream, most likely still playing catch. Satisfied she would nap for several hours, he gently laid her down in her bed and decided to phone William with the results from his morning appointment. He also wanted to ask William to give him Tasha's phone number. It was a breach of privacy, but Stephen wanted to make sure she was okay. Though to be honest, it wasn't just that. He really wanted to get to know her, and while the circumstances weren't optimal, it was an open door.

CHAPTER 25
BOULDER, CO

"SO, ARE you still taking children's portraits?" Winnie asked. "Yes, at least I was last week until I got a phone call that prompted me to go to my appointment this morning. I thought perhaps if everything worked out, I might be ready to go to work for someone else. The opportunity sounded so promising, and I am tired of taking pictures of the same thing day after day, year after year. But now, after seeing my photos on his walls, I don't know." Tasha looked stricken as she remembered her morning.

"What happened, dear?"

"Oh Winnie, I was so scared this morning, I actually prayed, even though as you noticed God and I haven't exactly been on speaking terms for a long time. I went to my appointment with a well-known photographer. It started out okay, though he seemed nervous, and I was too. Still, he seemed nice. He told me to go into the front room, and *my* photographs were on *his* walls, Winnie. I almost vomited right there on his beautiful floor. They were photos of my most private places, my sanctuaries. Places where I got lost in God's love and forgot what had happened to me … special places, and they were on *his* walls.

He explained that Dr. Guenther gave them to him and told him about me. I feel so betrayed. How can I go back there?"

Winnie didn't know what to say, but she did know how to give a good hug, so that's what she did now. Rising to her feet, it was worth the pops and pains her old bones complained more and more about lately. She wrapped Tasha in her loving arms and lightly caressed the young woman's tense shoulders. Oh, how good it felt to be needed again. *"Thank you for this day, Lord. You are so good. Use me, mold me, and make me into what you need me to be to serve this precious child of yours."*

"What should I do Winnie? I know we've just met, but you seem so kind and wise." Tasha's voice quivered with uncertainty and fear.

"Well, right now dear, we're going to tuck you in so you can get a good night's sleep. No decisions tonight. You've had an extremely long and emotional day, and difficult decisions need to be made with prayer and a clear head. A good night's sleep and a full stomach always help too, I say. I left an extra gown and toothbrush in the bathroom for you to use. I'll be right here should you need me in the middle of the night."

"Tomorrow we'll treat ourselves to some lovely rich dark coffee and blueberry pancakes and then go check on that cat of yours. How does that sound?" Winnie stated in her most matter-of-fact voice. This girl needed some grand-mothering. Tomorrow would bring a host of questions and hopefully some answers, but for right now, all Tasha needed was some good, solid loving.

It didn't take long before Tasha slept soundly, having listened to Winnie's sweet humming as she rocked back and forth next to her. Her last thought was a simple thank you to a God who answers prayers in the most creative and loving ways.

"That was delicious, Winnie. I just love blueberry pancakes!" Tasha gushed.

"Me too, aren't they wonderful?" Winnie agreed with a big smile.

Tasha was adorable with her freshly scrubbed face devoid of makeup and tousled curly hair. She looked like a teenager just after a sleepover.

"Why don't we get our little mess cleaned up, and I'll look at the bus schedule so we can go over to your apartment? When we're done, I'll have my son pick me up during his lunch hour, or after work if we're not done visiting yet. How does that sound?"

"Perfect, I think I can hear Penelope meowing pitifully from here, not that I know where I am or where here is," Tasha giggled. Her poor cat, this was the first time she had ever gone without a meal.

It didn't take long with the two of them working efficiently together to clean the small apartment. Winnie let her family know where she was off to and they almost skipped to the nearest bus stop. Both women felt like the trip was a grand adventure, and for the moment, Tasha was glad she didn't have to worry about yesterday. And, she had found a wonderful new friend.

They didn't have to wait long for the bus, and Tasha was grateful Winnie knew the schedules so well. After giving Winnie her address, the older woman studied a map and the bus schedules and got it all figured out before Tasha could get her clothes and shoes on. They only had one transfer, and Tasha hoped it was on the bus she normally rode so she could say hello to Jack, her favorite driver. It felt good to be in familiar territory again, away from Stephen Banks' questioning eyes and haunting front room.

The smells and sounds were the same on every bus she rode, and this one was no different ... except she had Winnie with her. Tasha realized she hadn't been afraid all morning, thankful Winnie was by her side. Maybe God really did answer prayers.

It was a beautiful day. Tasha felt a bit like she was playing hookie not going to work on a weekday. She arranged for vacation this week, anticipating having to make decisions and think about her career after the meeting with Mr. Banks, or rather Stephen.

"There's our bus transfer stop, dear," Winnie gathered her sweater and bag as the bus slowed to a stop. The brakes squealed and Tasha wondered if it was a factory specification that bus brakes had to squeal. Maybe it was a warning for oncoming pedestrians? Nothing looked familiar, and Tasha still didn't know where she was. But, she trusted Winnie. The neighborhood looked nice and they had 30 minutes before the next bus arrived. Winnie and Tasha both noticed the coffee shop on the corner at the same time and smiled mischievously at one another as they briskly walked towards the delicious aroma.

"One more cup won't hurt us, will it?" Tasha questioned, giggling again.

"Certainly not," Winnie replied in a matter of fact, all-knowing voice. "My mother would definitely approve, I'm thinking, and she knew everything, bless her soul."

They ordered their coffees to go, and after adding the appropriate amount of cream and sugar, walked back to the bus stop to enjoy the delicious beverage and the just as delightful warm sun and cool breeze. The bench for waiting passengers was full. Winnie smiled and thanked the two teenage boys who stood to let them sit down. It was nice to know some parents still taught manners to their children these days.

"Jack!" Tasha exclaimed as they boarded the bus. Was it only yesterday that she saw him, sad from his wife's Alzheimer's disease? It seemed like a lifetime ago. He looked brighter today. "I didn't know you drove other routes."

"Today was my day off, but I agreed to fill in for a co-worker. His wife went into labor early this morning with their first child. What are you doing over here on this side of town?"

"I don't even know where I am." Tasha mused. "But you'll get me home, won't you, Jack?"

"Yep, that would be the fifth stop on this route, about 10 minutes from now. How did your appointment go yesterday?"

"That's quite a long story best shared over lunch with you and Millie." She turned and smiled, "This is my new friend Winnie." Tasha guided the sweet lady up the stairs and dropped tokens in for both of them.

"We know each other, dear. Jack's wife Millie and I have been friends a long time. How's she doing Jack?"

"Good and bad days, the bad ones occurring more often now."

"I'm sorry Jack. If there's anything I can do … well you know, even to sit with her if she wants company. Will I see you in church this week?"

"Depends on Millie, but I hope so." He grinned, closing the bus door. "Got to get going to stay on schedule. You ladies take your seats now, okay?"

Tasha could tell Jack wanted to talk longer, but he had a bus full of passengers to deliver and more to pick up, on time.

Tasha and Winnie took a seat a few rows back and settled in for the ride. It was another beautiful day, and Tasha's artistic eye appreciated the vibrant colors and contrasts of spring. There were big white puffy clouds in the bright blue sky, and she wished she could go to her lake to see their reflection in the still water. Hmmm, she thought, I haven't wanted to go there for years. All she felt was peace and an anticipation to go back. Maybe she didn't need Joseph after all. God gave her Winnie and the desire to share her burden and set her free. Already, today she felt much different than yesterday.

"Oh, oh. I hear a very annoyed cat in there." Tasha searched for her keys. They were never in the same place in spite of her efforts to consistently put them in the front pocket of her purse. Maybe she should just put her keys on a chain around her neck like she saw many of the school teachers do. "Coming Penelope, hold on!"

"Tasha, this is just lovely. What a perfect setup, almost like my garage apartment. The yard and trees are so peaceful and relaxing." Tasha looked at the yard through Winnie's eyes. She was right. Her yard was very pretty. Everything looked new today. Her heart felt so light and she breathed a prayer of thanks.

"There they are." She exclaimed. Giving the deadbolt a quick turn, she opened the door to a very desperate cat. Penelope held her tail high, quivering back and forth while she both purred and meowed, threading her plump body between Tasha's legs. Tasha reached down and picked up the soft bundle of fur to cuddle her tight. Penelope sniffed her face, then gave her a quick nip on the nose. "Ouch! Why did you do that?"

"She's miffed and hungry, dear." Winnie laughed.

Tasha put Penelope down and rubbed her nose. Thank goodness a quick examination of her hand didn't show any blood. "Okay, let me get your dinner, breakfast and lunch. We'll call it brunch after a fast." She picked up the bowl from yesterday, licked clean, and added a new can of food, plus a sprinkling of Penelope's favorite treats on top. "That should make her happy." She was right. The cat forgot about her normal nonchalant attitude and rushed right over.

"Thank you for helping me to get home Winnie. More importantly, thank you for yesterday and last night. I know God used you to help me break through the terrifying, debilitating fear. I just don't know what's next?" Tasha's voice questioned.

225

"Well, I think the first thing we should do is go to the bath-room! Is the coffee affecting you the same as me?"

"Yes," Tasha laughed. "I only have one, so you go first. This apartment is so small, I doubt you'll have trouble finding it."

Winnie rushed off and soon Tasha heard water running, which certainly didn't help her painful coffee generated con-dition. The door opened, and Tasha felt tender toward her new friend as she watched Winnie walk through the tiny living area. Without her self-absorbed mind and eyes full of tears, she real-ized Winnie was quite old in the harsh light of day. Yet, she just hopped on the bus like a trip across town was something she did every day.

Tasha gave her a quick smile and walked into her room. Was it just yesterday she was deciding what outfit to wear to the interview? She quickly relieved herself and returned to the cozy kitchen where she found Winnie seated in one of the dining set chairs with a very happy cat on her lap.

"Are you ready to go home Winnie, or would you like to stay a bit?"

"Oh my, I think you must be plumb tuckered out. I don't mind staying dear, but perhaps you would like some time alone to pray and think? I have an opinion about what I want you to do, but it's God's plan that matters most."

"Winnie, where do you go to church? Do you think your pastor would pray with me and help me decide?"

"Actually, it's not too far from here, Living Waters Baptist Church. I can give him a call and see if he has time. It's within walking distance. Remember, dear, while the pastor can pray with you and give you words of wisdom, ultimately your answer needs to come from God. He can use people to help you decide, of course, just be sure and listen for the peace and reassurance from God, not man."

"I would like that Winnie. If you don't mind giving him a call, I'll make us a quick lunch of ham and Swiss cheese on sourdough with sliced fresh pineapple if that's okay with you. It's a beautiful day for a walk."

Tasha handed the cordless phone to the older woman and began her preparations. She decided to grill the sandwiches so the cheese would melt on the crunchy bread and add a bit of Dijon mustard to enhance the flavor.

"There, it's all settled. Pastor John is counseling someone right now, but he has nothing scheduled for the rest of the afternoon. It will take us about 10 minutes to walk over after we finish our lunch."

"Oh my, sweetheart, this looks wonderful. Do you mind if we eat outside on the cute little table I saw under the elm tree?"

"It's probably very dirty, I haven't been out all winter, but sure." Tasha replied, quickly grabbing an old cloth and a bottle of glass cleaner from under the sink.

"Winnie, do you mind pouring us some milk to go with our lunch? The glasses are in the cabinet next to the refrigerator."

Tasha rushed out the door and indeed saw a table under the big tree in the back yard. She didn't know it was an elm, and she had never noticed the table either. It was very nice, and once she wiped the leaves and dirt from the glass top and black wrought iron chairs, it looked inviting.

"I found some chocolate syrup in the fridge, I hope you don't mind I added some to our milk," Winnie chuckled.

Somehow, Winnie managed to carry both plates in one hand and three glasses in the other, one of which had a pair of garden shears resting inside.

"Wow, Winnie. You must have been a waitress, look at you!"

"Yes, I was in my younger days, I could actually carry four glasses in one hand and four plates in the other if I could get someone to load me up, but alas, no longer. This is about all I can manage now." Winnie put her load down on the freshly wiped table.

"Do you think your landlords would mind if I snipped a few roses from that bush over there?"

Tasha looked to where Winnie pointed. She hadn't noticed the roses either, and a memory of her childhood neighbor came flooding back as she gazed on their delicate blooms. What was his name? She remembered taking pictures of the roses and how he lovingly cared for them. Her mom was always having her carry a plate of food over to him. She turned her attention back to Winnie.

"The owners don't come back here, and the bush looks rather neglected, don't you think? I'm sure they won't mind."

"Oh good, this one is a Peace rose. See the yellow-pink blush? Smell it, the fragrance is delicate, not too overwhelming. It will be perfect for our impromptu picnic."

Winnie cut several blooms, mindful of the thorns, and arranged the pretty flowers in the glass.

"We'll get some water for them right after we eat and you can enjoy them on your kitchen table."

Tasha breathed in the fresh scent of spring and delicate fragrance from the roses. She looked up at the brilliant blue sky, filtered by new leaves, bursting forth from their winter hiding place. Why didn't she come out here more often? Maybe I'm like the leaves, it's time for me to emerge into my spring and blossom, Tasha mused.

"Shall we pray, dear?" Winnie interrupted her thoughts.

"Yes, Winnie, let's pray and eat. Then I'm ready to start my new life with you, my new friend, and get reacquainted with my old friend, God."

"Ah, home away from home." The building was small and somewhat run-down, not what Tasha expected from a church. In fact, it looked like an old house, and as an afterthought, someone stuck a hand-painted sign out front, otherwise she would never have guessed it was a church.

"I know it's not one of those big, new churches, but I love it here. The younger folk need to put on a fresh coat of paint, I suppose. What's more important is the inside, just like us," Winnie reflected as she saw the church through Tasha's eyes. "Dear, would you hold my arm while we climb the stairs?" Tasha felt both a wiry strength and a fragility that the small bone would easily break if she fell. It felt good to take care of someone else for a change.

Indeed, it was a house, with most of the inside walls removed to create a large open area that served as the sanctuary. There were posts placed here and there, Tasha supposed where the load-bearing walls used to be. Instead of pews, Tasha noticed chairs that looked like they might actually be comfortable. Now there's a novel idea, she thought. The chairs weren't in rows, rather in semi-circles around small round tables. On the tables haphazardly placed coasters, Bibles, notebook paper and a box of Kleenex waited to be useful. The windows were graced with stained glass, not of religious scenes, but bright flowers, trees and mountains. It looked quite inviting, and Tasha was tempted to take a seat and just sit for awhile.

She almost forgot Winnie was there until she heard her say, "Pastor John, I am pleased to introduce you to my new friend Tasha." Tasha turned around and though there were two men, her eyes locked with only one of them. Time stopped. He took a step forward, questioning without words. Her hand lifted on its own accord and he reached for it. Gently taking hold, without a word, they turned together and walked out.

Winnie's jaw dropped. In all of her advanced years, this was a new experience. "What was that about, John?" He led her to one of the tables and they sat down. "I don't know, Winnie. Who is she?"

"Tasha."

He smiled and said, "Stephen."

John reached for Winnie's hand and they bowed in silence.

They walked. And walked. And walked. For the second time in two days, Tasha had no idea where she was. She didn't care. Her cat was fed, she was on vacation and this intriguing man was at her side. No questions. No answers. No fear. No anger. No distrust. Her response to him confused her. Why, after meeting him just yesterday, did she feel like this today?

For now, nothing mattered except his hand encompassing hers. He smelled clean, like the outdoors. Every few moments she felt enveloped in his scent and breathed him in, deep, as far as her lungs would expand. Then it would fade and she felt a loss until she noticed the warmth from his hand radiating up her arm. There was no way she was letting go first. Impossible.

The shadows were longer, and Tasha felt a chill when Stephen guided her through a gate to a house that looked familiar. "William?" she questioned, brows lifted. Her voice sounded strange, distant.

"Yes."

Stephen opened the door without knocking and walked in, surprising the old teacher. He handed William a set of keys and said, "Go feed my puppy."

William chuckled, shook his head, and muttered, "No respect from young kids anymore, no respect at all," and grabbed the keys, his coat and headed out the door.

"Wait," Tasha exclaimed. William turned, "Yes?"

Reaching into her pocket, "Here's my keys too, will you please feed my cat?"

"Certainly, since you asked nicely, Tasha," and he gave Stephen a mock scowl and left.

Tasha looked down at her hand, small in comparison to Stephen's, still surrounded in his protective and secure grip. No, she thought, I'm not letting go. Pulling him toward the couch, she fell back and sank into its comfort, smelling him, feeling his warmth, his strength next to her. He pulled her closer and using his other hand, gently pressed her head against his shoulder and stroked her hair. Stephen put his feet up on the coffee table and laid his head back against the worn cushions. When William returned after his pet-sitting duties, he found them both sound asleep.

"Rise and shine, sleepyheads. Dinner."

"I'm very angry with you William. How could you? I trusted you." Tasha stormed back and forth across his small living room. "You are supposed to be professional, a trusted professor, and you treat your students like this? Stealing their work?" Pounding on the table, Tasha continued, "My work, William, mine. Not yours. Mine. How dare you? Do you know how I felt yesterday, seeing my work on Stephen's walls? Not just any work, my most intimate sanctuaries. And on a stranger's walls." Tasha dropped back to the sofa, and Stephen reclaimed her hand, giving it a reassuring squeeze.

"You don't look like strangers," William pointedly looked at their joined hands. "Does this mean we're not going to eat dinner?"

"You're impossible, both of you." Tasha shook her head as she saw the two men smiling at one another. She felt betrayed and started crying and hated herself for it. Did they have a clue? No heart at all? Oh, she was mad, madder than when she found out she was adopted. Was she doomed to be the victim of deception her entire life? Glaring at both of them, Tasha jerked her hand out of Stephen's and ran for the door. They didn't get it, not at all. Were they that insensitive?

Rushing out into the cold air, she ran, tears streaming down her face. The nerve. How dare they? She decided right then and there to cancel her vacation and tell her boss she was available to take school pictures for the rest of her life, starting tomorrow. Her shoes pounded on the sidewalk, and in her anger, the repetitious rhythm was comforting. Why did she think she needed anyone? It hurt too much.

Finally, she stopped, gasping for breath, Tasha felt the fear return. It was dark. "Where am I? Oh God, now what?" Sounds at night became amplified, creepy. She felt a touch on her shoulder and screamed. Terrified, she whimpered, "Don't hurt me, please," and dropped to her knees, waiting for the inevitable.

Stephen's heart broke at her vulnerability and felt tears on his own face. He reached down, gathering her small frame in his arms, "No Tasha, I'm not going to hurt you. I'll never hurt you. Don't shut me out. Give me a chance." She trembled in his arms and his heart broke. Stephen sat down on the cold pavement, rocking back and forth. He held her like he would a child. What happened to her? She reminded him of a broken doll he had seen in an antique store, beautiful even though damaged. The brokenness brought out protective feelings for her he didn't know he had.

She sniffed, "We're a mess, aren't we?"

"A beautiful mess. I'm sorry William and I didn't give you the consideration you deserve." Stephen made a vow to himself to never intentionally hurt or let go of this woman, to do whatever it took to love her, unconditionally.

CHAPTER 26
BOULDER, CO

"I CAN'T BELIEVE you're quitting," Tasha's supervisor moaned. "School is getting ready to start, and you're the best photographer we've got."

"I've accepted another position, doing freelance work. I'm sorry." Tasha felt horrible, she knew this put them in a bind, but now she had the opportunity to realize her dream, and with Stephen. They were spending a lot of time together, something Penelope was entirely disgusted about. When Stephen brought Annie over, Penelope hissed at the puppy and was quite satisfied at the small drops of blood resulting from a sharp smack to her curious little nose.

"But now, can't you wait a few months?"

"Now is a perfect time. If I wait, you'll procrastinate on hiring another photographer, and I'll feel stuck. You've got a month to advertise and interview. Call the local colleges and universities. Many starving students would appreciate a good job."

"I suppose you're right."

It felt strange, not having a regular job to show up to every day. Stephen started her salary last week, quite generous considering she hadn't been given an assignment yet. He told her to get used to the studio and dark room, to play around a bit and get comfortable. This afternoon they had a meeting to discuss his current projects, specifically how she would work both alongside him and independently. Tasha wondered how she would tell him she was afraid to go out alone, especially to places she'd never been before or in crowds filled with terrifying people.

Tasha hung up the phone, glad the unpleasant task was over. She hated to let people down. She knew she was a people pleaser and avoided conflict at all costs. Well, I guess I'm growing, she mused, proud of her little accomplishment. She'd never quit a job before. She was resolved to conquer her fear once and for all … with God's help.

Excited and apprehensive about her meeting with Stephen, Tasha willed her stomach to calm down. Too much coffee, again. She checked Penelope's automatic feeder, making sure there was enough food for a few days, just in case. The cat showed her displeasure over the disgusting dry food, but at least Tasha knew she wouldn't starve if she ended up at Winnie's house again. She grabbed her purse and a coat slung over the kitchen chair. Turning, she didn't see the cat dash out from under the chair and just as Tasha took a step forward, Penelope darted between her legs. The fall was in slow motion, and in the distance she heard Penelope's howl as her purse went flying and her head hit the sharp corner of the table.

"I wonder what's keeping Tasha," Stephen said aloud. Annie heard his voice and recognized an opportunity to play. "Not now, you delinquent puppy, I'm still irritated at you after discovering my favorite slippers in shreds." Stephen didn't know Tasha well, but so far she was always prompt when they had a date or appointment. Checking his watch again, he frowned and noted that it was now an hour past when she said she would be over. Not wanting to worry, he called Annie, "Okay, you win little girl, where's your ball?" The puppy woofed and her whole body wiggled. Running to her mat for the ball, Annie's tail sent coasters and a candle crashing to the floor. Stephen swore the puppy actually smiled at him, completely oblivious to the mess she just made.

Rubbing his tired arm, Stephen wondered how many times he threw the ball. Annie wasn't ready to quit yet. Her energy amazed him. Dog slobber mixed with dirt covered his hand. It was so disgusting he didn't want to wipe the frothy mess on his favorite Levis. "Come on girl, time for your nap." Stephen went inside and washed up while Annie slurped from her water bowl, making yet another mess. Drool dripping from her muzzle, Annie loped over to her mat, plopped down and within minutes was softly snoring.

Stephen glanced at the clock, two hours late. Now he was worried. No messages on the answering machine. This was not like Tasha, at least what he knew of her from their short time together. He dialed her number and got a fast busy signal. That was odd. Her phone must be off the hook. Dialing her cell, it went straight to voice mail. "Tasha, where are you?"

"Annie, you stay." The dog didn't wake up, feet twitching in her dream. Stephen rushed out the door and in minutes was at Tasha's house.

He rang the bell and waited for what seemed like forever, and rang it again. He heard the bell, but tried knocking anyway. Where was she? He turned the doorknob and found it locked. Of course. She always kept her door locked. And dead-bolted. She told him what happened to her, and he didn't blame her, in fact, it made him angry ... again, just to think about it. But right now, he wanted in. He whispered a mild expletive and walked around the side to peer in the kitchen window. Penelope was meowing, loudly. Not a "I want food," or "You're a despicable dog," meow, it sounded more urgent.

Stephen cupped his hands around his face to reduce the glare in the window. He didn't see Tasha anywhere. He tapped on the window and called her name. If she was here, he didn't want to scare her, especially now that she trusted him. Penelope meowed again, even louder if possible. The cat jumped up on the table and leaped over to the counter, her beautiful eyes looking right at him through the window. "What is it, girl? What are you trying to tell me?"

"Meooooow!"

Oh, this is crazy, Stephen thought, his heart racing over a stupid cat's meow. He thought he heard a groan. Peering inside the window again, he looked left, right and finally down. There she was, her small body crumpled on the floor, and a small pool of blood beneath her head.

"Oh, Tasha," Stephen moaned. Crippled with fear, he frantically considered his options. 911. He remembered the last time a policeman called him, the morning his mom died. She's not my mom, and she's not dead. She just made a noise.

"911 Operator, what is your emergency?"

"My friend, she's lying on the floor with blood under her head."

"Can she talk to you?"

"I don't know, I'm outside, looking through the kitchen window. Her door is locked."

"What is the address?"

Stephen realized he didn't know Tasha's address, it was a guest house in the back yard. He told the operator.

"Leave your phone on, we've got a trace on you and an ambulance is on their way."

"How long?"

"Just minutes. Are you okay?"

"No, I'm not okay. I want to break the door down and hold her."

"Then we'll have two injured people. Stay calm."

Calm? Was she insane? Tasha was lying on the floor bleeding and unconscious. Calm? What a stupid word. Stephen heard the sirens in the distance and felt a huge sense of relief. He didn't know how they would get inside, but figured they had the right tools for the job.

An older woman approached him, concern etching her face.

"Is everything okay? I couldn't help but notice you looking in the window and yelling into your phone. Where's Tasha?"

"No, she's inside lying on the floor. Who are you?"

"I'm her landlord, I live right here in the house. Who are you? Tasha *never* has visitors."

"I'm Stephen Banks, her new employer and a friend of one of her professors. Do you have a key?"

"Sure, and Tasha keeps one buried under the 12th brick stepping stone."

Stephen breathed, "Thank you, Lord," and realized he never asked God for help, but he sent it anyway.

Lifting the brick stone, sure enough, there lay a small rusted metal box, the kind people stuck to their cars that thieves found quite convenient. Stephen pried the lid open with his pocket knife and found the key inside. He ran to the front door and opened first the deadlock and then the doorknob. Both were locked, just as he expected. The sirens were louder now, and the landlord hurried to the street to greet them.

Penelope meowed again, quieter this time. Stephen rushed into the kitchen and fell to the floor. He wanted to pull Tasha into his arms but knew he shouldn't move her. He had a few precious seconds before the chaos began. Brushing her hair back, he saw a nasty gash on her temple. The bleeding had stopped, but there was a huge knot the size of a golf ball on her head. His heart filled with tenderness.

"Tasha, can you hear me?"

Her eyelids fluttered, and she moaned.

"It's okay, don't move, help is on the way." He continued to stroke her silky hair and reached for her hand. Giving it a slight squeeze, he was reassured when her fingers moved slightly. At least she was conscious. Penelope pressed against his leg and climbed into his lap, her purr exaggerated in the silence of the moment. The cat had actually thanked him.

Chapter 27
Boulder, CO

"IT'S ONLY been two months, Tasha. There's no reason to rush this."

"Stephen, I'm ready. Will you please stop babying me?"

"Just wait until tomorrow. I'll go with you. I don't understand why you have to do this today. You don't have a deadline and the display will be set up for a few more weeks."

"You know it's not about a deadline. It's about me proving to myself that I can be a successful freelance photographer without having to rely on you."

"When was the last time you were dizzy?"

"Yesterday. But, just for a few seconds, and it was because I got up too fast after picking up Annie's toys. Again. We really need to teach her how to put her own toys away," Tasha teased.

Stephen felt the gnawing start deep inside his stomach, the place where worry originates and grows. He wanted to call someone, anyone to talk Tasha out of this since she obviously wasn't listening to him. He remembered her abduction and was scared. What if it happened again? Who? William? No, he would only encourage Tasha to pursue her dream after years of hiding. Sadly, he realized there was no one else. How could a person be so alone? Her mom was in the final stages of early

on-set Alzheimer disease and no longer knew her daughter. He
hadn't met Tasha's parents yet, but from what she had told
him, they truly loved each other. Her dad refused to leave her
mom's side, as he was the only one who could comfort her. The
grandparents on both sides of her family were in assisted living
homes. Tasha hadn't visited them in years.

Stephen was glad she started going to church with him
and seemed to be making new friends, though she still clung
to his hand from the moment they walked in until they left.
She seemed so much more confident lately, as long as she
was in a public place. Wait, what about Winnie? Tasha trusted
the old dear.

"How about Winnie? Will you let me call her? Tasha, you
know I would reschedule this appointment if I could, but our
client is heading back to Europe tomorrow, and this is an opportunity I've been waiting for a long time."

"Stephen, of course I don't want you to reschedule, and I'm
not going to call Winnie. She's old, and besides, her grandson
has a football scrimmage this afternoon she doesn't want to
miss. I told you I would take a taxi, not the bus, and the shoot
is in a mall for goodness sake. There will be a ton of people
around. Why anyone would want to set up a pumpkin patch
in the center of the town mall is beyond me. It's such a mess.
Anyway, along with the mall commission, this assignment is
perfect for my contrast work. They've already agreed to let
me use my photos in anything else I submit, as long as I credit
where they were taken."

"I'm going to compare the commercial use of pumpkins for
Halloween and Thanksgiving with scenes from a traditional
Thanksgiving in the country. For that shoot, you're invited to
join me, of course, since I need your knowledge of the surrounding area, and your chauffer service since I am not cleared
to drive yet. Annie can come too. She's a perfect prop."

"Oh, and thank you for saying 'our' client. I don't know if it was intentional or if the word slipped, but I love it. You are the best, you know?"

Stephen relished the way she leaned into his embrace, breathing in her scent and kissing her soft hair. He sighed and wondered where the fearful woman he met just a few months ago went. She was much more independent now, and while he was happy for her, he still worried, especially after her accident. The doctor expected a full recovery, but said the dizzy spells might last up to a year. He felt so protective over her, this love of his, one he never expected. The thought of losing her filled him with dread. He wondered if he would ever fully get over his mom's tragic death.

"No guarantees, right God?" He shook his head and sighed again.

"It will be fine, Stephen, really. Stop worrying. I know you'll be busy, but I'll text you when I get there and again when I leave, okay?"

"I guess that will have to do. If you get the least bit dizzy, find a place and sit down. Please don't take a tripod and extensive lighting equipment, just the Canon, extra batteries and an external flash."

"Okay, your way."

She loved how protective and attentive he was toward her and knew it was a huge part of her regained confidence. The fall was definitely a scare, but Stephen found her. He rarely left her out of his sight except for the hours each evening after dropping her off at her apartment until seeing her the next morning at the studio. She still insisted on taking the bus in the morning. Tasha loved the church. She had some new friends and a growing relationship with God. This time it felt different, more mature … real. She remembered Joseph and talking to God now was like talking to Joseph. The love overwhelmed her at times.

He watched Tasha gather up her equipment and call the taxi service, trying to ignore the nagging feeling that something would go wrong.

"God, be with her. I love her so much."

She wanted to tell him she loved him, but it seemed so soon. In her heart she knew, the first day she saw him, head bowed, praying for her.

"God, he's the one, isn't he?"

Her heart filled with warmth and she smiled, giving him a quick kiss on the cheek and gently extracted herself from his arms, trying not to hurt his feelings. This was something she needed to do. On her own.

The taxi driver was kind and drove cautiously as Stephen requested he do. They arrived at the mall and Tasha thanked him, requesting the fare.

"No problem. Do you need a ride back?'

"I don't want to make you wait. I'll probably be awhile."

"Tell you what, here's my card. If I'm in the vicinity, give me a call, and I'll pick you up right here. That will be $10.80 for your ride here, and if you call me for your ride back, I'll give you a discount."

Tasha gave him $15.00 and told him to keep the change or use it for a deposit on the ride home. She thought about how some people were so nice, and others were downright grumpy and mean. What's the difference, Lord? Some Christians I know are mighty grumpy and some who've never set a foot in your house are kind and generous. Pondering the thought, she heaved the camera bag over her shoulder, texted Stephen and headed into the mall.

Wow, it's been awhile. She spotted the pumpkin patch right away. The wide variety of stores, and the art and tasteful decorations on the walls drew her in. What a perfect place to begin her adventure. The people were fabulous ... colorful and animated. Strolling down the aisle, she smelled aromatic coffee, earthy candles and cheap perfume among other scents. The cinnamon rolls made her mouth water, but Tasha resolutely passed them by, thinking of all the clothes in her closet that still didn't fit. Embarrassed by the women's clothing, she looked down at her own modest top and decided she wasn't the type to bare her cleavage or slightly rounded stomach.

Okay, time for work. Tasha returned to the pumpkin patch and found a corner to unpack her gear. Still shots would be fine, but if she knew children, and she did from her years as a school photographer, it wouldn't be long before she had subjects in her photos too. Sure enough, a harried looking mom rushed after her toddler intent on climbing to the top of the pile.

The hay bales were stacked in such a way that should a child fall, it would only be to the next bale. Tasha snapped a quick photo of the mom reaching out and catching the child directly in front of the sign that said, "NO CLIMBING!" Giggling, the little boy pointed at the scarecrow, who until this moment, Tasha didn't know was real. The scarecrow gathered some loose straw and threw it in the air, making the child giggle harder. The transformation was amazing, and Tasha caught it all on film. The once harried mother joined in the laughter as life stopped for a moment. She sat down and cuddled her squirmy child in the midst of scratchy hay, big fat orange pumpkins and a hilarious scarecrow.

Tasha pulled out a release form and asked the mom if she could publish the photos, offering to send copies if she included her address. The next few hours rushed by before Tasha felt her stomach growl. Sitting down on one of the hay bales, she put her equipment back in the bag and smiled. This morning could be the definition of her perfect day. The scarecrow approached and asked if he could join her.

"Sure."

"I've never had so much fun being a silly scarecrow in a mall, just watching you."

Surprised, Tasha smirked, "What made today any different?"

"You. The utmost joy in your face, engaging with people, taking delight in simple everyday moments."

Pleased, Tasha softly replied, "Thank you. I did have a wonderful time."

"I look forward to seeing your pictures. It's my break time. Can I buy you lunch?"

Startled, Tasha laughed, and shook her head no. "Thank you for the offer, but I want to get these developed, and I have a special someone waiting for me."

"Can't blame a guy for trying," the man grimaced slightly. "Even if I am dressed like a scarecrow."

"Well, thank you for the offer, and just for the record, I think you make an excellent scarecrow." She laughed as he stood and skipped off humming the song "If I Only Had a Brain" from *The Wizard of Oz*.

Tasha pulled the card out of her pocket and called the taxi driver. He said he would be there in 15 minutes, so she purposely walked the longer direction away from the cinnamon roll place and picked up a chef salad and black coffee to go from a deli. While waiting, she texted Stephen that she would be back at the studio in about a half an hour. He quickly replied, writing that he would see her soon and was thankful that she was safe and in one piece. Tasha felt all warm inside. She had someone who cared about her, and she had to admit, while she wasn't remotely interested, it was nice to have someone attracted to her, even if he was dressed up like a scarecrow.

"Ready?"

Stephen wondered just how long they were going to be out taking pictures of pumpkins based on the size and weight of the picnic basket he loaded into the car.

"Almost, one more bag." Laughing at the long-suffering look on his face, she replied, "It's for Annie!"

"Oh, well in that case, anything for Annie." Grinning, Stephen asked, "Just curious, is Annie *your* dog or my dog?"

"She is *our* dog, silly."

"Well, I can't tell that by her actions. She is completely devoted to you."

"As she should be." Tasha was secretly pleased that Annie decided it was her full-time job to take care of her. She knew without a doubt that Stephen was happy about it too. It put his mind at ease when they weren't together. Annie went on most solo photo shoot locations with her, and the teenager was learning to sit somewhat quietly on her mat while Tasha worked. Otherwise, it was in the crate, and Annie did not like being in the crate, as attested to by her pathetic howls.

As much as Annie didn't like the crate, Penelope had the same aversion to the exuberant dog. She stood her ground, back arched high, with ready sharp claws, but it often meant being stepped on, slapped in the face with a tail or a disgusting lick across her perfectly groomed fur. Tasha wondered if they were trading pets. Stephen knew just where to rub Penelope under her chin to get her to purr the loudest.

"Okay, that's everything."

"Where's Annie going to sit?" Stephen shook his head. Between the camera gear, lunch items, blankets, an umbrella for shade and extra water, there was no room for the dog. So much for minimalism.

"On my lap."

She was serious.

"Annie, come on girl."

Sure enough, the dog jumped right up, wiggled around a little and settled in. Her tongue had already slobbered up the window before Tasha had a chance to roll it down half way for the ultimate in Annie's life ... to stick her head out of a moving car's window. Annie's ears would flap wildly, she sneezed often and her eyes watered, but every time they got in the car, her head went out the window in anticipation of the delicious smells to come.

Tasha read that a dog's sense of smell is at least 10,000 times that of human's. What did Annie process in that pretty head of hers ingesting all the different odors? Oh, if a dog could talk, what would it say? After a complete sniffing down, probably something like, "Where have you been all day, and why do you smell like other dogs?"

Stephen felt his heart swell with happiness for this special woman in his life. He truly enjoyed spending time with Tasha. She was a breath of fresh air and he had to admit, he was smitten. She made him laugh out loud, and he found himself touching her every time he walked by, just a gentle squeeze of her shoulder or caress of silky hair. He loved to hold her hand when they walked, even if it was just from the parking lot into a store. And her scent, when they hugged he lowered his lips to her hair and breathed her in, a combination of a mountain meadow, fresh rain and a hint of rose. Uniquely Tasha. And ... she liked him!

"You're staring at me."

"I can't help it. Do you know how beautiful you are?"

Embarrassed, she blushed and buried her face in Annie's neck.

"Tasha," he gently lifted her chin.

Looking up, she saw his eyes well with tears. She placed her hand over his own, moving her face to place a small kiss inside the palm of his hand.

He felt, more than heard, her small prayer of thankfulness, her lips moving against his palm.

"Woof!"

They both laughed and self-consciously wiped their eyes.

"Annie, are you ready to go on a picnic?"

"Woof, woof!"

Soon they were passing cars and Tasha took more pleasure in watching the passengers laugh at Annie's pure delight of the wind in her face than in the dog herself. It was too bad the camera bag was inaccessible. The shots she could have got in the side mirror were hilarious.

"Stephen, this is absolutely perfect! However did you find this place?"

Looking around she saw an old red barn, vintage tractors, piles of hay, and mounds of every kind of pumpkin Tasha could imagine. Some were huge, large enough to be a fine carriage for a certain princess. There were bright orange, red, green, yellow and white, some striped and spotted, others smooth and round or misshapen and covered in wart-shaped bumps. There was a cornfield maze, a big fire pit for roasting hot dogs and marshmallows, and a cauldron filled with steaming hot apple cider. Everywhere she looked there were families with children. Annie was beside herself, quivering in anticipation.

"We need a bigger car."

"Why?"

"I want to take a bunch of pumpkins for our studio steps."

"You can, they just need to be in the form of photos," Stephen teased.

"Yeah, well next year can we get an Outback for the business after I start selling some of my work and publish my book of contrasts?"

"We can get one now, Tasha. The business is doing quite well, especially with you on board. Our customers are very pleased with your commissioned work. I have every confidence your freelance work will start selling soon, but that's your money. Come on, let's meet George and Judy, the owners of the farm. I did an article on them while working for the magazine, and they gave me an open invitation to come by anytime … which I have every fall for the last several years. Judy makes chocolate chip cookies to die for, but we'll be sure to leave room for our picnic later."

Clipping a leash on Annie's collar, lest the excited dog slobber all over the children, Tasha opened the door and watched Annie's nose get right to work. It really was fascinating, and again she wondered at what the dog registered from all the scents. The air did smell good, it was a crisp fall morning in the Colorado countryside, but Annie's nose was to the ground amidst cow manure. Tasha thought Annie's preference in smells was much different from hers, though she had to admit there was something earthy about the smell of fresh cow manure.

After meeting George and Judy and enjoying warm, fresh baked chocolate chip cookies in their homey country kitchen, Stephen and Tasha got to work. They tag teamed different angles of taking shots, whether it was a lone child running through the corn maze, Annie sitting amidst a group of children in the middle of the pumpkin patch or parents playing hide and seek in the hay bales with their kids. He made suggestions or merely pointed and she was on it, and she did the same for him. Their synergy worked like magic, and Tasha thought with amazement that she was actually paid to do something she loved with someone she truly enjoyed spending time with.

Stephen and Tasha took a break from their work to make a homemade pumpkin pie from scratch, an activity unique to George and Judy's farm. George built two large outdoor ovens, one for baking pumpkins and the other for baking pies and seeds. When families arrived, they picked their pumpkin and took it to a table, cut it in half and placed it on a roasting pan, cut side down. Their pumpkin baked for 30 minutes while they explored and went to the barn to collect fresh cream and chicken eggs. Stephen got the best shots of Tasha peeking into the nesting boxes, especially the one where she surprised a hen in the middle of laying an egg. She was so apologetic and felt horrible that she interrupted the sweet little lady in the middle of her gallant task.

Reading the fact sheet George posted about farm animals, Tasha asked, "Can you imagine, Stephen? Every 28 hours a hen can lay an egg. Giving birth every 28 hours? That's incredible. I am so glad I'm not a chicken."

Stephen agreed and held her free hand as they walked back to retrieve their pumpkin. His heart quickened at how small and natural it felt next to his. Her hair had golden highlights in the sun and blew gently in the breeze, giving glimpses of cute little ears with small pearl earrings on the lobes. Tasha had a huge smile on her face and her cheeks were flushed a rosy pink. Dark lashes framed her sparkling eyes. Even her brows were pretty. He thought of his mom and wondered if she could see how happy he was. She would have loved Tasha.

Arriving back at the pumpkin oven, they found their pumpkin cooked and ready for the next step. Stephen scraped the seeds out, placing them back on the pan with a little olive oil and salt to roast. The stringy part of the pulp went into a bucket to feed the farm animals or composted. He scooped the warm pumpkin flesh into a large bowl while Tasha added the milk, eggs, sugar and spices and stirred it all together with an old-fashioned hand beater until the concoction was smooth and creamy.

Together they learned how to make a perfect homemade pie crust from ice cold real butter, flour, salt and water. Neither had ever made a pumpkin pie before, and were surprised at how thin the pie filling was as they poured it into the crust. They carefully took their pie and seeds back to the oven to bake.

Judy's job was to watch Annie and hold their cameras while they made the pie. She snuck several shots of the adorable couple working together. Capturing them through the lens, her heart warmed at how happy they were. She got some of Annie looking with adoration at her mistress and quizzically at all the new and fascinating things on the farm. Perhaps they would let her put some of the shots on their web page.

"I'm hungry. Are you ready for our picnic, Tasha?"

"Now that you mention it, my stomach is growling, and the smell of baking pumpkin pies is making my mouth water. We have turkey, smoked Gouda cheese and avocado on sourdough with carrot sticks and ranch dip in the cooler. Do you think if we eat our sandwiches and veggies we can have two slices of pie?"

"Absolutely. I like the way you think."

"I hope we get to make homemade whipped cream to go with it."

"It wouldn't surprise me, knowing Judy and her love for Jersey cows."

Stephen went to get the cooler while Tasha filled two home-made pottery mugs with hot apple cider. She found a quiet spot under a heavily laden apple tree. Judy brought Annie over and tied her leash to the tree while Tasha placed the mugs out of the dog's reach on a flat rock. The sun peeked through the branches and felt good on her back and Annie's soft golden coat. Tasha leaned into the dog and they both fell backwards in the soft grass. Annie wagged her tail slowly and made no move to get up. Tasha put her head on the dog's shoulder and felt her eyes get heavy as she succumbed to a luxurious nap.

Stephen found Tasha cuddled up to Annie, both of them sound asleep after the busy morning. He sat down next to her and picked up one of the abandoned mugs. Sipping the still warm cider, he looked at her peaceful face and daydreamed about the possibility of a lifetime of days like this one with Tasha at his side. What would it be like to share his life with this beautiful woman? He thought about them sharing an evening meal and talking about their day, perhaps sipping a glass of wine under the stars before going upstairs to bed. Would she cuddle with her head nestled in his shoulder, hair tickling his nose and their legs entwined as they fell asleep together? Or, did she prefer to spoon? He wondered when he woke in the middle of the night if he would reach out just to make sure she was warm and safe. He thought about her adorable mussed hair and sleepy eyes as he brought her morning coffee, a little sugar and enough cream to make the hot liquid the color of a Jersey cow.

He reached down and stroked her soft hair and she stirred slightly. Leaning over, he lightly brushed a kiss against her temple and rather than wake her, decided to join them. A nap would feel good. He slowly and gently lowered his body and spooned her back and legs, breathing in her lovely scent. Stephen matched his breathing to hers and for the second time today, a tear came to his eye.

"Oh, please God. I want to follow your plans, but I am going to be broken all over again if this doesn't work out. Why would you put her in my life if it wasn't meant to be? I'm really trying to trust and be patient. You know me, you know Tasha, and you know our future. Please let it be together."

He drifted off, the prayer in his mind.

"Woof!"

Annie jumped up and started barking at the tree above them, then biting at the offending apple on the ground. It must have fallen and startled her.

Tasha started laughing, and then quieted as she realized Stephen was lying next to her. She gave a sigh of pleasure and nestled her back against his solid chest, laying her head on his outstretched arm, using it as a pillow. She didn't want to wake him and end this moment. Suddenly she thought about the pie and abruptly sat up.

"Oh no, the pie!"

"It's okay, George gets them out of the oven when they are done." Stephen murmured.

"You're adorable when you sleep, you know?"

"I wouldn't know because I can't see myself sleeping. But, thank you." Tasha blushed. "Am I adorable when my stomach is growling?"

"Even more so." Stephen winked at her. "Let's eat our lunch, and then we can go get our pie. Judy also gave me a smoked beef marrow bone for Annie. Hopefully that will keep her busy for a while."

Chapter 28
Boulder, CO

"**P**ASTOR JOHN gave another great sermon."

Not quite ready to leave the cozy church, Stephen asked, "Would you like another cup of hot coffee? Even though it's a beautiful spring day, there's still a bit of winter lingering."

"Sure, not that I need one, but it's so good."

Tasha relaxed into the comfortable chair and continued reading the passage Pastor John referred to in the sermon.

"Do not let any unwholesome talk come out of your mouths, but only what is helpful for building others up according to their needs, that it may benefit those who listen. And do not grieve the Holy Spirit of God, with whom you were sealed for the day of redemption. Get rid of all bitterness, rage and anger, brawling and slander, along with every form of malice. Be kind and compassionate to one another, forgiving each other, just as in Christ God forgave you."[11]

It was a good reminder to think first before speaking, and how to treat people with kindness and compassion. The memories were fading, but it was still difficult to think about forgiving her birth mother and Harley. In her heart, she knew that forgiveness brings healing for the forgiver regardless of the response from the transgressor. Of course, she couldn't offer forgiveness in person to dead people, but she could still say the prayer and offer it the Lord. Pushing the thought aside like countless times before, she continued with the next verse.

"Follow God's example, therefore, as dearly loved children and walk in the way of love, just as Christ loved us and gave himself up for us as a fragrant offering and sacrifice to God. But among you there must not be even a hint of sexual immorality, or of any kind of impurity, or of greed, because these are improper for God's holy people."[12]

Tasha squirmed. She found her thoughts about Stephen were increasingly going places reserved only for the marriage bed. She longed to feel his lips on hers, trailing down .... "Stop! You're in church for goodness sake," Tasha told herself, sure her face was beet red for how warm it felt. Just last night when they were watching a movie while snuggled up on her couch, it led to kissing. When she started moaning, Stephen broke the kiss, got up and moved to a chair on the other side of the room. Neither said a word, knowing he was the stronger of the two, but she could tell he was frustrated. After a moment of silence, they gave up on the movie and went outside to sit in their separate chairs and look at the stars. She thought about how her heart warmed when Stephen talked to God about the beauty and thanked him for bringing her into his life.

The past winter was amazing. Her photography blossomed under Stephen's mentoring, and many photographic journals raved about their work together. There was a synergy between them that flowed, turning their work into exquisite art. She finished her book of contrasts, and the publisher was anxious for her to start on another one. Often, they forced themselves to leave their cameras behind and just have fun without stopping every few minutes to snap a photo. There was so much to do in Colorado, and it made Tasha sad she hid herself away so many years. Downhill and cross-country snow skiing were by far her favorite winter activities, and they had plenty of places close by to choose from. Annie loved it when they went cross-country skiing because with her little snow boots, she got to go along. The dog had so much energy!

"Your coffee, pretty lady, just the way you like it." He set her cup down and brushed an errant lock of hair from her cheek. "What are you reading?"

"The verse from this morning's service, but I went on to the next chapter."

"What does it say?"

Still flushed, Tasha gently pushed the book towards him and pointed at the verse.

"Wow, God sure knows when to put a verse right in front of a man when it's exactly what he needs to read." Shaking his head, he took her hand and placed it on top of the verse, his own hand warmly covering hers.

"You're not alone. I needed to read it too."

"This is getting more difficult isn't it?"

"Yes, I don't think I can trust myself to be alone with you anymore."

"What are you saying, Tasha?"

"Just that, I don't trust myself. I really like you, Stephen, I can't stop thinking about you, and if I'm honest with myself, I know I'm in love with you." Tasha's eyes filled.

"I've felt that way about you since the first day we met, Tasha. I love you, I like you, I adore you, and I can't imagine life without you. Do you really love me?"

"Yes, but I am afraid."

"Me too."

"We're not supposed to be afraid, Stephen. We've both read the Bible and come to church, we say we trust in God, we pray, yet we both admit we're afraid."

"What are you afraid of, Tasha?"

"That something will happen to you. After my fall, when you found me, and since then, you are so attentive and protective over me, I am no longer afraid. What if something happens to you and I am alone again? The longer we're together, the more I rely on you, and I feel vulnerable. It doesn't make sense, I know. My life was 'safe' before you even though I lived in constant fear because I never went anywhere except schools to take photos. Now that I'm with you, I'm no longer afraid, but if something happens to you, I'll be right back where I was. It was easier being there and not having to worry about losing something so precious."

"Tasha, I'm not going to lie to you and promise that nothing will ever happen to me. I don't have control over that. I can promise that I will live my life for God and that includes doing everything in my power to not do something careless that will put me at risk. I'll even wear sunscreen, eat my vegetables and get a yearly physical." Stephen winked and lovingly squeezed her hand still resting on the Bible.

"What are you afraid of, Stephen?"

"The same thing, losing you. Putting you in the taxi and watching you drive off to do the photo shoot in the mall was very difficult, as is knowing you are home alone at night. I don't trust anyone to take care of you as well as I can. However, that means never letting you out of my sight and stifling your creativity. If I didn't have you in my life to love, I wouldn't have to worry about a drunk driver killing you by his selfishness and stupidity. That also means that I'm not living the life God intends for me. I have so much love to give and share, and I want that in return. This life is very short, and I want to spend it with a very special lady."

"I love you, Stephen. I do." Tasha's tears started falling in earnest.

"This isn't the way I planned it, but I've been waiting to say and hear those beautiful words."

Stephen turned towards her, gently took her other hand and looked deep into her eyes. "Tasha, will you be my wife, companion, soul-mate, helper, friend and lover for the rest of our lives?" His own eyes brimmed with tears and his stomach turned while he anxiously awaited her answer.

"Oh Stephen, I'm broken, I'm a mess, how could you honestly want me?"

"We're all broken, sweetheart. The book right here under our joined hands is filled with stories about broken people. But, God is our healer and our savior. With him, we can become whole if only we ask. Do you want to ask him?"

"I do. I'm so tired of not liking myself and fighting my fears and doubts when I think about living a life without you, even though in my head I know you can't replace God. I haven't forgiven those who hurt me. They are often still present in my thoughts, and it makes me angry to think about what they took from me. I don't know how to say the words."

"Pastor John and Winnie are here, as am I. Though you don't need us Tasha, this is between you and God, it's your decision. We can give you the words, but you just said them yourself. All you need to do is say them to God instead of me. There are no specific right or wrong words. God already knows your heart. He made you."

"Really, that's all there is to it? I was raised in a church, and I prayed the sinner's prayer to be saved. I know the mechanics, but honestly, this is the first time that it feels real, that I really could be healed and have a future free of anxiety and fear when I'm alone."

Stephen smiled at her, the tears now falling freely down his face. He remained silent and bowed his head, still gently holding her hands. There was no hurry, no rushing this life-changing moment. He felt his mind and heart connect with God … no words were necessary. When Tasha started praying aloud, a warmth filled his hands connected with hers and through his body. Her voice was exquisitely sweet as she prayed the exact words she just spoke to him. She renewed her vows to trust and believe in Christ and asked him to help her forgive those who hurt her.

Tasha continued her prayer.

"God, you heard the question Stephen just asked me. I know he wouldn't have asked me without checking with you first. Do you want me to marry this man, God? Will he follow you the rest of his life and put you first in our home? Will he protect and lead me in your ways, and if you bless us with children, will he teach them about you?"

Stephen felt his heart beating in the complete silence as she waited for her answer. She actually said the word children, the desire of his heart second only to a sweet wife. The seconds felt like hours, and the warmth continued to emanate through his body. There were no words, but he could feel how pleased their Lord was with their submission and obedience.

The one whispered word was so quiet, Stephen wasn't sure he heard correctly until he lifted his head, opened his eyes and saw the most beautiful woman in the world nodding yes, all the while whispering, "Yes, yes, yes," over and over again. He pulled her into his arms and held her tight, burying his face in her soft hair. She could feel his tears on her neck and heard him say, *"Oh thank you, Jesus. Thank you."*

Tasha felt so light, and all the colors were brighter than she could remember seeing in a very long time. The coffee smelled wonderful, and she noticed the roses on the table, their delicate scent tickling her nose. Everything was intensely vibrant, all of her senses felt alive … especially the feeling of Stephen's arms around her. Pulling back, she kissed him gently on the cheek, and whispered in his ear, "I hope Pastor John's calendar has an opening very soon."

John and Winnie witnessed the entire scene, and while not intentional, were both honored to be included in this special moment.

"What does your calendar look like, Pastor John?" Winnie teased.

"Oh, I think there is plenty of room first for pre-marital counseling, then a wedding. Tasha is going to be a stunning bride if she looks even half as radiant as she does now."

The next morning when Tasha got on the bus, Jack took one look at her and asked, "What has you smiling so brightly this morning, pretty lady?"

Blushing, Tasha gushed, "Stephen asked me to marry him, and I said yes!"

"Oh, Tasha, I am so happy for you. He is a fine man and well deserving of a special lady like you."

Jack unbuckled, got out of his seat and gave her a big hug. "The fare is on me this morning, congratulations Tasha!"

Everyone stood and the bus erupted in applause. Tasha bowed her head in embarrassment. Some of the faces were familiar, but most she didn't know and the attention was overwhelming. She looked at Jack helplessly.

"Alright everyone, sit down or we won't stay on schedule." Jack bellowed.

Thankfully, there was an available seat in the first row and Tasha dropped into it, face still burning.

"Young love is a beautiful thing, so full of promise, a lifetime ahead of you filled with joy and a bit of pain too."

Tasha looked over at her seatmate. He was very old with a humped back, smelling of stale cigar smoke and dressed in a fine tweed jacket and wool slacks.

"I knew of such a love once."

A single tear fell down his wrinkled cheek.

"I would do it all over again. The joy far outweighed the sorrow. Focus on the joy so you'll have the memories when you need them," his gravelly voice exhorted.

The tears came in earnest now and he turned his body toward the window.

"Thank you, kind sir. Was she sweet and loving?"

He didn't reply and stared at the people on the sidewalk as they drove by, lost in his thoughts, no doubt of the love he had once and lost.

"Downtown, 27th and Mapleton," Jack called out.

"That's my stop." Tasha said, hoping the old man would reply. As she got up from her seat, he turned and demanded, "Live your life well young lady. You only have one."

"Thank you. I will sir," she said with conviction.

"Have a great day, Jack. Thank you for the fare."

Tasha fairly skipped down the street in order to get to work quickly and see Stephen. Yesterday was the best day of her life, and she would spend today with her *fiancée*.

Stephen was waiting on the inviting porch when she opened the gate. Would this be her house too? Her heart surged at the thought. She loved this house from the moment she set eyes on it.

"Good morning, beautiful," Stephen spoke shyly. Was this exquisite woman really going to be his wife? Stepping down off the porch, he welcomed her into his arms under the maple trees and tucked a fragrant white gardenia into her hair.

"Good morning, Stephen. Did yesterday really happen?" Tasha looked up into his handsome face wondering if she was in a dream.

"It did, future Mrs. Washington Banks. Do you have any doubts after sleeping on it last night?"

"Not a one. Especially if it means that Annie will have two full-time parents."

"She already does, silly. That dog chose you from the start. You should see her every night when you go to your apartment, it's pathetic. She goes right to her mat and mopes, giving me a sad questioning look about why you left." Wrapping his arm around her waist, they went up the stairs to their future home together.

"Hungry?"

"Always, especially for your delicious cooking. I hope you'll teach me your secret recipes, but that doesn't mean that you're off the hook for making me breakfast every day."

"Absolutely, but before we eat, I have some bad news."

"What is it?" Tasha frowned.

"Tasha, your dad called this morning. Your mom is dying." He didn't want you to hear the news while you were alone.

"She's been dying for quite some time now, Stephen. She doesn't even know me. It tears me apart when I think about it, and I don't want to see her like this. I want to remember her before this awful disease changed my mom into a woman I don't even recognize ... and one who doesn't know me."

"When is the last time you've seen her?"

Tasha felt guilty. "Over a year ago, last Thanksgiving. I took the bus. It's only a little over 30 miles, but it still takes two hours to get there with the transfers. My dad and I tried to have a nice dinner at the convalescent home, but my mom just sat there and drooled with a vacant look in her eyes. I don't know how he does it every day."

"The doctor thinks it will be any day."

Tasha gulped. She knew her dad would appreciate her coming. It was much easier to stay away and not think about it. A thought filled her mind, "Isn't that what you usually do about anything that makes you uncomfortable?"

"Will you go with me, Stephen?"

"I wouldn't have it any other way, Tasha. I love you. I am here for you and I still want to ask your father for his blessing on our marriage. I should have asked him first. It will be an opportunity for you to tell your mom, even if she doesn't understand. Let's look at our calendar and see what appointments need rescheduling. I have a few things to finish up today, and we can leave tomorrow morning. Do you mind making the calls?"

"Of course, thank you, Stephen. I don't know what I would do without you."

As they finished their breakfast Annie whined, pulling both of their attention to her adorable face. She was lying on the kitchen floor, head resting on her feet with her soft brown eyes looking up at her favorite people.

"Do you think she's asking to go with us or wants the left-over bacon?" Stephen asked as he softly cupped his hand on her cheek and winked to lighten the moment.

"Probably both, actually, I would love to take her with us. I'll take her shot records so she can go into the convalescent home. My dad can meet her, and she'll be a hit with the other patients. You know Stephen, along with trusting God and your protection, having Annie with me all the time really does help me feel safe and calm."

"I think God had a plan when he brought Annie and you into my life, Tasha, almost at the same time. You were meant to be together. And, I must say you've been doing a great job training her. I really appreciate that. It's getting so we can take Annie almost anywhere if we bring her mat so she knows where to stay put. I really like how you have her lie down when children want to pet her. It lets her know it's time to be still, and because she's a large dog, petting her is not so intimidating for the children. I don't know how you taught her to take a treat so gently, either. She used to about take my fingers off, and now look at her." Stephen invited Annie over and gave her a bite of bacon.

"Oh, we have our secrets, don't we Annie girl? You are such a good dog!" Tasha rubbed the beautiful dog's soft ears and she could swear Annie smiled.

"Okay, girl, let's get busy and make those phone calls."

CHAPTER 29
LOVELAND, CO

"WELL, WHO do we have here?" Tom laughed when Annie bolted from the car almost knocking him over.

"Dad, I've missed you so much." Tasha fell into his arms, breathing in his familiar scent and feeling his scratchy wool sweater against her cheek. Tears filled her eyes, and again she wondered why she stayed away so long. He felt so good.

"I've missed you too, honey." He brushed the tears from her cheeks, and said, "You look beautiful, and softer. The haunted look in your eyes is gone."

"Oh, Dad. I am so happy, and yes, I am much better."

"I can't wait to hear what you've been doing. Now, introduce me to this fine young man."

"Dad, this is Stephen, my boss and uh …." Stephen shook his head slightly and winked at her.

Stephen quickly stepped forward to shake Tom's hand. "Sir, I am glad to meet you in person. Your daughter is an amazing woman and gifted photographer. I am very fortunate to have her both in my employment and my life."

Returning the young man's firm handshake, Tom replied, "I am glad to meet you too, Stephen. I look forward to spending some time together. I've seen some of your work. Even from my untrained eye, I think it's exceptional."

Tom turned to see his daughter fairly glowing as she looked at Stephen, and he remembered the same look in Joan's eyes when she looked at him a lifetime ago. It made him happy to know she had found someone special. He missed his someone special.

Joan was a completely different person, one that on most days he didn't recognize. He didn't blame Tasha for not visiting very often in the past few years. The disease ravaged Joan's mind to the point that she no longer knew him. He still loved her, but if he was honest with himself, admitted that he had to rely on memories to keep the promise he made to her on their wedding day. Sighing, he said, "I suppose we should go see your mom. She doesn't have much time left. She probably won't respond, but we can hope, and it will give you an opportunity to say goodbye. If you like, we can walk. The convalescent home is less than a mile from here, and I'm sure your pup would enjoy a walk after her car ride."

Tasha hesitated and Stephen squeezed her hand. "It's okay, I'm here." Leaning down, she hugged Annie and clipped on her leash.

"Okay, Dad, I don't think I'll ever be ready so we might as well just go now."

It was a beautiful day for a walk. Tasha pointed out houses where her friends had lived and places she frequented as a child. Pointing her elbow up to Stephen, "This scar is from falling out of that huge tree. It wasn't as big then, and I climbed up to one of the bottom branches and promptly fell, catching my arm on a branch on the way down."

Tom chuckled, "Honey, that's not the only scar you have from your adventures growing up. I hope you're not as accident prone now. Buying gauze bandages and tape was a weekly item in our budget."

Stephen thought of her fall, "Sir, I'm not sure that is the case."

"Oh you two! I am much better than I used to be."

The men exchanged looks, their expressions full of doubt.

Annie spotted a squirrel in the park and lunged toward it.

"Annie heel," her mistress commanded.

The dog stopped and dropped back to Tasha's side.

"Good girl." She leaned down and stroked the dog's soft ears.

"Wow, that was impressive, Tasha. You've grown up into quite an accomplished woman, a published photographer and a dog trainer."

"Just don't judge when you come to visit and see my cat," Tasha smirked. "She's untrainable."

They quickly arrived at the convalescent home and Tasha gave Stephen a copy of Annie's shot records to give to the aide at the information counter. Annie busily greeted all the residents in the lobby, going from one to another to get a pat and compliments on her gorgeous fur and good manners.

"I think we're going to have a difficult time getting her to go home with us," Stephen laughed after getting authorization to take the dog to her mom's room.

"This is a nice place, Dad. The furnishings are attractive and comfortable, and the paint colors and decorations feel happy. It's quiet and smells nice too."

"They really try hard. It's expensive, but worth it for your mom. Many convalescent homes are understaffed, so the nurse's assistants don't have enough time to adequately care for the residents. This one has enough staff to take their time bathing, changing their bedding and clothes daily, and importantly when a resident needs their adult brief changed, they are on it right away."

There are fresh flowers brought in every day throughout the home, and they open the windows when it's not cold outside. Each caregiver also wears a pager that notifies them with a quiet beep and vibration when their resident needs assistance.

They silence the alarm, and a light in the resident's room notifies them that their caregiver is on their way. I work off some of the cost by maintaining the lawns and gardens outside, as do many of the other family members. The residents that are able and want to help are encouraged to participate and help grow fresh fruits and vegetables for their meals. The food here is very good, it's healthy, served hot and not overcooked, another challenge for understaffed facilities. In fact, I usually eat with your mom and help feed her when she wants to eat. She is quite frail now. It sounds odd, but I will miss this place after she goes. They are like family to me. I'll come down to Boulder and take you to lunch sometimes if you don't mind. I need to get back into church too. I'm a little worried about what I'll do when I don't have your mom to care for.

"Here we are," Tom entered a cheery room with sheer yellow curtains billowing from the fresh breeze in the open window. Bright orange and red tulips adorned the hickory chest of drawers. Her mom's favorite antique rocking chair stood in the corner with a bright colored throw across the padded seat. Tasha forced herself to look at the bed. There was a slight mound under the down filled comforter, certainly not large enough to be a person?

"Joan, you have some special visitors. Tasha and her friend Stephen came from Boulder on this fine day just to see us." Tom pulled the comforter down a bit to kiss his wife on her cheek. Her head rested on a white down pillow, barely nestled into its softness, eyes closed and twitching slightly. Her wispy hair was white, and her skin was almost translucent. She was so ... small.

Annie whined, pushing against Tasha's leg to move her closer to the bed. Stephen still held her hand and gave it a slight squeeze and a little tug. Between the two of them, Tasha found the strength to go closer to the strange looking person that could not be her mom. Then she caught it, breathing deep, the faint smell of roses that her mom always wore filled her senses.

265

It brought back memories of their neighbor's roses. When they were in bloom, she always had them in vases on the kitchen counter. A sense of calm and peace flowed over her. *"Thank you, Jesus."*

"Mom? It's me, Tasha."

She wasn't sure, but thought she saw a slight smile on the pale lips.

"I love you, Mom."

The shallow breathing continued, not even enough to raise the comforter. Tasha kissed the soft, downy cheek. It was cool, but the smell of roses remained and now, curiously, the smell of fresh rain. It was so comforting. Her lips parted, and words that didn't feel like her own spilled forth, "Mom, you can go now if you're ready. Dad and I will be fine." She leaned closer to her mom's ear, cheek to cheek, and barely whispered, "I met someone, Mom. We are in love, and he is going to care for me and protect me, just like Dad does for you. I'm going to be okay."

If possible, her mom's breathing slowed even more, but when Tasha looked back at her face, there was definitely a dreamy smile and her eyes even crinkled up a little.

Annie whined again and Tasha reluctantly pulled away, leaning into Stephen's strength.

"Goodbye, Mom. I'll see you again someday. I love you so much."

The tears now came, little shudders, yet it was good. She walked to the door with Stephen and Annie by her side and took one last look back. Her dad was kissing her mom, gently loving her as he had consistently all their lives, and Tasha knew deep within how blessed she was that they chose her to be their daughter.

The walk back to her childhood home was quiet, and when they got there, Tasha begged off to take a nap. She felt exhausted. Annie promptly plopped down on her mat next to Tasha's bed, still covered in the same flowered spread she had as a teenager. Looking around her room, her favorite childhood things brought comfort. Her mom hadn't changed a thing. She remembered the Christmas morning when her dad pretended to be a bear and smiled. Her eyes grew heavy while good memories lulled her to sleep.

"Would you like something to drink, Stephen? I don't have much in the house. I have coffee, tea or apple juice."

"Coffee would be nice, with just enough cream to make it look like a Jersey cow and one teaspoon of sugar."

Tom jerked his head toward the young man. "What did you say?"

Stephen laughed, "I know, that's exactly how Tasha likes her coffee, with a little less sugar now that we're supposedly adults. We got a kick out of that when we discovered it. It's like we were meant to be."

Tom nodded.

"Mr. McCleary, I need to ask you a very important question, and I hope you say yes. You don't know me well, but I love your daughter from the depths of my heart. I want to love, protect and care for her for the rest of our lives. I'm not perfect, but I love our Lord Jesus Christ and will do my very best to lead our family as he shows me through the Bible, regular attendance at our church and prayer. May I please have your blessing to marry your precious daughter?"

Tom looked down at his shoes with a slight smile and wiped a tear from his eye. He waited a moment and finally said, "I had a feeling you might need these." Reaching into his pocket, he pulled out Joan's engagement and wedding ring. "Tasha may not want to wear these, but if she does, both her mom and I would be honored. I took the rings home when they fell off her finger, not wanting to lose them. Welcome to our family, Son."

"Thank you so much, sir. I will do my very best to make you proud." Choked up, he reached out to shake the older man's hand, but found himself embraced in a bear hug instead.

"Now, that's enough of the sir. Please call me Dad or Tom, whichever you prefer, and sooner is better than later. I've always wanted a son." Winking, he said, "I wouldn't mind being called Grandpa someday in the future too if it's in the Lord's plans."

Epilogue
BOULDER, CO
One Year Later

"TASHA, THERE is no need to be drying your hair at a time like this. Please get down here right now!"

"The contractions are still five minutes apart, and we are just a few miles from the hospital. You know what a mess my hair is when I let it dry naturally. Ouch, that one hurt. Oh oh, Stephen, can you bring me some dry clothes? My water just broke."

Rushing up the stairs he yelled, "That's it, you are going with wet hair. Now. Here's your bathrobe. They're going to put you in one of those fancy gowns anyway."

"Woof, woof!"

"Not now, Annie, you stay and guard the house. It's okay."

The dog obviously knew it was not okay. Her mistress was in pain, and the floor smelt weird. She panted and paced back and forth.

"I'll call William. He can come sit with her."

"Okay, bring an extra towel, will you? I don't want our new Subaru seats to get stained."

"Subaru seats, Tasha! Oh, why did we decide to start a family so soon? I don't think I can handle the stress. I did enjoy our honeymoon though, very much."

"Me too," she reached toward him for a lingering kiss and an awkward hug. "God blessed us, Stephen. We're fine." Gasping, "Ohhhh. I think you're right. We need to leave right now, this contraction was only two minutes from the last one."

"Aren't first babies supposed to come slowly?" he exclaimed. "Hold my arm so I can help you down the stairs."

"Stephen, I'm sorry to tell you this, but you need to take me to our bedroom and call an ambulance. This baby is coming now! I can feel the head and have this huge desire to push. Do you remember our class? They said when I want to push it's time for the baby. We're not going to make it to the hospital, Stephen."

"You are so in trouble, all for pretty hair."

"Now is not the time, get me to our room and make that call! And, unlock the front door so they can get in."

Annie leaned into Tasha and whined.

"Annie, on your mat, I don't need to trip over you."

Settled into their bed, Tasha thought their pretty sheets were going to get stained. Oh well, they could buy more.

"God, I could really use some help right now. I'm scared that we are not prepared to deliver this baby, much less raise it. But, it's a gift from you, and I trust you. Please help us."

"The ambulance and William are on their way and the front door is unlocked."

"William?"

"Yes, for when we go to the hospital."

"Oh, right. Stephen?"

"Yes?"

"Get ready. I'm going to give a big push, and you are going to catch our baby."

"What?"

"Yes, now. Oh my. Gosh, this really hurts. No one said how much it would hurt! It feels like someone has a vice grip on my whole stomach. Ohhhhh."

"You're right, Tasha, I can see our baby's hair. Oh wow, the whole head is out now."

"I think you probably need to support the baby's neck, Stephen."

"Oh God, please help us!" They both cried at the same time.

"Whew, okay, another contraction is coming. I can feel it, and I'm going to push again hard, get ready, Stephen!"

"God I really need your help now. Our baby is being born, and I have no idea what to do. I'm so worried about my wife and child."

"Ahhhhh! Stephen, what's happening?"

"The shoulders just came out. And here comes the rest."

"Oh God, help me now, I don't want to drop him."

"This little guy is really slippery. Tasha?"

"Yes?"

"We have a little boy."

"Is he breathing, Stephen?"

"He's making a very angry face, but I don't think he's breathing. What do I do Tasha?"

"Rub his back. Quickly, Stephen."

"He's still not breathing."

"Again."

"Waah, waah, waah!"

"Oh what a relief. That was scary. He's really mad, Tasha."

"Of course he is, wouldn't you be? Wipe his nose and mouth if you see any liquid or mucous, then put him on my chest and cover him with the blanket. Just leave the umbilical cord attached but don't pull on it. The placenta has to come next." Tasha tried to keep her breathing even and voice calm in spite of being scared. She could feel her heart pounding and didn't want to scare the baby or Stephen. She rubbed little circles on their baby's back and he stopped crying.

"Where is that ambulance? I don't think I can do this, Tasha."

"You can Stephen. You're doing great!"

"Oh, Stephen, he's absolutely perfect. Do you think Carl will be pleased we chose to name the baby after him? Well, hello little Carl Thomas Washington Banks," she crooned.

"Yes, it's an honor he well deserves. Tasha, our little family of two, plus Penelope and Annie, is now three! I am so relieved you and the baby are fine. Do you know that I love you more than life itself? If something would have happened to you ...." He struggled to keep from sobbing as the emotions overcame him.

"I know, Stephen, I feel the same way about you. But, we're not done yet and we can get gushy later, okay? The placenta is coming now. Will you please go get a clean towel from the bathroom and wrap it up?"

She pushed again at the next contraction and felt something warm slide down between her quivering legs.

Stephen got himself under control and hurried back, "Wow, this thing is amazing, Tasha."

"I know. It nourished and fed our baby for nine months. It's a miracle the way God designed procreation."

"Yes, it is. Oh, I think I hear the sirens now."

"Stephen?"

"Yes."

"Come here and look at our son. Soon, we're going to have a ton of people around us, and I want to enjoy this moment with just us."

"Oh, sweetheart, you're right. Carl Thomas, you my little man, are absolutely perfect." Their baby had wispy light brown hair and olive skin. His tiny nose looked just like a miniature of Tasha's. Carl looked up at his mom and dad, blue eyes wide open as if to say, "So that's what you look like." They both laughed and cried and stared at their baby in amazement. He opened his tiny mouth and Tasha placed their son on her breast. He easily found the nipple and started to suckle. Overwhelmed, Stephen kissed his bride's hair, eyes, nose, cheeks and finally her mouth. Gazing deep into her eyes, he said, "You are the most beautiful wife and mother in the world."

Taking hold of Tasha's hand, Stephen prayed, *"God, we thank you for blessing us with each other and this child. Guide us with your wisdom as we raise him. Please protect him from sickness and harm. You are so good to us, we love you."*

Looking at his son again, he said, "Wait until Sarah, Carl, Tom, Winnie, Pastor John and Rich see you. They're going to love you, almost as much as we already do."

"Woof, woof!"

"Of course, and you too, Annie. Would you like me to teach him how to throw a ball and swim with you at our lake cabin?"

"Woof!"

AUTHOR NOTE

Dear Reader,

Thank you for taking the time to read *The Lens of God*. My sincere hope is that you not only enjoyed the story, but that it inspired you. You may ask, "Inspired? How?" That depends on you.

Do you have a dream or passion that you put aside or are afraid to try? Both Tasha and Stephen took risks that were uncomfortable for them, but they prayed and were willing to try. Do you want to write a book, take a pottery class, learn a musical instrument or get back to playing your favorite sport? What is keeping you from doing it? I've found that if I'm willing to try something, I'm either good at it or I'm not. Or perhaps I find it easy, but I don't like it, knitting for example. Alternatively, I like the activity, but struggle so I have to practice more, as in playing the piano.

Perhaps your inspiration was how my characters regularly talked to God, as if he were sitting right next to them. It was natural for them in their day-to-day thoughts and concerns to include God. Many of us were taught that prayer is what we do before we sit down to eat a meal or during times of worship in church. God wants us to include him in every aspect of our lives. He made us to be in a relationship with him.

Or maybe you read this book and thought of a friend or relative who needs to hear its message. Please pass it on and pray for them.

Know that I am praying for your eyes and heart to see through God's lens and that you experience his amazing love.

I would love to hear your thoughts about the book or if you would just like to chat.

My email address is carrie.dugovic@gmail.com if you have a moment to jot a line or two.

Blessings!

Carrie

Bible Verse References

1 1 John 4:18
2 Jeremiah 29:11-13
3 Philippians 4:6
4 Jeremiah 6:16
5 Mark 11:25
6 3 John 11
7 John 8:3-8
8 Psalm 23
9 Ephesians 6:1-3
10 Psalm 67: 1-2
11 Ephesians 4:29
12 Ephesians 5:1-3

CPSIA information can be obtained
at www.ICGtesting.com
Printed in the USA
LVOW07s1236091017
551752LV00011B/1089/P